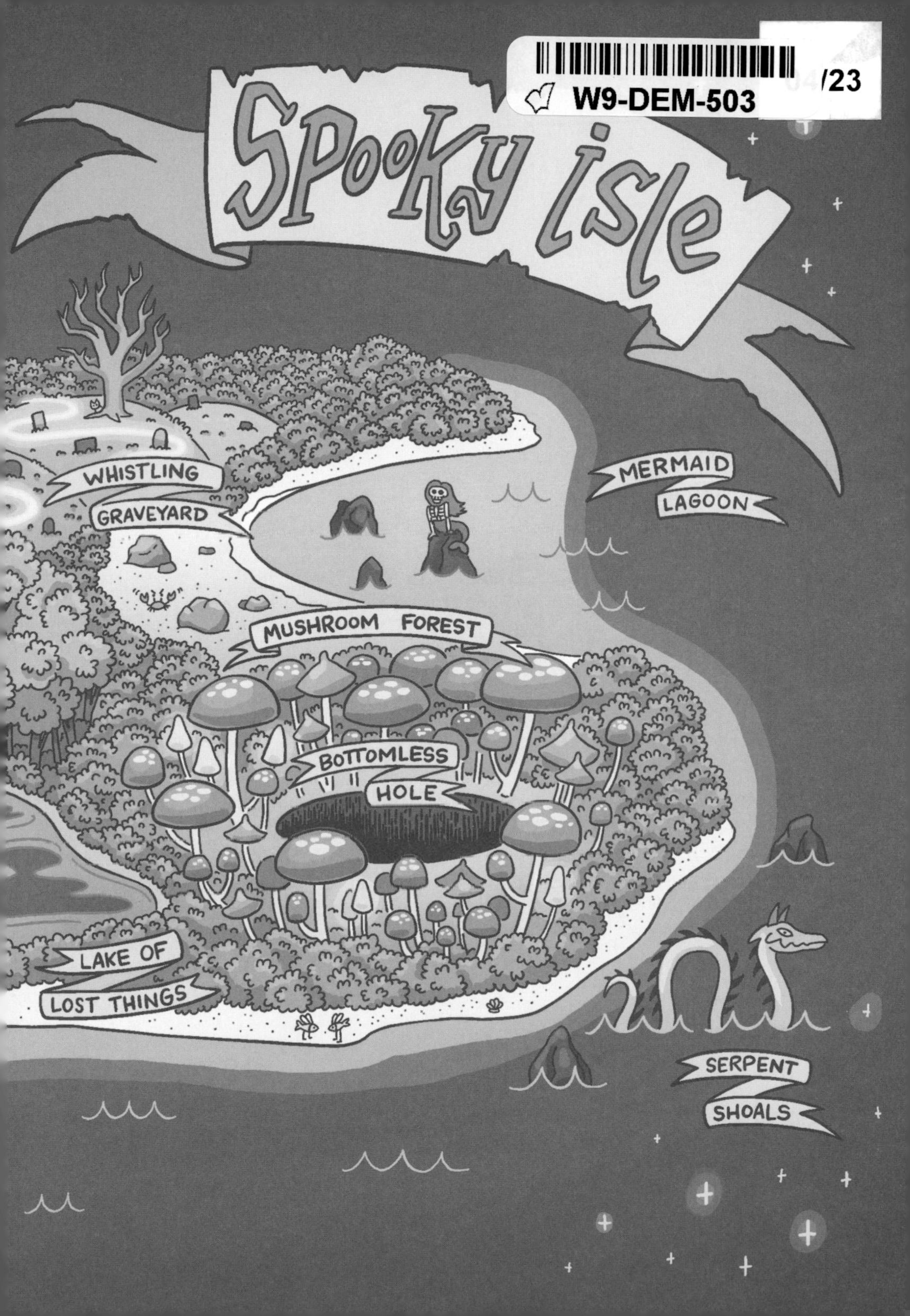
Spooky Isle
WHISTLING GRAVEYARD
MERMAID LAGOON
MUSHROOM FOREST
BOTTOMLESS HOLE
LAKE OF LOST THINGS
SERPENT SHOALS

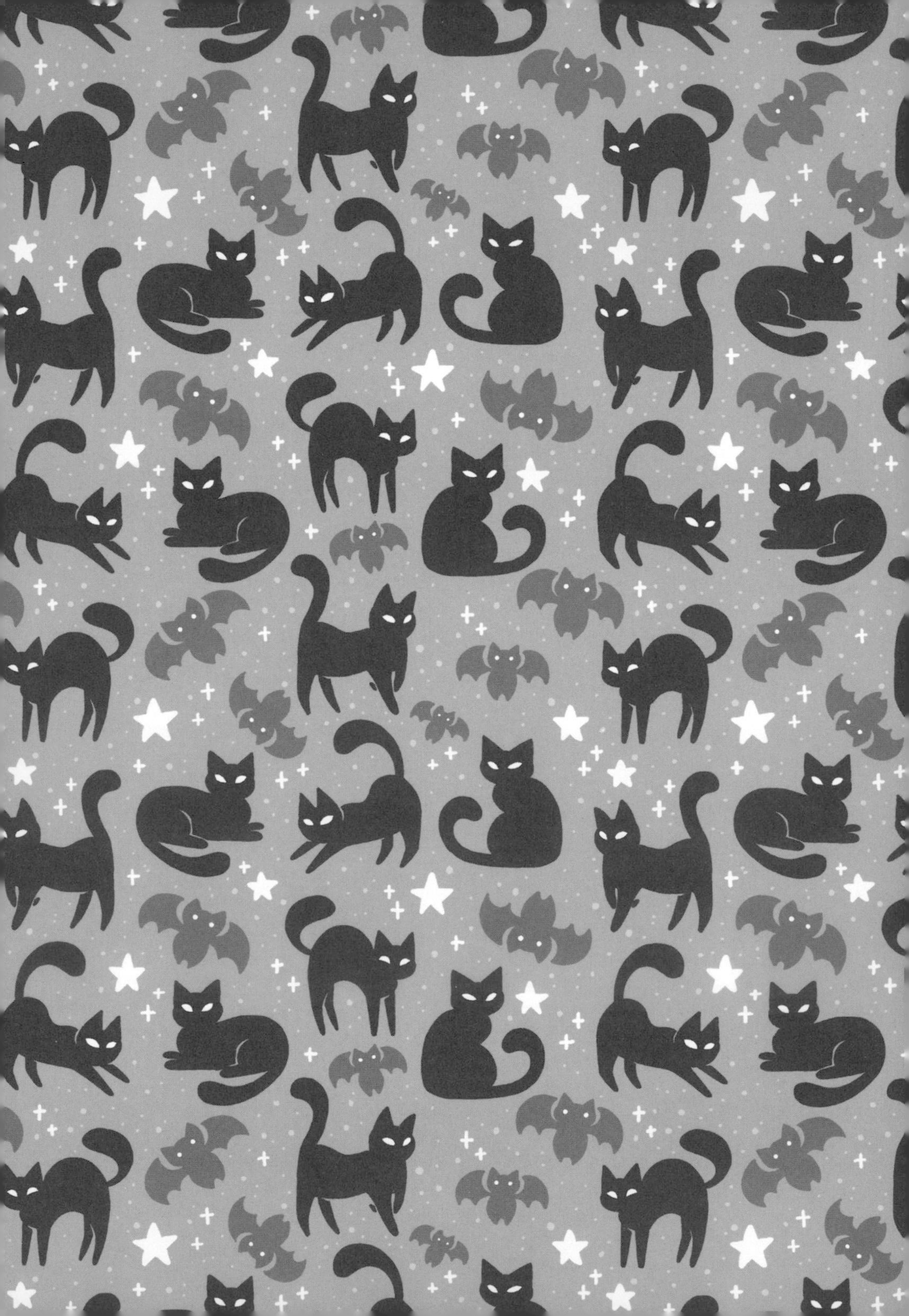

by **MEGGIE RAMM**

AMULET BOOKS • NEW YORK

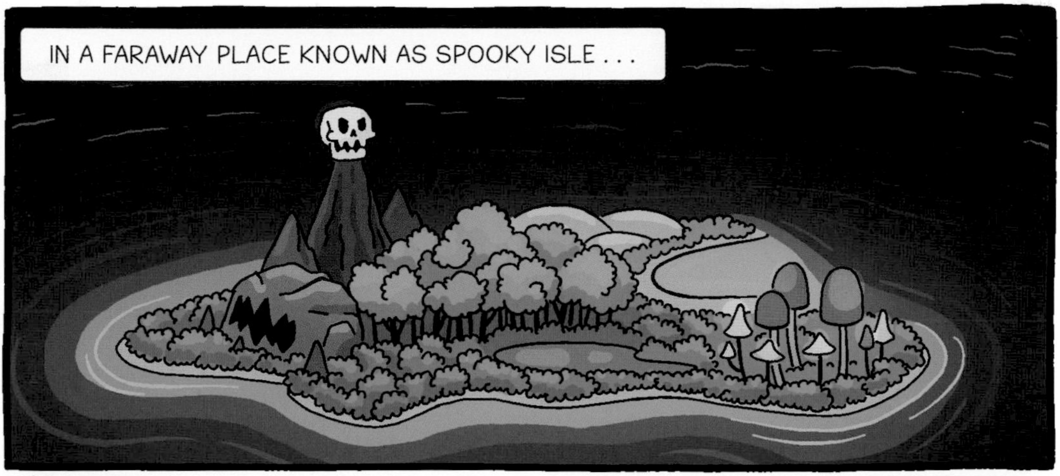
IN A FARAWAY PLACE KNOWN AS SPOOKY ISLE . . .

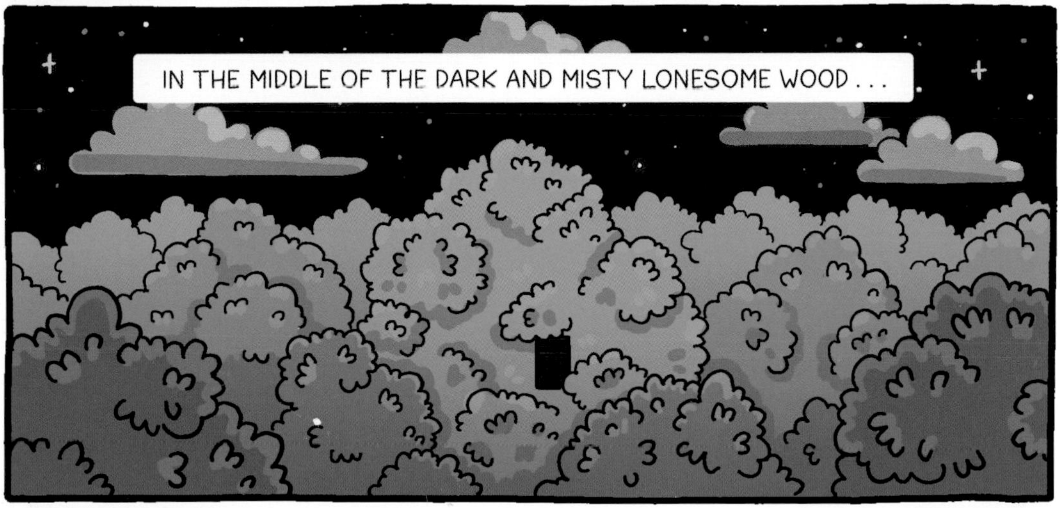
IN THE MIDDLE OF THE DARK AND MISTY LONESOME WOOD . . .

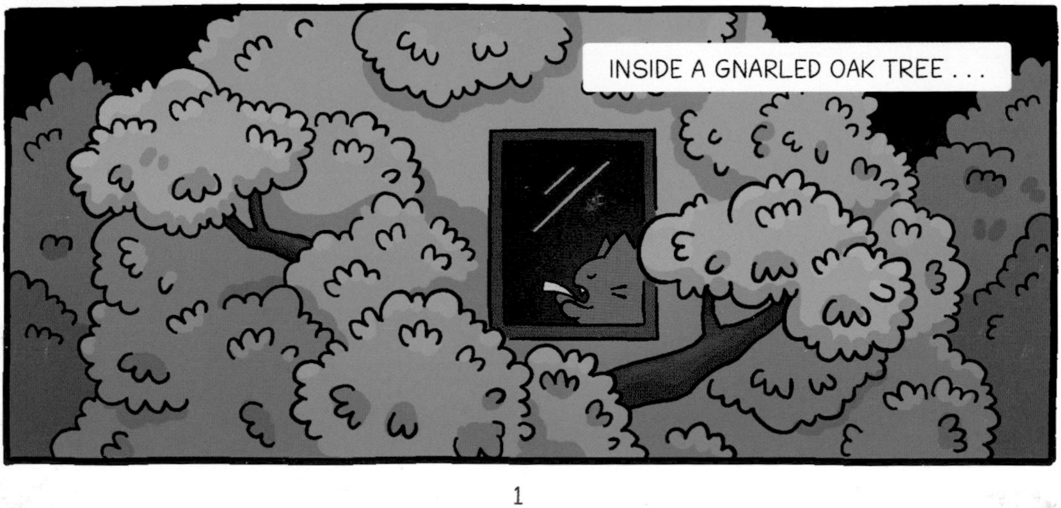
INSIDE A GNARLED OAK TREE . . .

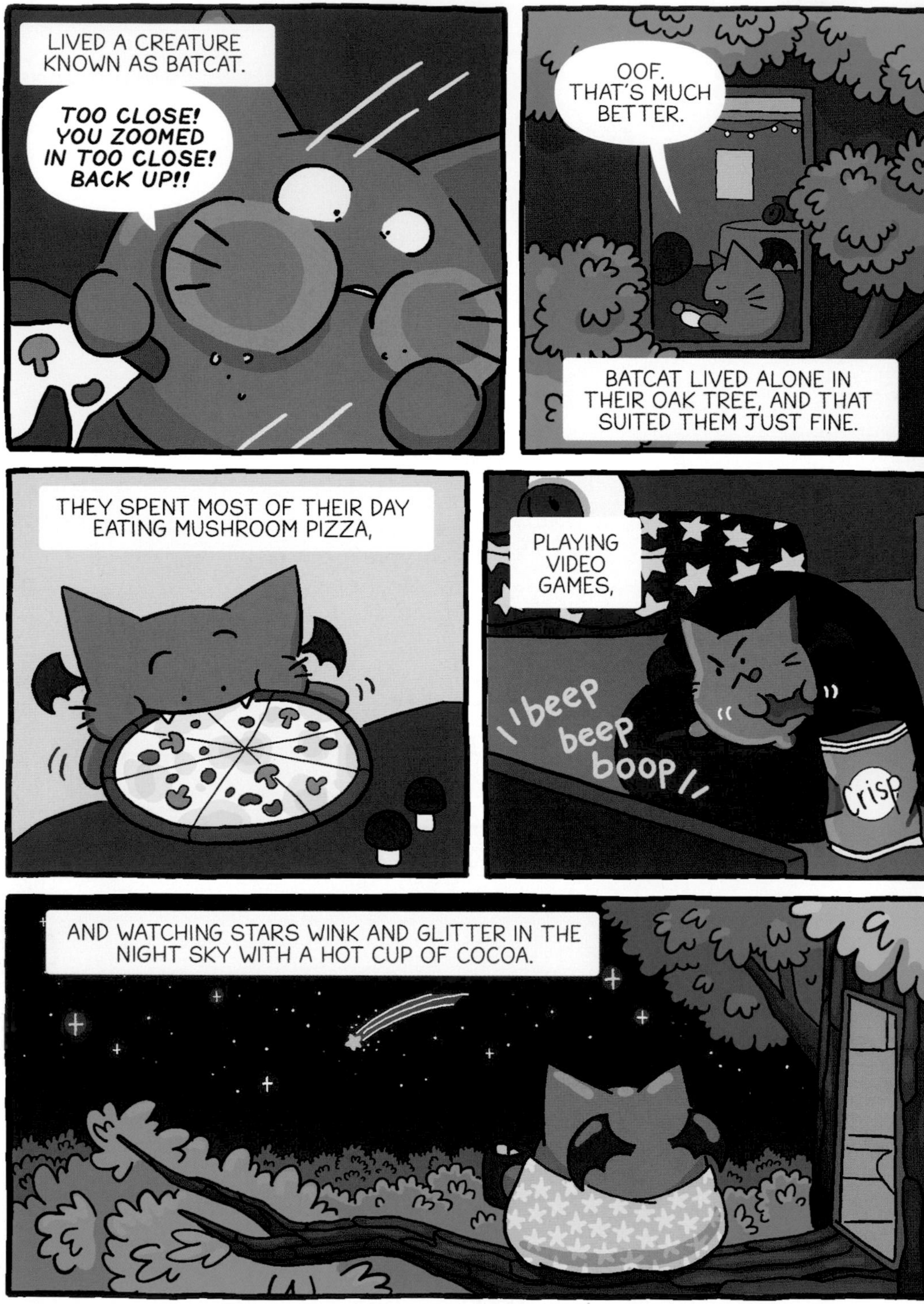
LIVED A CREATURE KNOWN AS BATCAT.
TOO CLOSE! YOU ZOOMED IN TOO CLOSE! BACK UP!!
OOF. THAT'S MUCH BETTER.
BATCAT LIVED ALONE IN THEIR OAK TREE, AND THAT SUITED THEM JUST FINE.
THEY SPENT MOST OF THEIR DAY EATING MUSHROOM PIZZA,
PLAYING VIDEO GAMES,
beep beep boop
Crisp
AND WATCHING STARS WINK AND GLITTER IN THE NIGHT SKY WITH A HOT CUP OF COCOA.

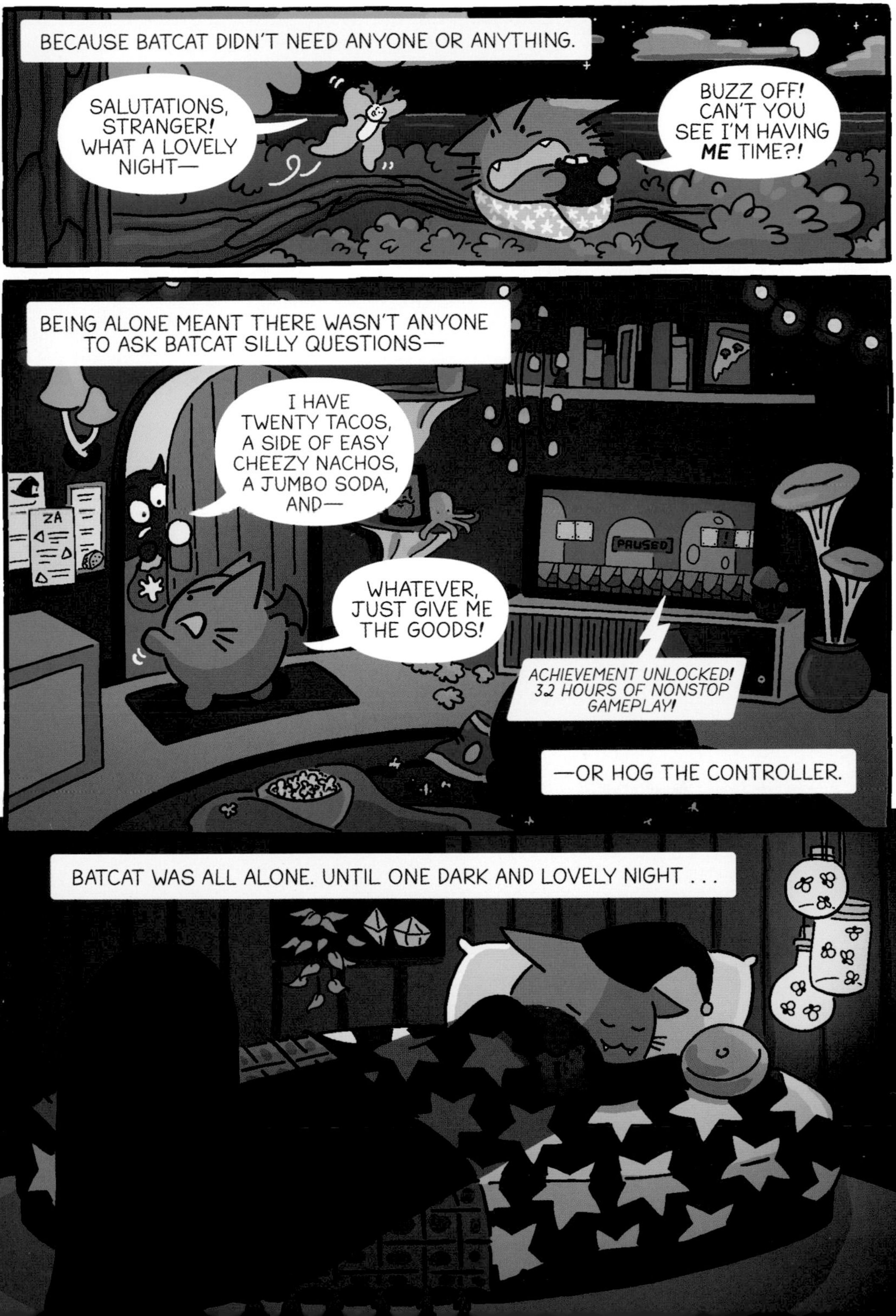
BECAUSE BATCAT DIDN'T NEED ANYONE OR ANYTHING.
SALUTATIONS, STRANGER! WHAT A LOVELY NIGHT—
BUZZ OFF! CAN'T YOU SEE I'M HAVING **ME** TIME?!
BEING ALONE MEANT THERE WASN'T ANYONE TO ASK BATCAT SILLY QUESTIONS—
I HAVE TWENTY TACOS, A SIDE OF EASY CHEEZY NACHOS, A JUMBO SODA, AND—
WHATEVER, JUST GIVE ME THE GOODS!
ZA
PAUSED
ACHIEVEMENT UNLOCKED! 32 HOURS OF NONSTOP GAMEPLAY!
—OR HOG THE CONTROLLER.
BATCAT WAS ALL ALONE. UNTIL ONE DARK AND LOVELY NIGHT . . .

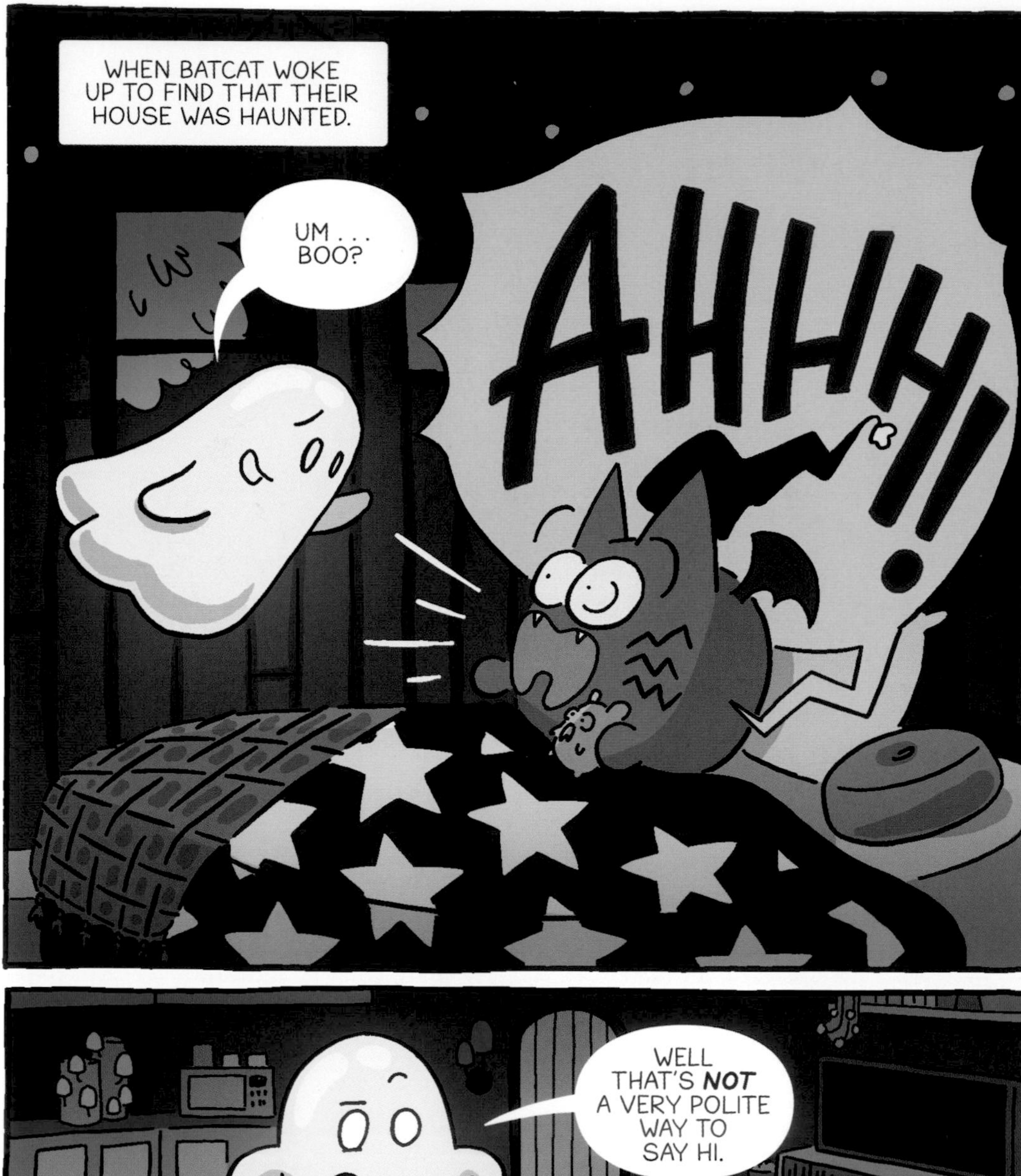
WHEN BATCAT WOKE UP TO FIND THAT THEIR HOUSE WAS HAUNTED.
UM . . . BOO?
AHHH!!

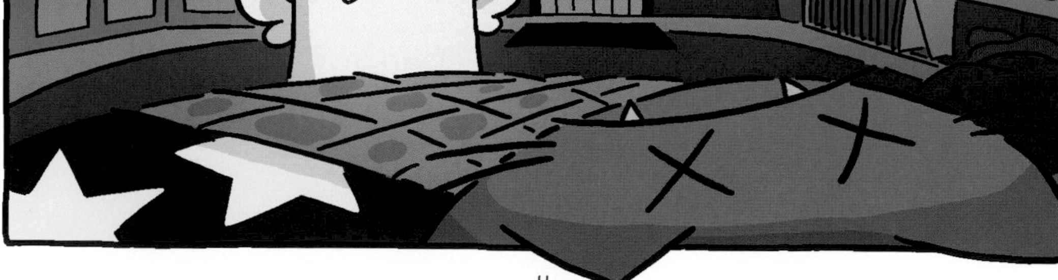
WELL THAT'S **NOT** A VERY POLITE WAY TO SAY HI.

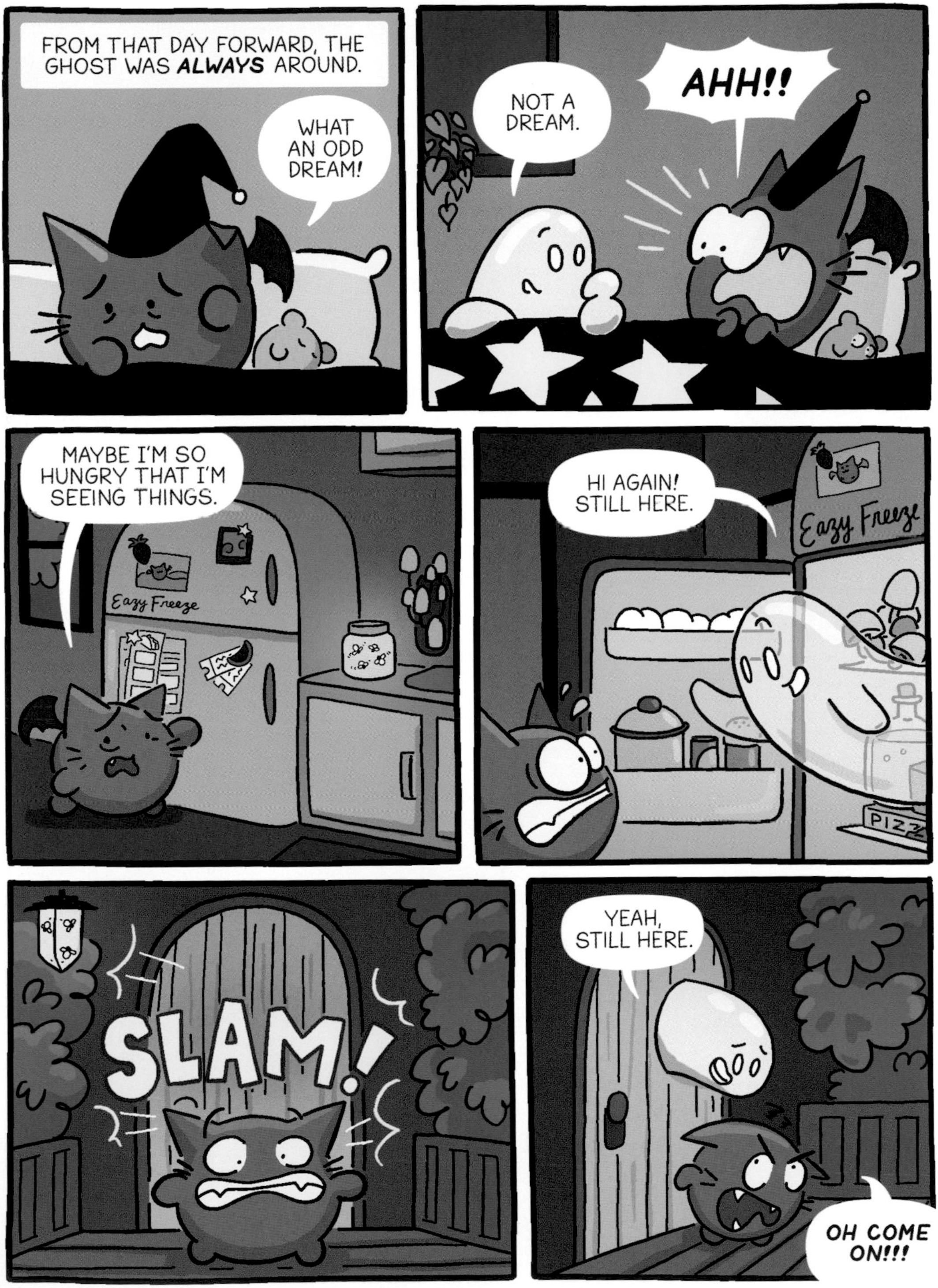

FROM THAT DAY FORWARD, THE GHOST WAS **ALWAYS** AROUND.
WHAT AN ODD DREAM!
NOT A DREAM.
AHH!!
MAYBE I'M SO HUNGRY THAT I'M SEEING THINGS.
Eazy Freeze
HI AGAIN! STILL HERE.
Eazy Freeze
SLAM!
YEAH, STILL HERE.
OH COME ON!!!

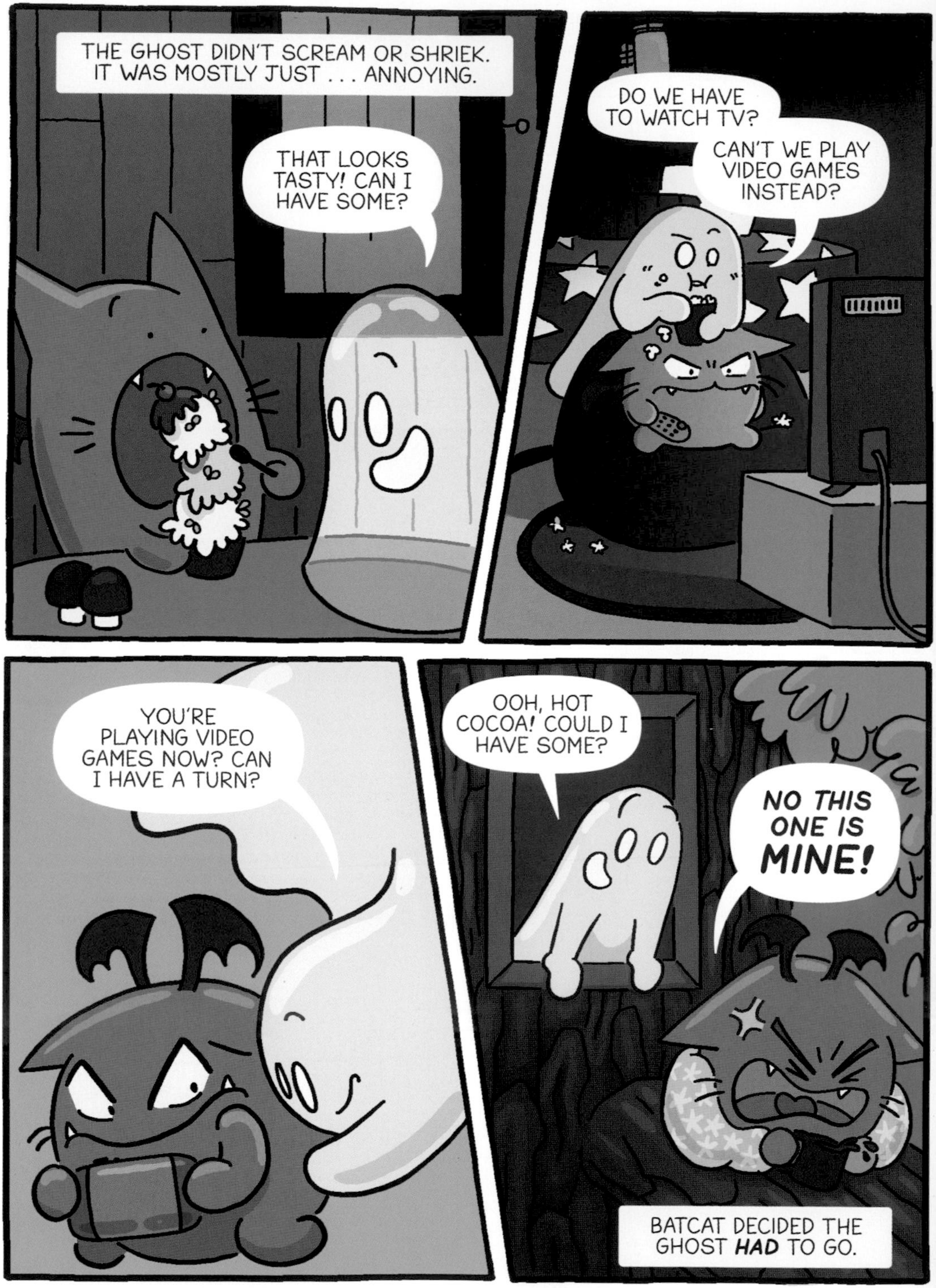
THE GHOST DIDN'T SCREAM OR SHRIEK. IT WAS MOSTLY JUST . . . ANNOYING.
THAT LOOKS TASTY! CAN I HAVE SOME?
DO WE HAVE TO WATCH TV?
CAN'T WE PLAY VIDEO GAMES INSTEAD?
YOU'RE PLAYING VIDEO GAMES NOW? CAN I HAVE A TURN?
OOH, HOT COCOA! COULD I HAVE SOME?
NO THIS ONE IS MINE!
BATCAT DECIDED THE GHOST HAD TO GO.

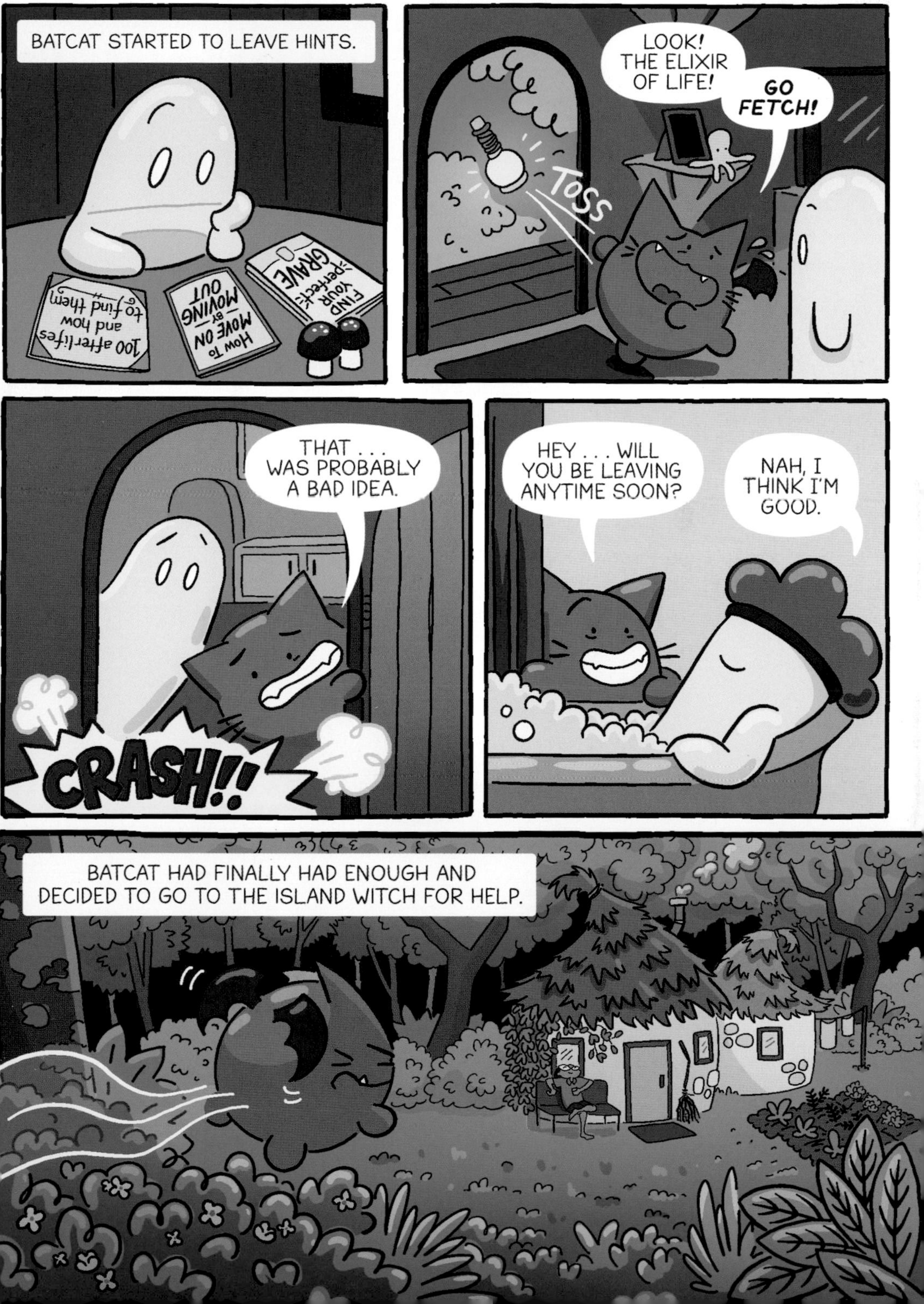
BATCAT STARTED TO LEAVE HINTS.
100 afterlifes and how to find them
How To MOVE ON BY MOVING OUT
FIND YOUR perfect GRAVE
LOOK! THE ELIXIR OF LIFE!
GO FETCH!
TOSS
THAT . . . WAS PROBABLY A BAD IDEA.
CRASH!!
HEY . . . WILL YOU BE LEAVING ANYTIME SOON?
NAH, I THINK I'M GOOD.
BATCAT HAD FINALLY HAD ENOUGH AND DECIDED TO GO TO THE ISLAND WITCH FOR HELP.

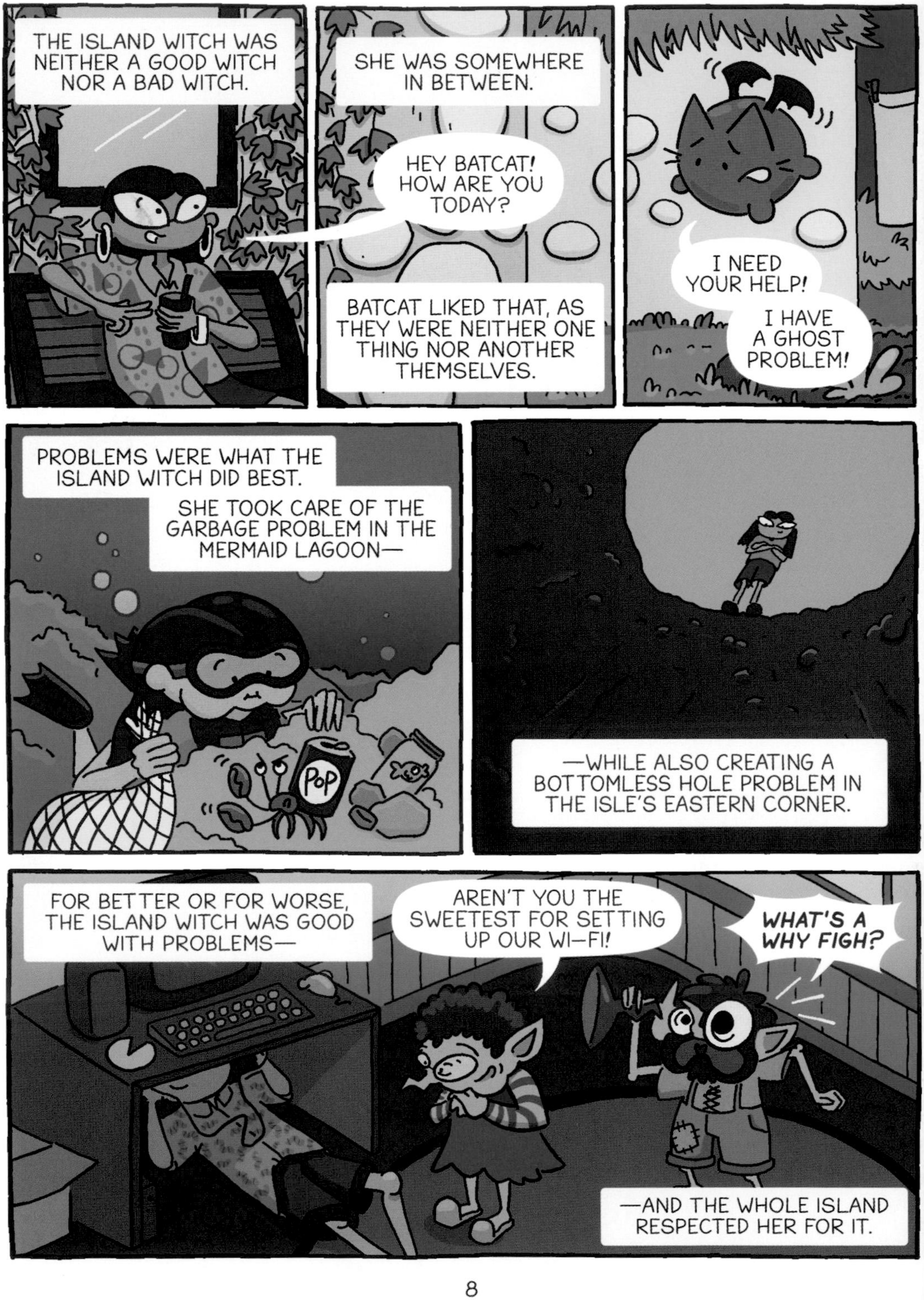
THE ISLAND WITCH WAS NEITHER A GOOD WITCH NOR A BAD WITCH.
SHE WAS SOMEWHERE IN BETWEEN.
HEY BATCAT! HOW ARE YOU TODAY?
BATCAT LIKED THAT, AS THEY WERE NEITHER ONE THING NOR ANOTHER THEMSELVES.
I NEED YOUR HELP!
I HAVE A GHOST PROBLEM!
PROBLEMS WERE WHAT THE ISLAND WITCH DID BEST.
SHE TOOK CARE OF THE GARBAGE PROBLEM IN THE MERMAID LAGOON—
POP
—WHILE ALSO CREATING A BOTTOMLESS HOLE PROBLEM IN THE ISLE'S EASTERN CORNER.
FOR BETTER OR FOR WORSE, THE ISLAND WITCH WAS GOOD WITH PROBLEMS—
AREN'T YOU THE SWEETEST FOR SETTING UP OUR WI-FI!
WHAT'S A WHY FIGH?
—AND THE WHOLE ISLAND RESPECTED HER FOR IT.

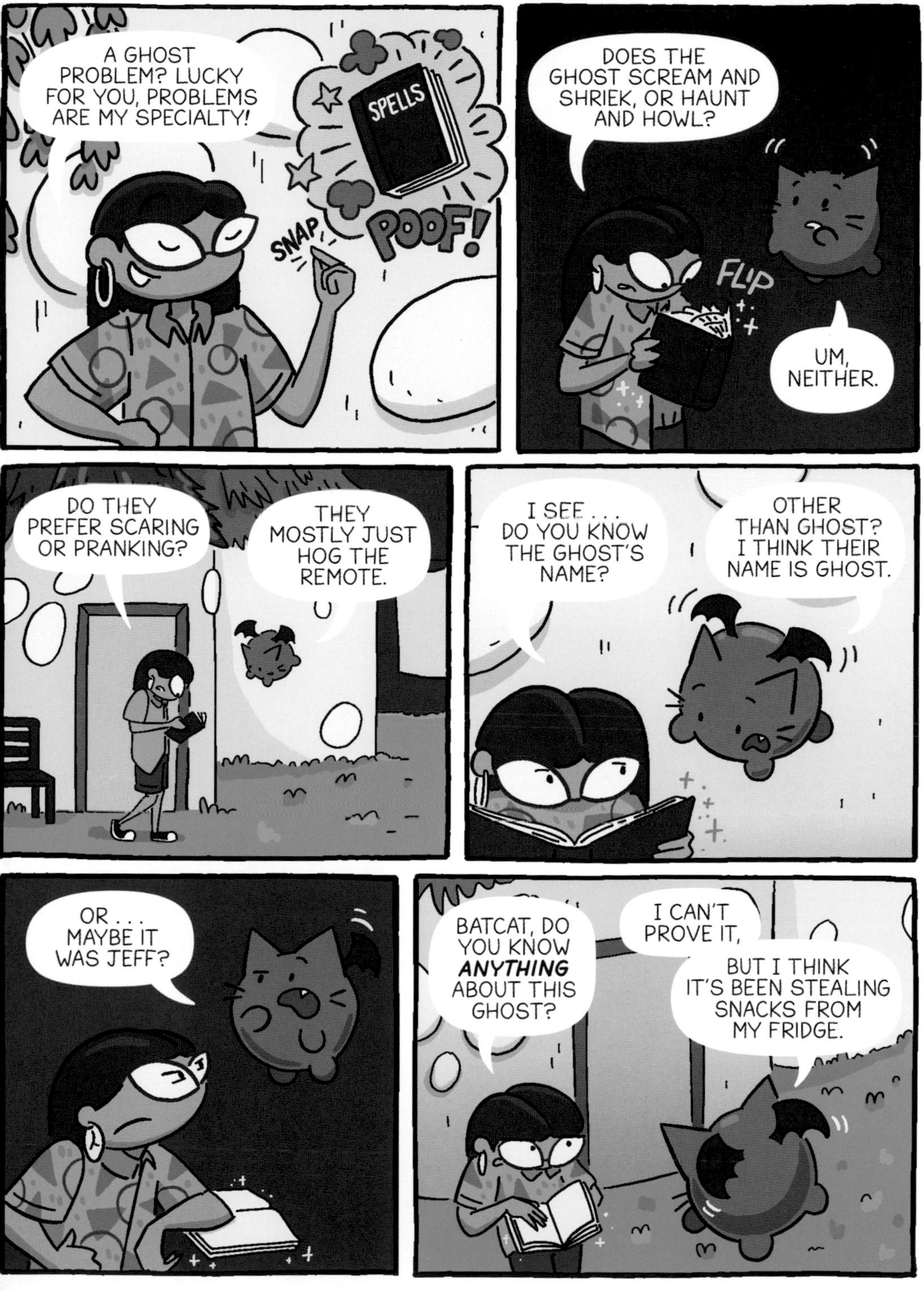
A GHOST PROBLEM? LUCKY FOR YOU, PROBLEMS ARE MY SPECIALTY!
SPELLS
SNAP
POOF!
DOES THE GHOST SCREAM AND SHRIEK, OR HAUNT AND HOWL?
FLIP
UM, NEITHER.
DO THEY PREFER SCARING OR PRANKING?
THEY MOSTLY JUST HOG THE REMOTE.
I SEE . . . DO YOU KNOW THE GHOST'S NAME?
OTHER THAN GHOST? I THINK THEIR NAME IS GHOST.
OR . . . MAYBE IT WAS JEFF?
BATCAT, DO YOU KNOW **ANYTHING** ABOUT THIS GHOST?
I CAN'T PROVE IT,
BUT I THINK IT'S BEEN STEALING SNACKS FROM MY FRIDGE.

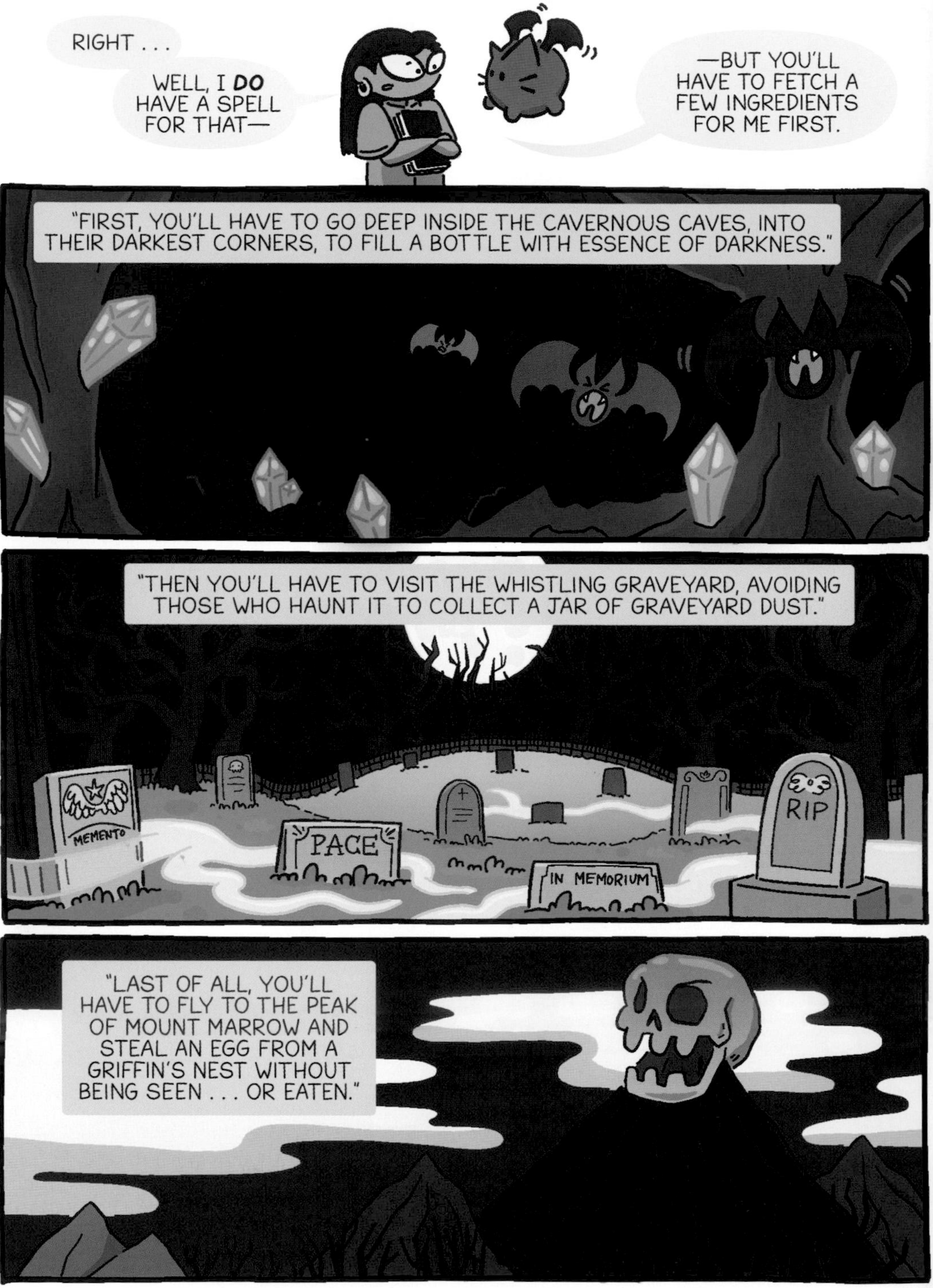
RIGHT . . .
WELL, I **DO** HAVE A SPELL FOR THAT—
—BUT YOU'LL HAVE TO FETCH A FEW INGREDIENTS FOR ME FIRST.
"FIRST, YOU'LL HAVE TO GO DEEP INSIDE THE CAVERNOUS CAVES, INTO THEIR DARKEST CORNERS, TO FILL A BOTTLE WITH ESSENCE OF DARKNESS."
"THEN YOU'LL HAVE TO VISIT THE WHISTLING GRAVEYARD, AVOIDING THOSE WHO HAUNT IT TO COLLECT A JAR OF GRAVEYARD DUST."
MEMENTO
PACE
IN MEMORIUM
RIP
"LAST OF ALL, YOU'LL HAVE TO FLY TO THE PEAK OF MOUNT MARROW AND STEAL AN EGG FROM A GRIFFIN'S NEST WITHOUT BEING SEEN . . . OR EATEN."

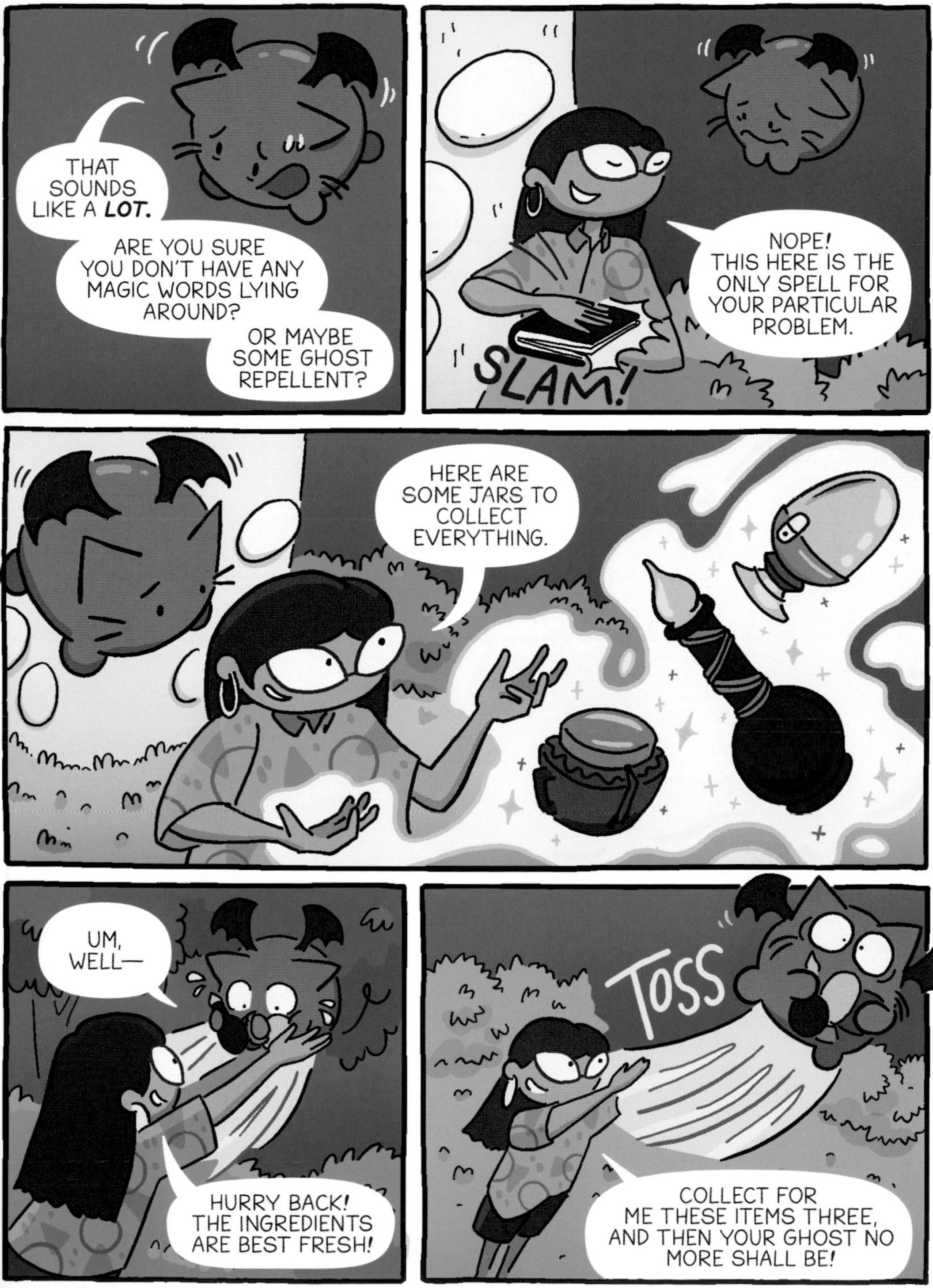
THAT SOUNDS LIKE A **LOT.**
ARE YOU SURE YOU DON'T HAVE ANY MAGIC WORDS LYING AROUND?
OR MAYBE SOME GHOST REPELLENT?
NOPE! THIS HERE IS THE ONLY SPELL FOR YOUR PARTICULAR PROBLEM.
SLAM!
HERE ARE SOME JARS TO COLLECT EVERYTHING.
UM, WELL—
HURRY BACK! THE INGREDIENTS ARE BEST FRESH!
TOSS
COLLECT FOR ME THESE ITEMS THREE, AND THEN YOUR GHOST NO MORE SHALL BE!

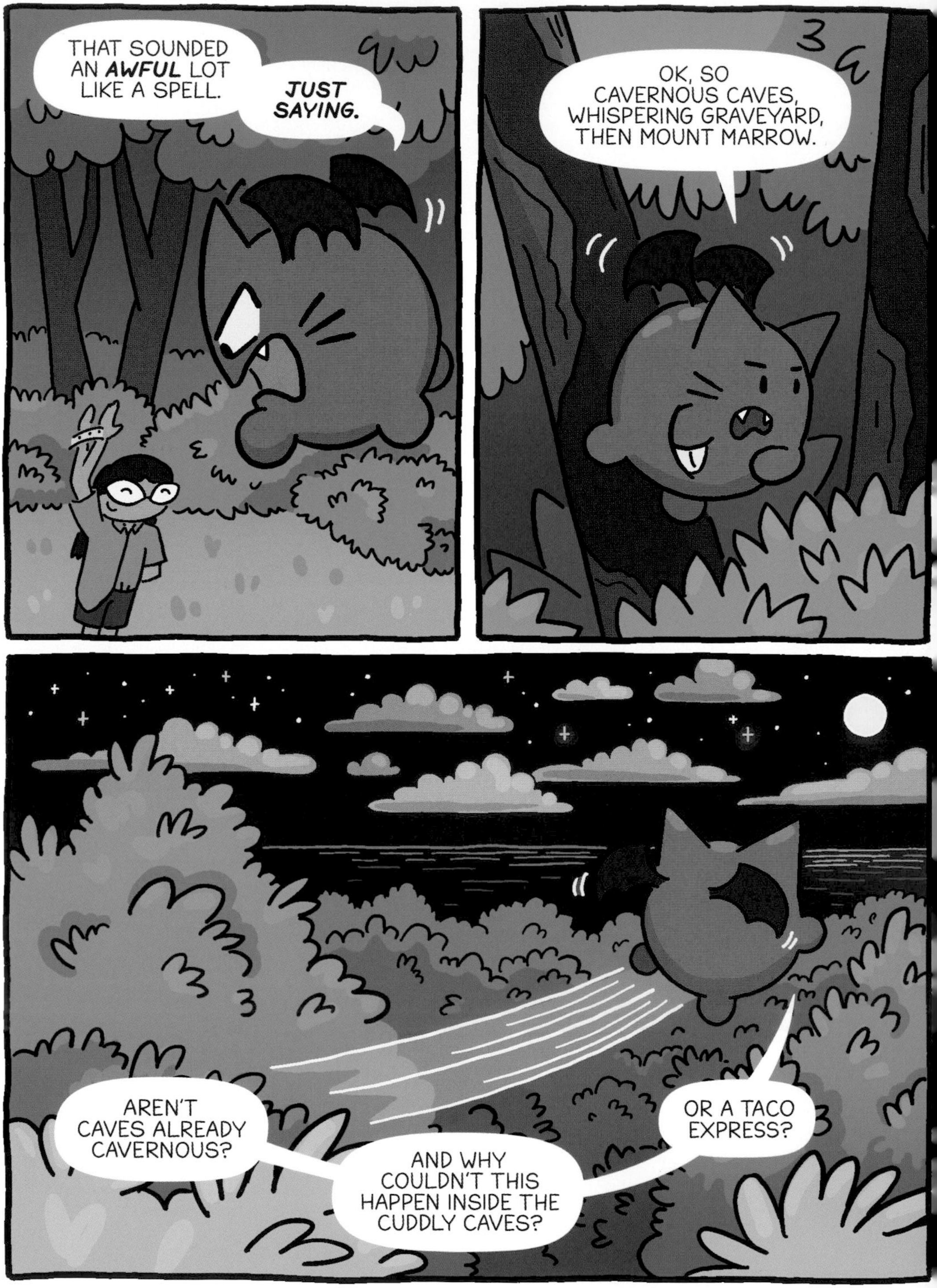
THAT SOUNDED AN **AWFUL** LOT LIKE A SPELL.
JUST SAYING.
OK, SO CAVERNOUS CAVES, WHISPERING GRAVEYARD, THEN MOUNT MARROW.
AREN'T CAVES ALREADY CAVERNOUS?
AND WHY COULDN'T THIS HAPPEN INSIDE THE CUDDLY CAVES?
OR A TACO EXPRESS?

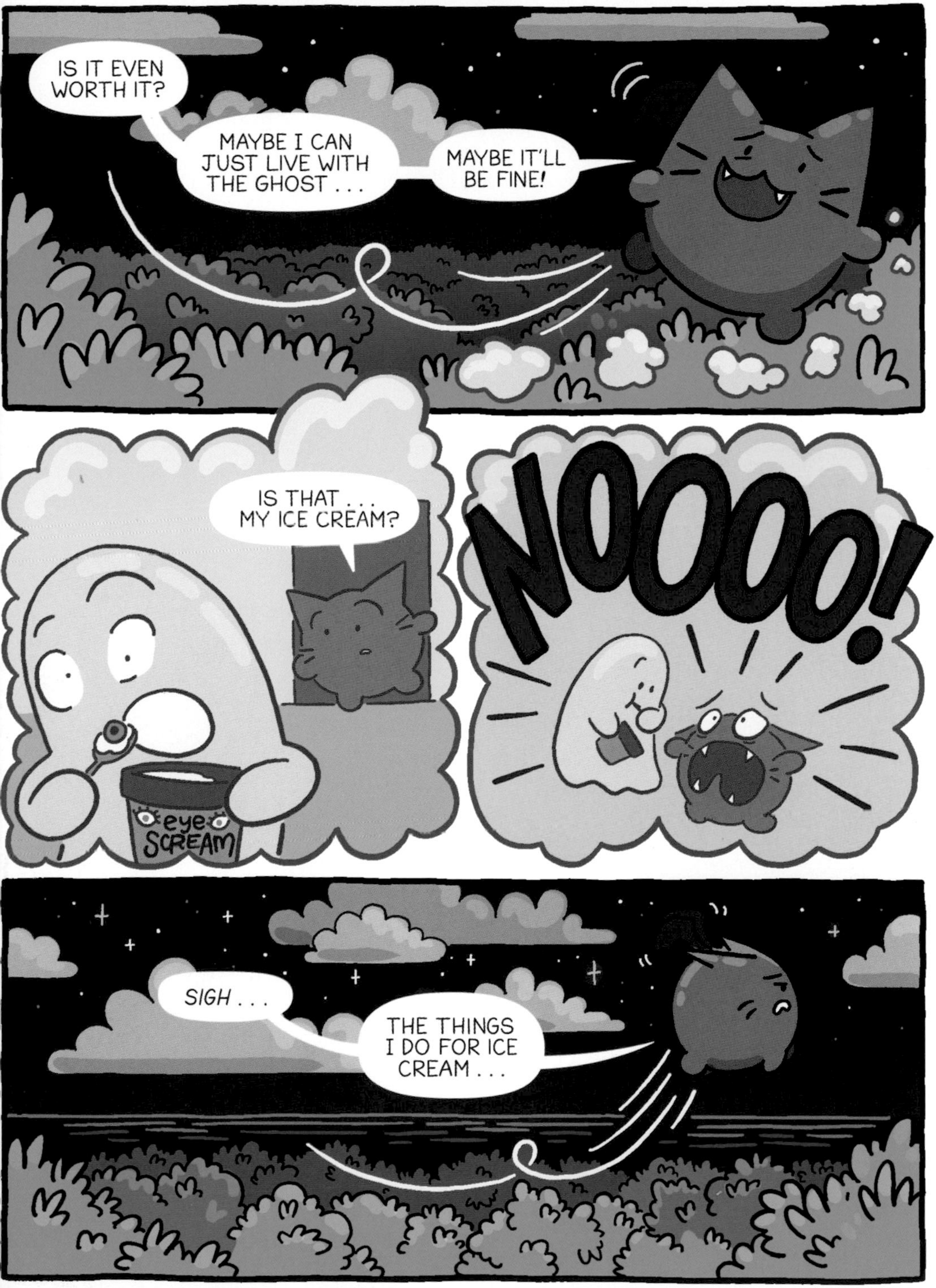

IS IT EVEN WORTH IT?
MAYBE I CAN JUST LIVE WITH THE GHOST . . .
MAYBE IT'LL BE FINE!
IS THAT . . . MY ICE CREAM?
eye SCREAM
NOOOO!
SIGH . . .
THE THINGS I DO FOR ICE CREAM . . .

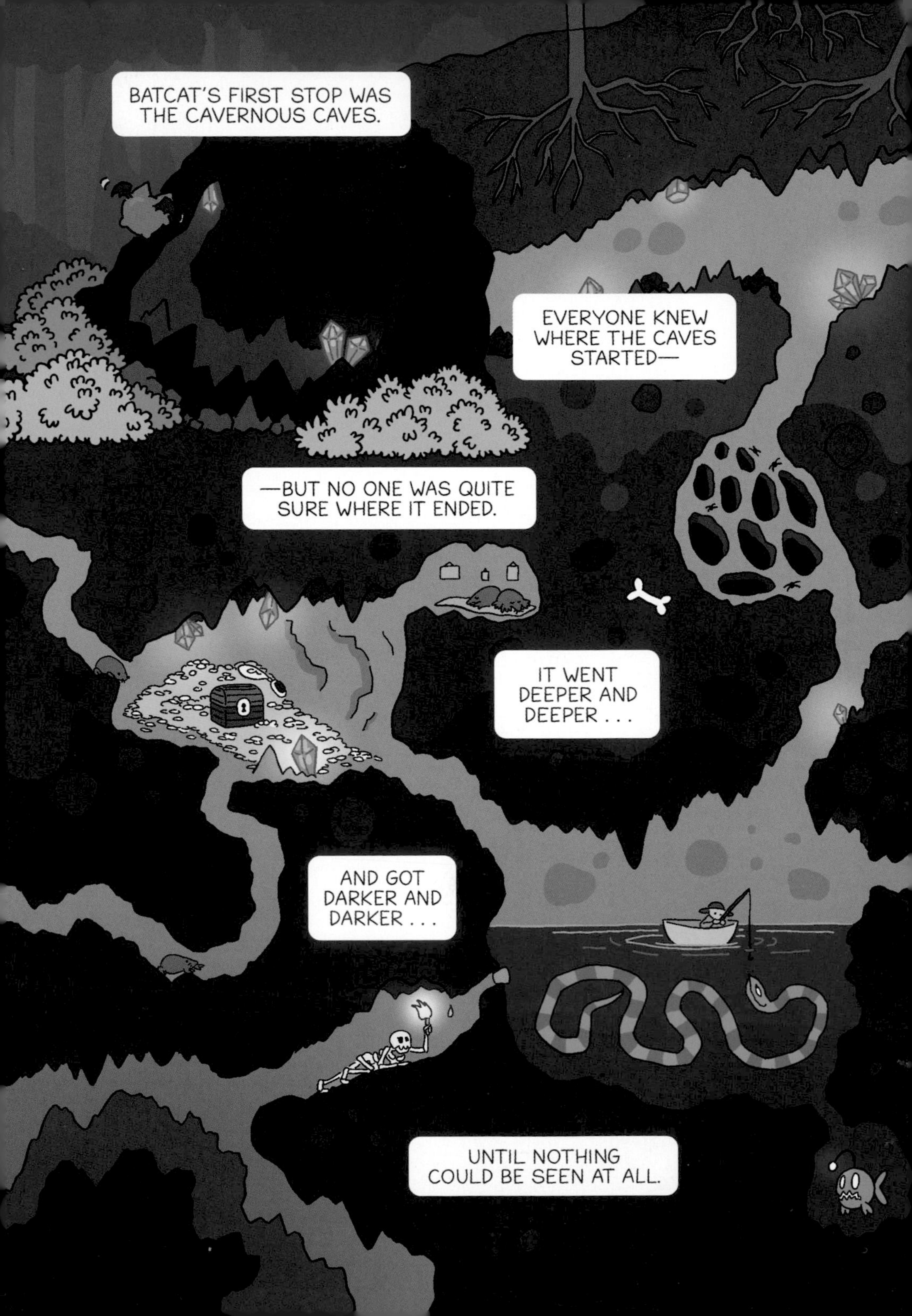
BATCAT'S FIRST STOP WAS THE CAVERNOUS CAVES.
EVERYONE KNEW WHERE THE CAVES STARTED—
—BUT NO ONE WAS QUITE SURE WHERE IT ENDED.
IT WENT DEEPER AND DEEPER . . .
AND GOT DARKER AND DARKER . . .
UNTIL NOTHING COULD BE SEEN AT ALL.

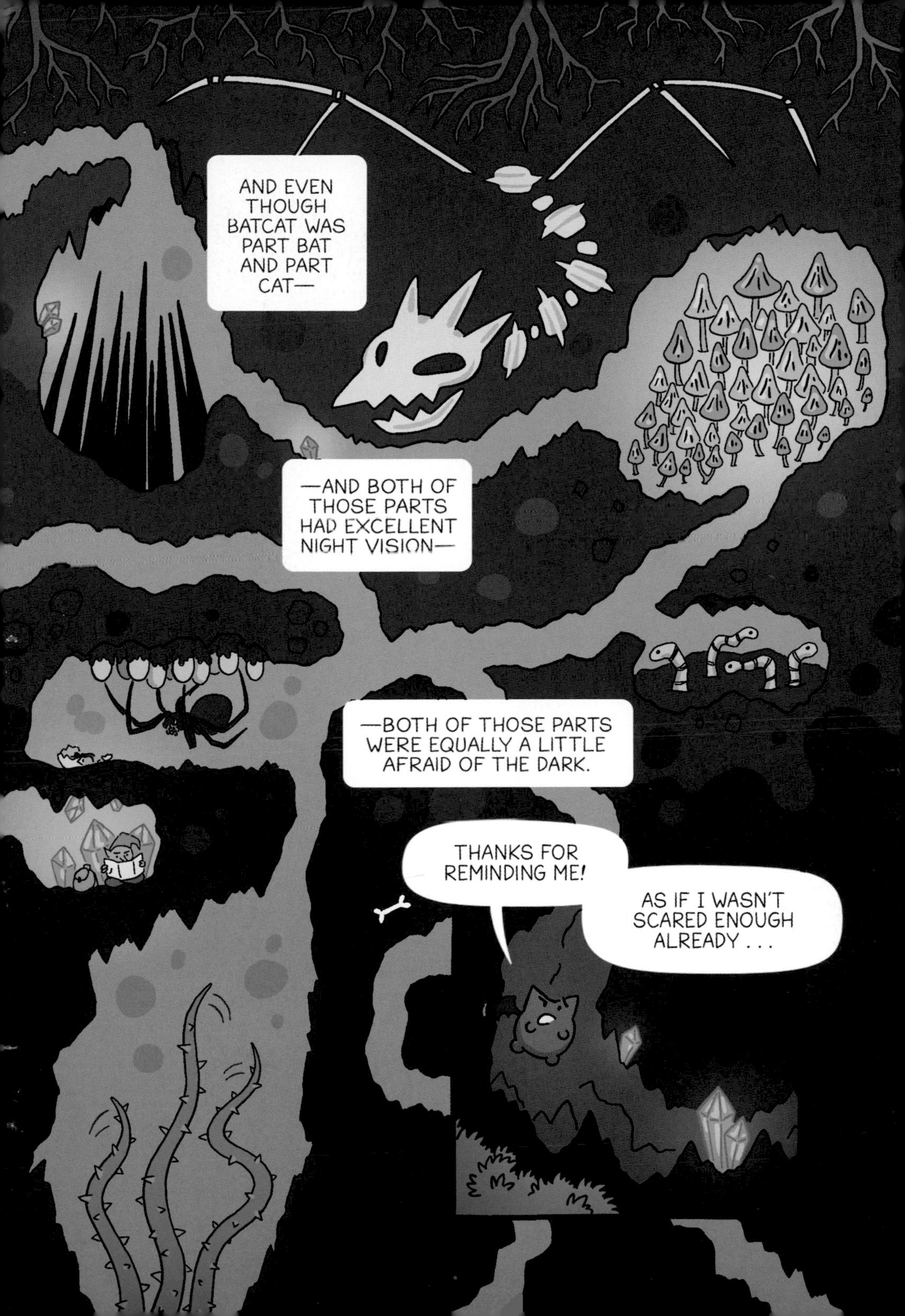
AND EVEN THOUGH BATCAT WAS PART BAT AND PART CAT—
—AND BOTH OF THOSE PARTS HAD EXCELLENT NIGHT VISION—
—BOTH OF THOSE PARTS WERE EQUALLY A LITTLE AFRAID OF THE DARK.
THANKS FOR REMINDING ME!
AS IF I WASN'T SCARED ENOUGH ALREADY . . .

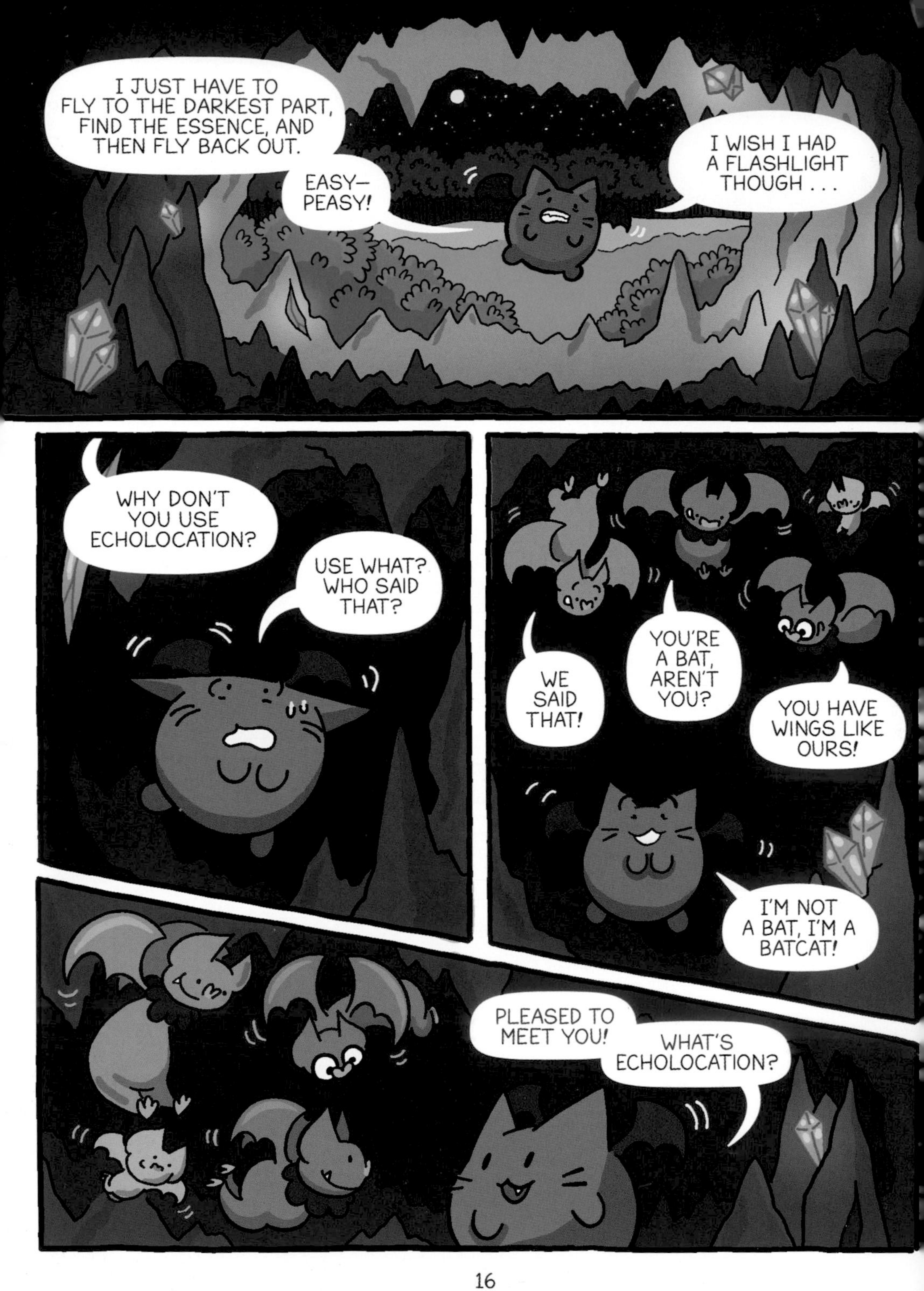
I JUST HAVE TO FLY TO THE DARKEST PART, FIND THE ESSENCE, AND THEN FLY BACK OUT.
EASY—PEASY!
I WISH I HAD A FLASHLIGHT THOUGH . . .
WHY DON'T YOU USE ECHOLOCATION?
USE WHAT? WHO SAID THAT?
WE SAID THAT!
YOU'RE A BAT, AREN'T YOU?
YOU HAVE WINGS LIKE OURS!
I'M NOT A BAT, I'M A BATCAT!
PLEASED TO MEET YOU!
WHAT'S ECHOLOCATION?

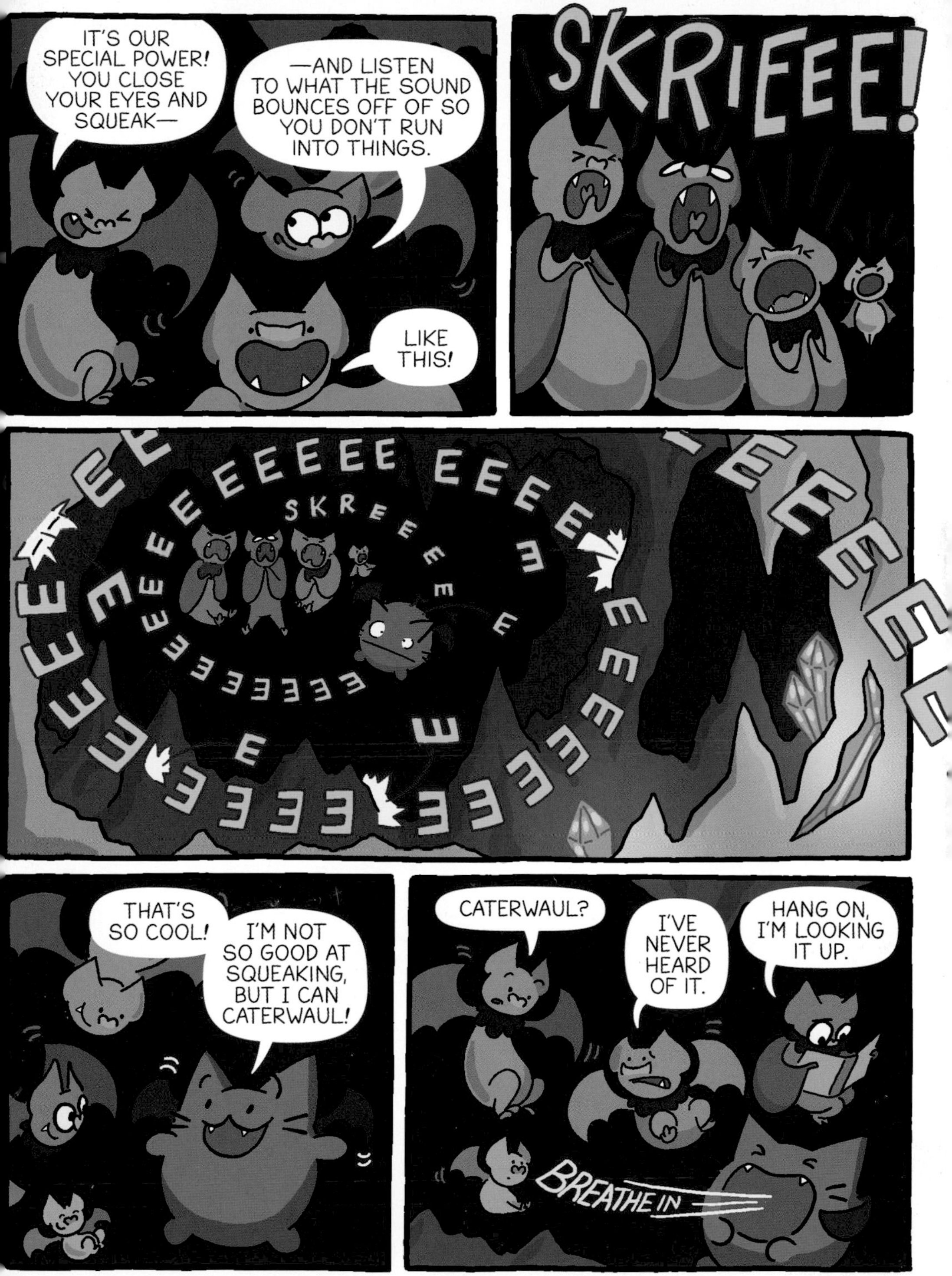
IT'S OUR SPECIAL POWER! YOU CLOSE YOUR EYES AND SQUEAK—
—AND LISTEN TO WHAT THE SOUND BOUNCES OFF OF SO YOU DON'T RUN INTO THINGS.
LIKE THIS!
SKRIEEE!
SKREEEEEEE
THAT'S SO COOL!
I'M NOT SO GOOD AT SQUEAKING, BUT I CAN CATERWAUL!
CATERWAUL?
I'VE NEVER HEARD OF IT.
HANG ON, I'M LOOKING IT UP.
BREATHE IN

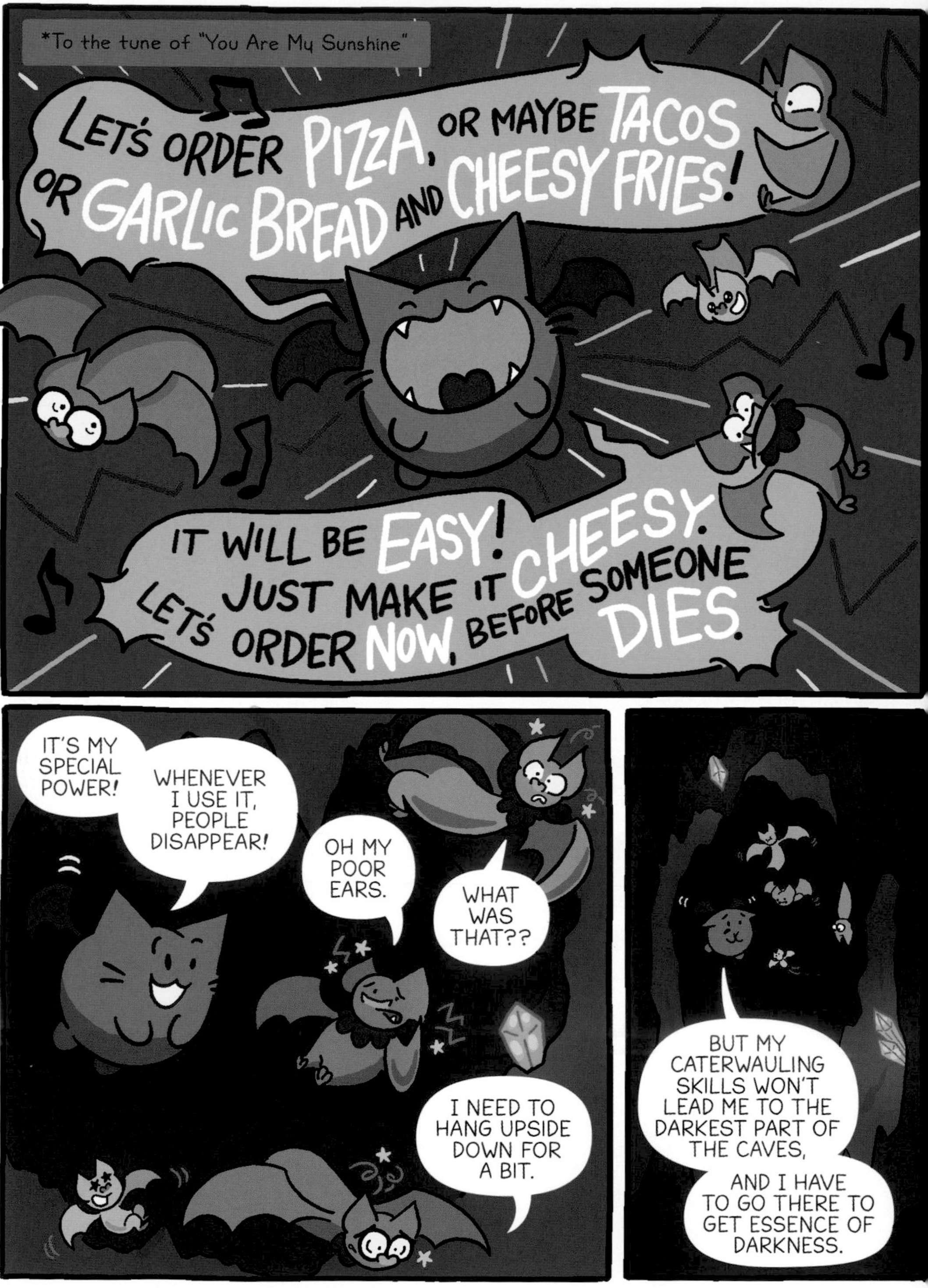

*To the tune of "You Are My Sunshine"
LET'S ORDER PIZZA, OR MAYBE TACOS OR GARLIC BREAD AND CHEESY FRIES!
IT WILL BE EASY! JUST MAKE IT CHEESY. LET'S ORDER NOW, BEFORE SOMEONE DIES.
IT'S MY SPECIAL POWER!
WHENEVER I USE IT, PEOPLE DISAPPEAR!
OH MY POOR EARS.
WHAT WAS THAT??
I NEED TO HANG UPSIDE DOWN FOR A BIT.
BUT MY CATERWAULING SKILLS WON'T LEAD ME TO THE DARKEST PART OF THE CAVES,
AND I HAVE TO GO THERE TO GET ESSENCE OF DARKNESS.

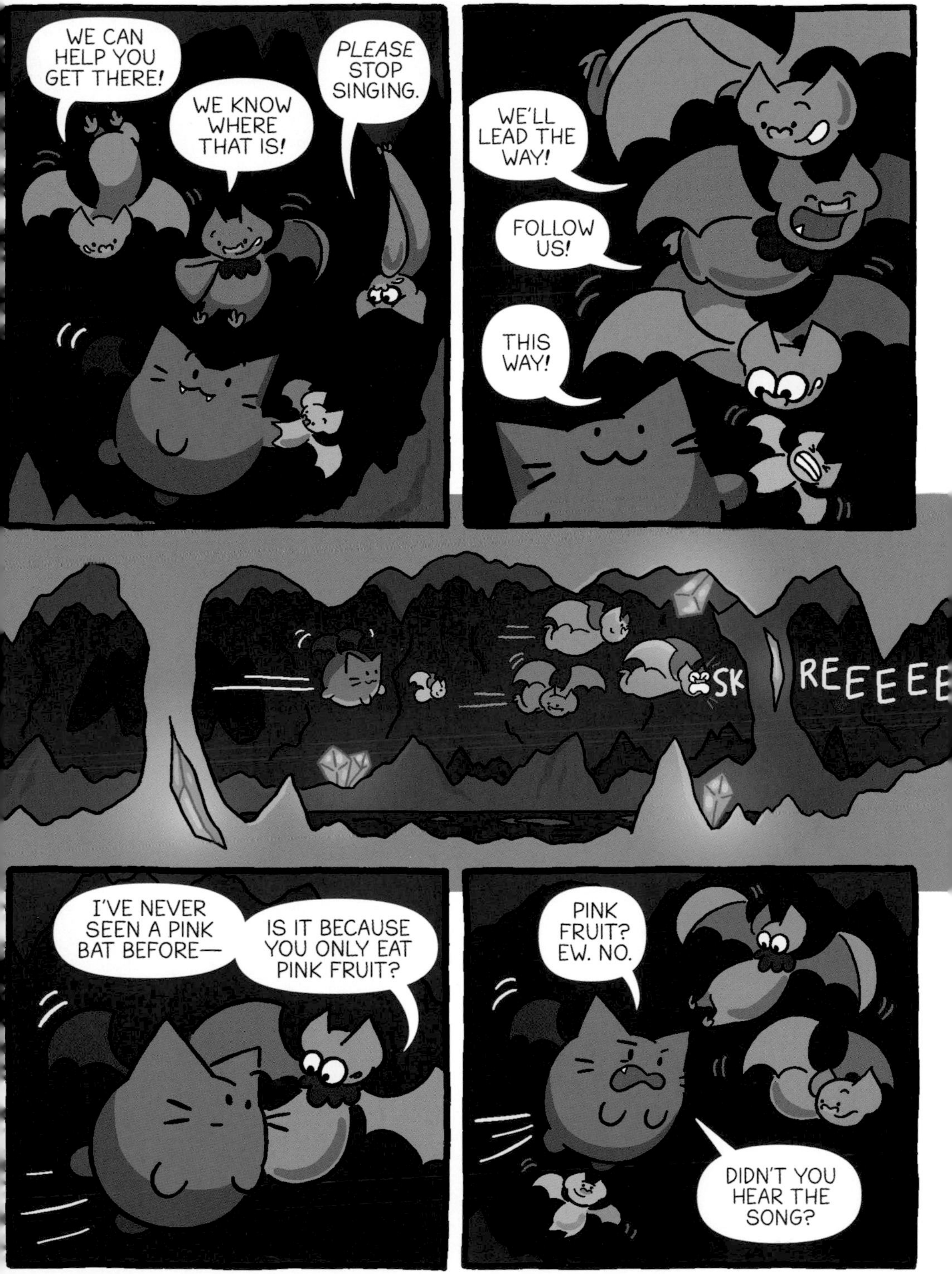
WE CAN HELP YOU GET THERE!
WE KNOW WHERE THAT IS!
PLEASE STOP SINGING.
WE'LL LEAD THE WAY!
FOLLOW US!
THIS WAY!
SK
REEEEEE
I'VE NEVER SEEN A PINK BAT BEFORE—
IS IT BECAUSE YOU ONLY EAT PINK FRUIT?
PINK FRUIT? EW. NO.
DIDN'T YOU HEAR THE SONG?

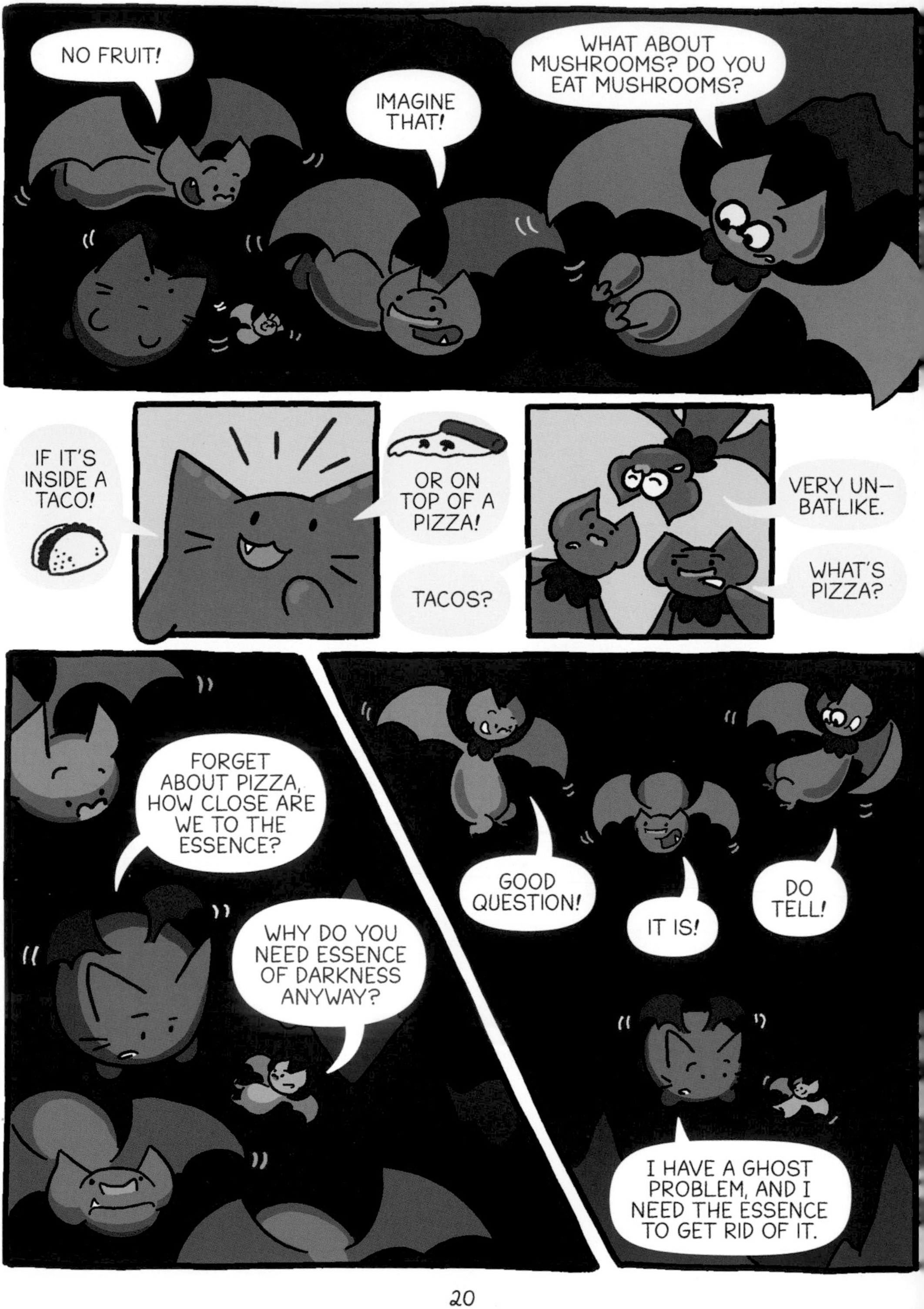
NO FRUIT!
IMAGINE THAT!
WHAT ABOUT MUSHROOMS? DO YOU EAT MUSHROOMS?
IF IT'S INSIDE A TACO!
OR ON TOP OF A PIZZA!
TACOS?
VERY UN-BATLIKE.
WHAT'S PIZZA?
FORGET ABOUT PIZZA, HOW CLOSE ARE WE TO THE ESSENCE?
WHY DO YOU NEED ESSENCE OF DARKNESS ANYWAY?
GOOD QUESTION!
IT IS!
DO TELL!
I HAVE A GHOST PROBLEM, AND I NEED THE ESSENCE TO GET RID OF IT.

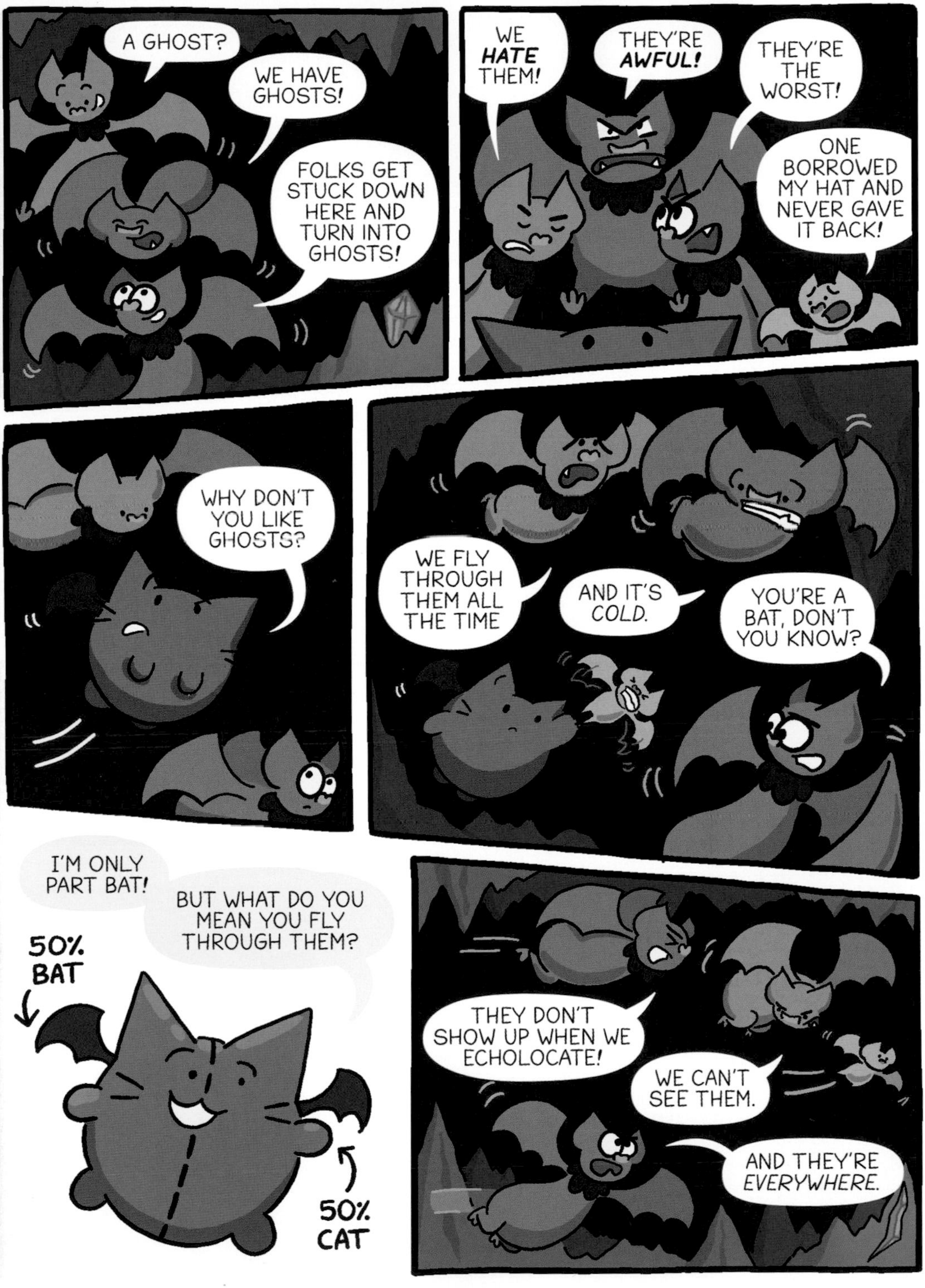
A GHOST?
WE HAVE GHOSTS!
FOLKS GET STUCK DOWN HERE AND TURN INTO GHOSTS!
WE **HATE** THEM!
THEY'RE ***AWFUL!***
THEY'RE THE WORST!
ONE BORROWED MY HAT AND NEVER GAVE IT BACK!
WHY DON'T YOU LIKE GHOSTS?
WE FLY THROUGH THEM ALL THE TIME
AND IT'S *COLD*.
YOU'RE A BAT, DON'T YOU KNOW?
I'M ONLY PART BAT!
BUT WHAT DO YOU MEAN YOU FLY THROUGH THEM?
50% BAT
50% CAT
THEY DON'T SHOW UP WHEN WE ECHOLOCATE!
WE CAN'T SEE THEM.
AND THEY'RE *EVERYWHERE*.

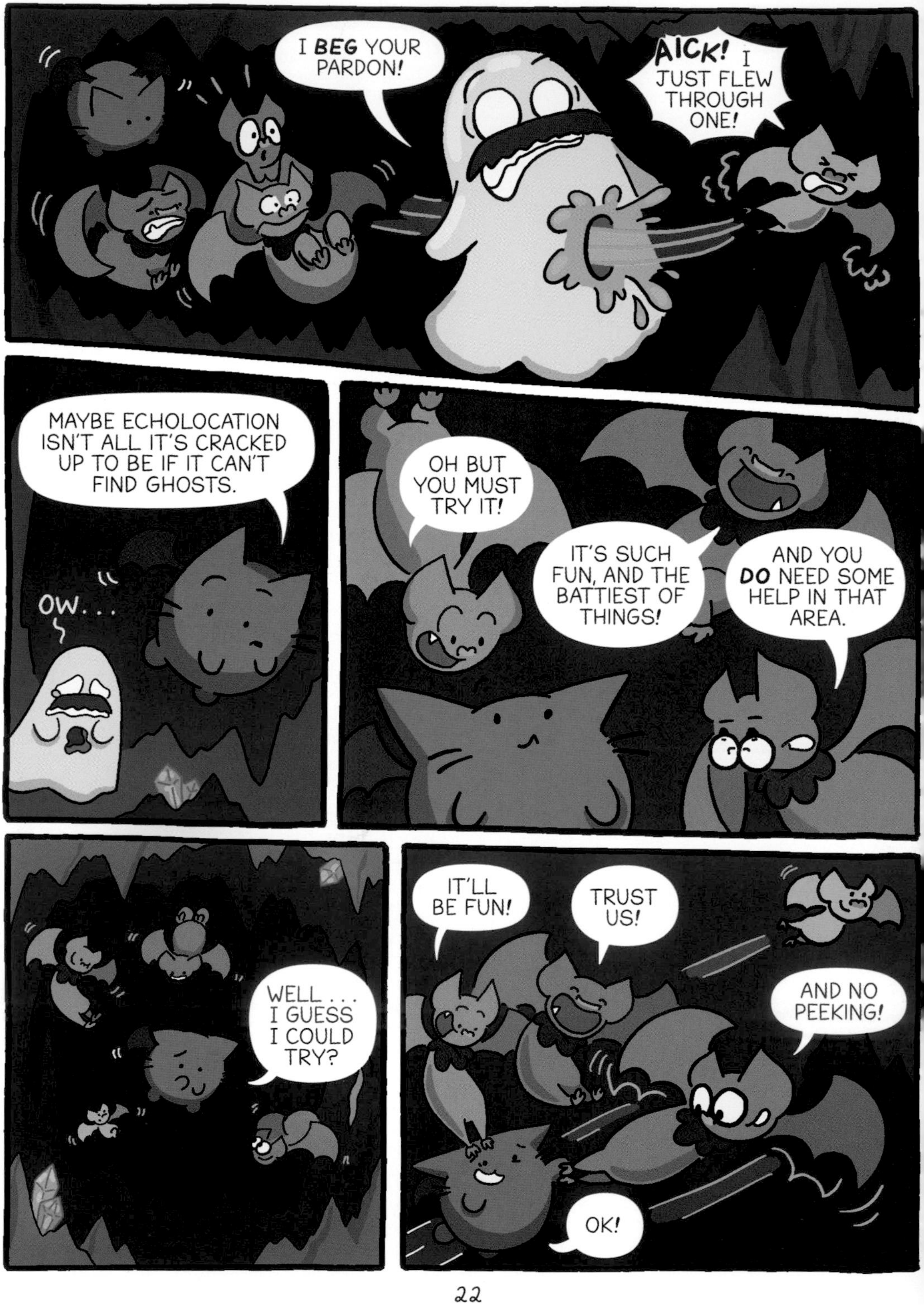
I **BEG** YOUR PARDON!
AICK! I JUST FLEW THROUGH ONE!
MAYBE ECHOLOCATION ISN'T ALL IT'S CRACKED UP TO BE IF IT CAN'T FIND GHOSTS.
OW...
OH BUT YOU MUST TRY IT!
IT'S SUCH FUN, AND THE BATTIEST OF THINGS!
AND YOU **DO** NEED SOME HELP IN THAT AREA.
WELL... I GUESS I COULD TRY?
IT'LL BE FUN!
TRUST US!
AND NO PEEKING!
OK!

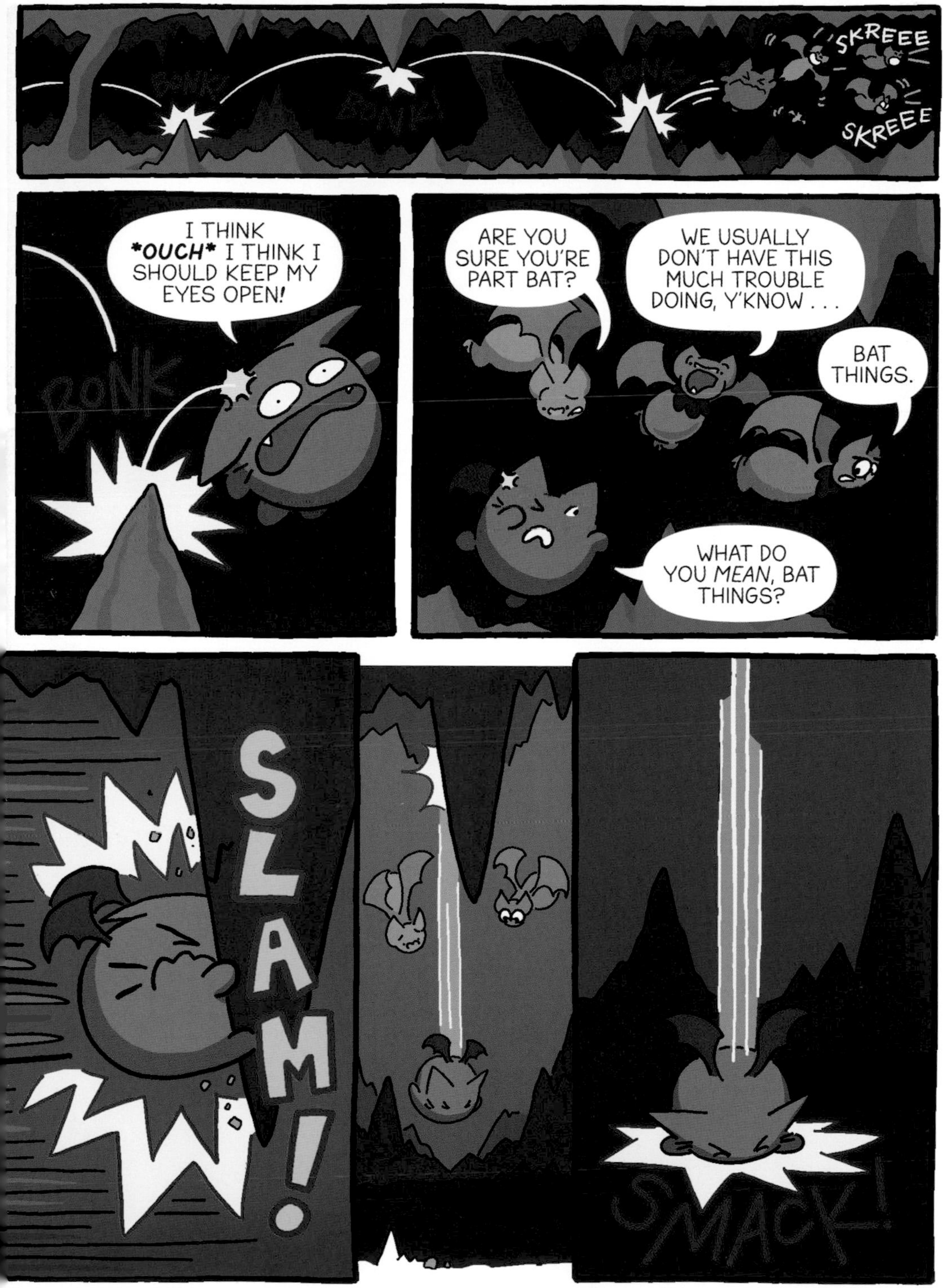
BONK!
BONK!
BONK!
SKREEE
SKREEE
I THINK *OUCH* I THINK I SHOULD KEEP MY EYES OPEN!
BONK
ARE YOU SURE YOU'RE PART BAT?
WE USUALLY DON'T HAVE THIS MUCH TROUBLE DOING, Y'KNOW . . .
BAT THINGS.
WHAT DO YOU MEAN, BAT THINGS?
SLAM!
SMACK!

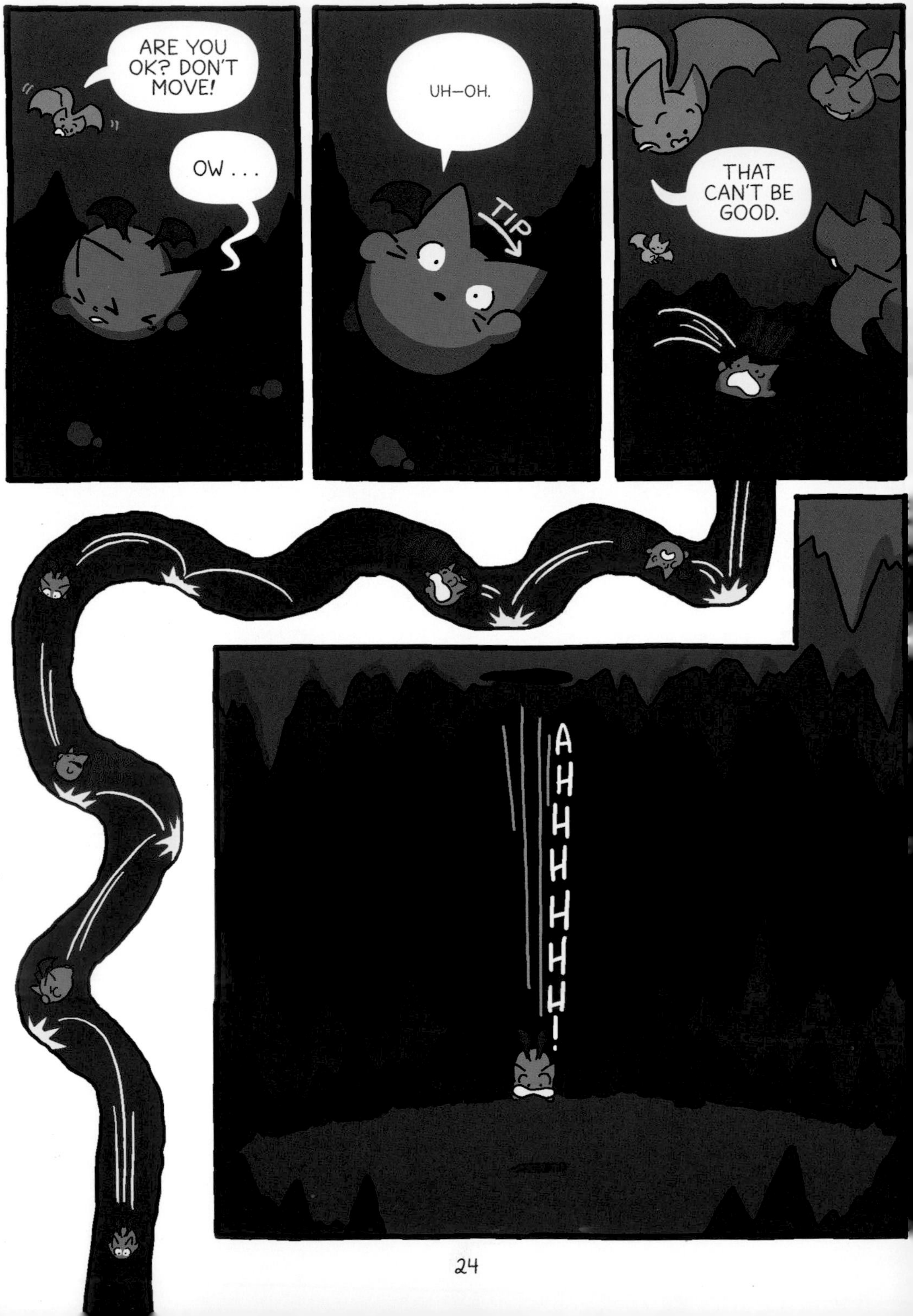
ARE YOU OK? DON'T MOVE!
OW . . .
UH-OH.
TIP
THAT CAN'T BE GOOD.
AHHHHHHH!

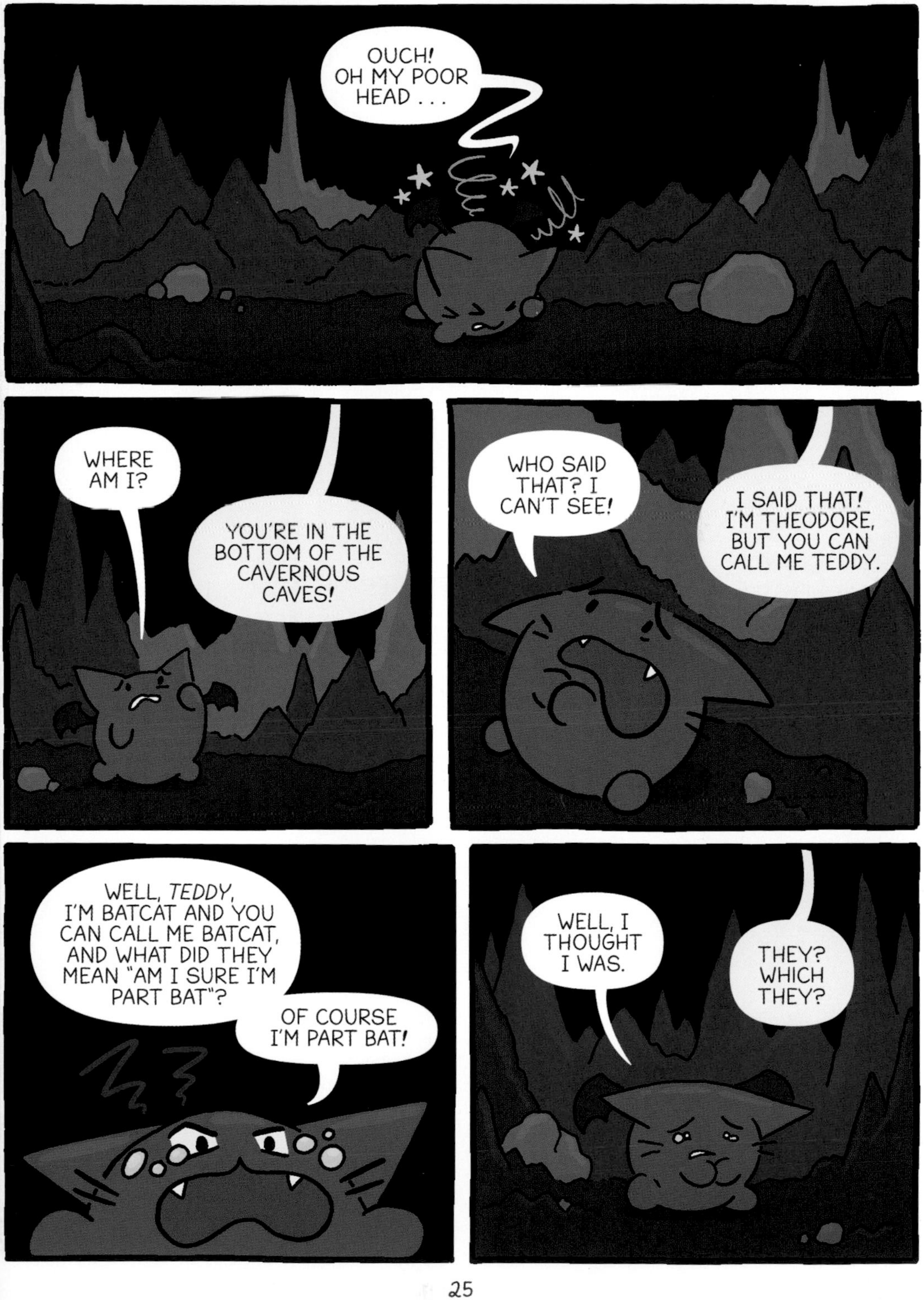
OUCH! OH MY POOR HEAD . . .
WHERE AM I?
YOU'RE IN THE BOTTOM OF THE CAVERNOUS CAVES!
WHO SAID THAT? I CAN'T SEE!
I SAID THAT! I'M THEODORE, BUT YOU CAN CALL ME TEDDY.
WELL, *TEDDY*, I'M BATCAT AND YOU CAN CALL ME BATCAT, AND WHAT DID THEY MEAN "AM I SURE I'M PART BAT"?
OF COURSE I'M PART BAT!
WELL, I THOUGHT I WAS.
THEY? WHICH THEY?

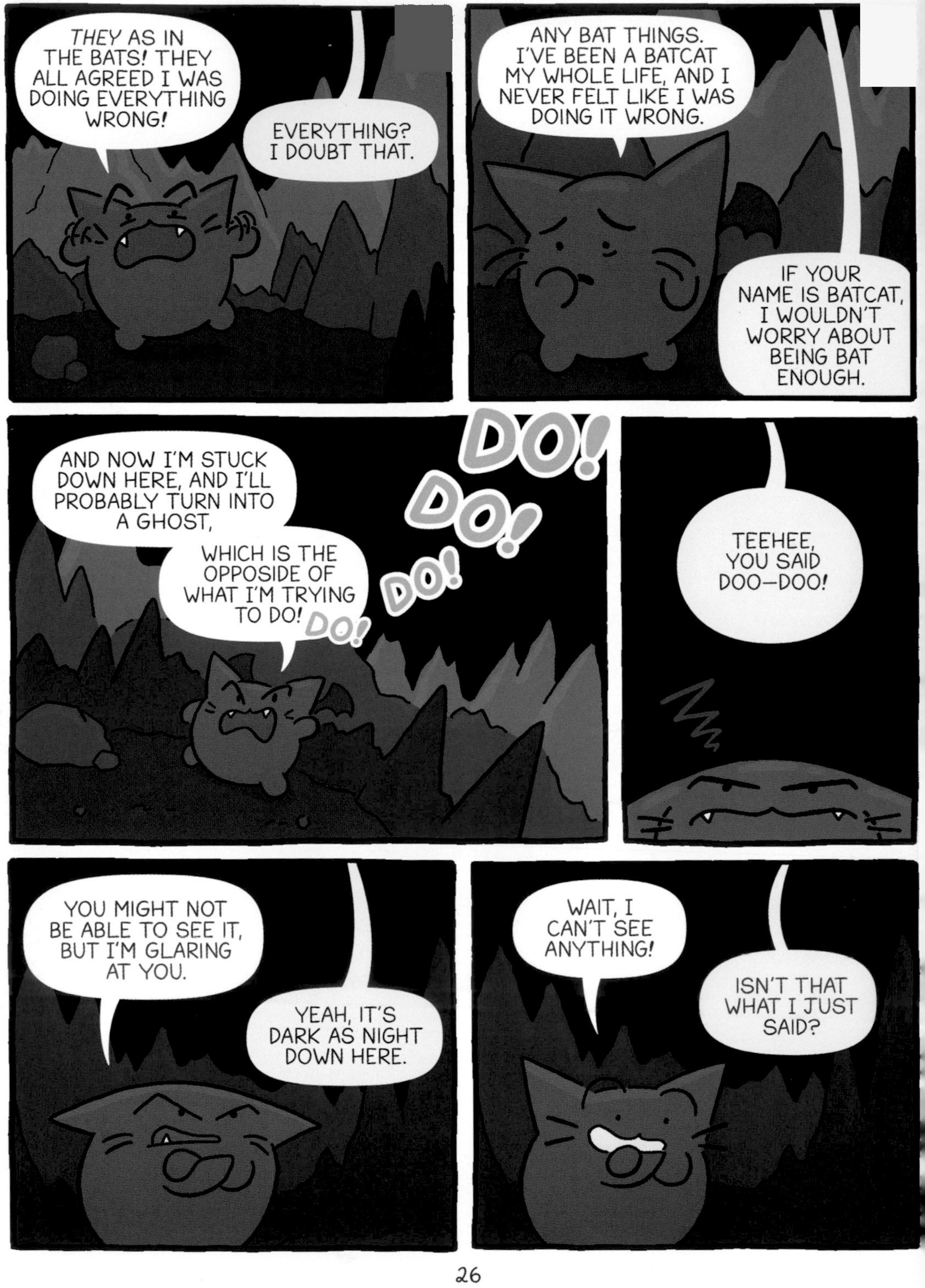
THEY AS IN THE BATS! THEY ALL AGREED I WAS DOING EVERYTHING WRONG!
EVERYTHING? I DOUBT THAT.
ANY BAT THINGS. I'VE BEEN A BATCAT MY WHOLE LIFE, AND I NEVER FELT LIKE I WAS DOING IT WRONG.
IF YOUR NAME IS BATCAT, I WOULDN'T WORRY ABOUT BEING BAT ENOUGH.
AND NOW I'M STUCK DOWN HERE, AND I'LL PROBABLY TURN INTO A GHOST,
WHICH IS THE OPPOSIDE OF WHAT I'M TRYING TO DO!
DO!
DO!
DO!
DO!
TEEHEE, YOU SAID DOO-DOO!
YOU MIGHT NOT BE ABLE TO SEE IT, BUT I'M GLARING AT YOU.
YEAH, IT'S DARK AS NIGHT DOWN HERE.
WAIT, I CAN'T SEE ANYTHING!
ISN'T THAT WHAT I JUST SAID?

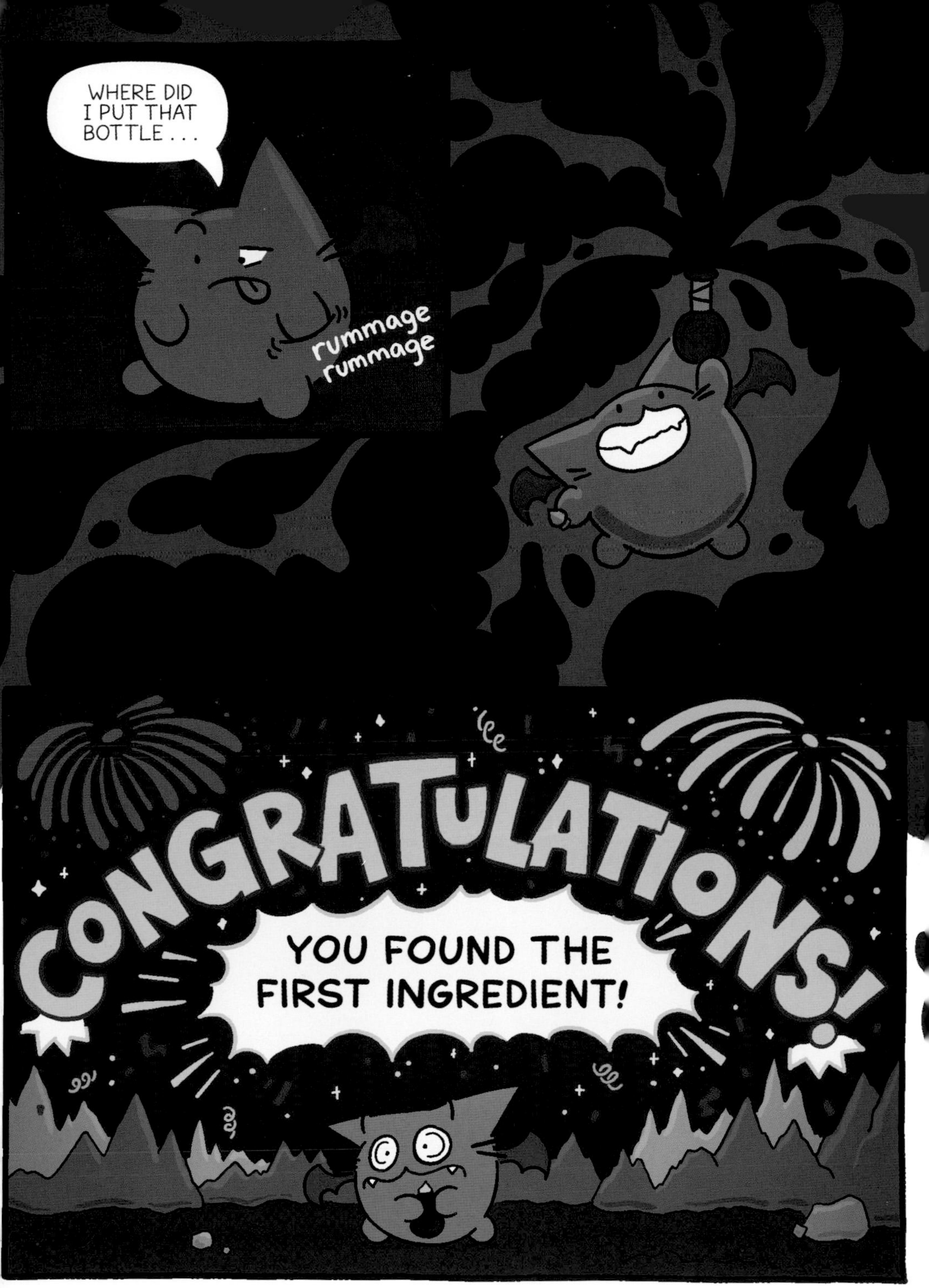

WHERE DID I PUT THAT BOTTLE . . .
rummage rummage
CONGRATULATIONS!
YOU FOUND THE FIRST INGREDIENT!

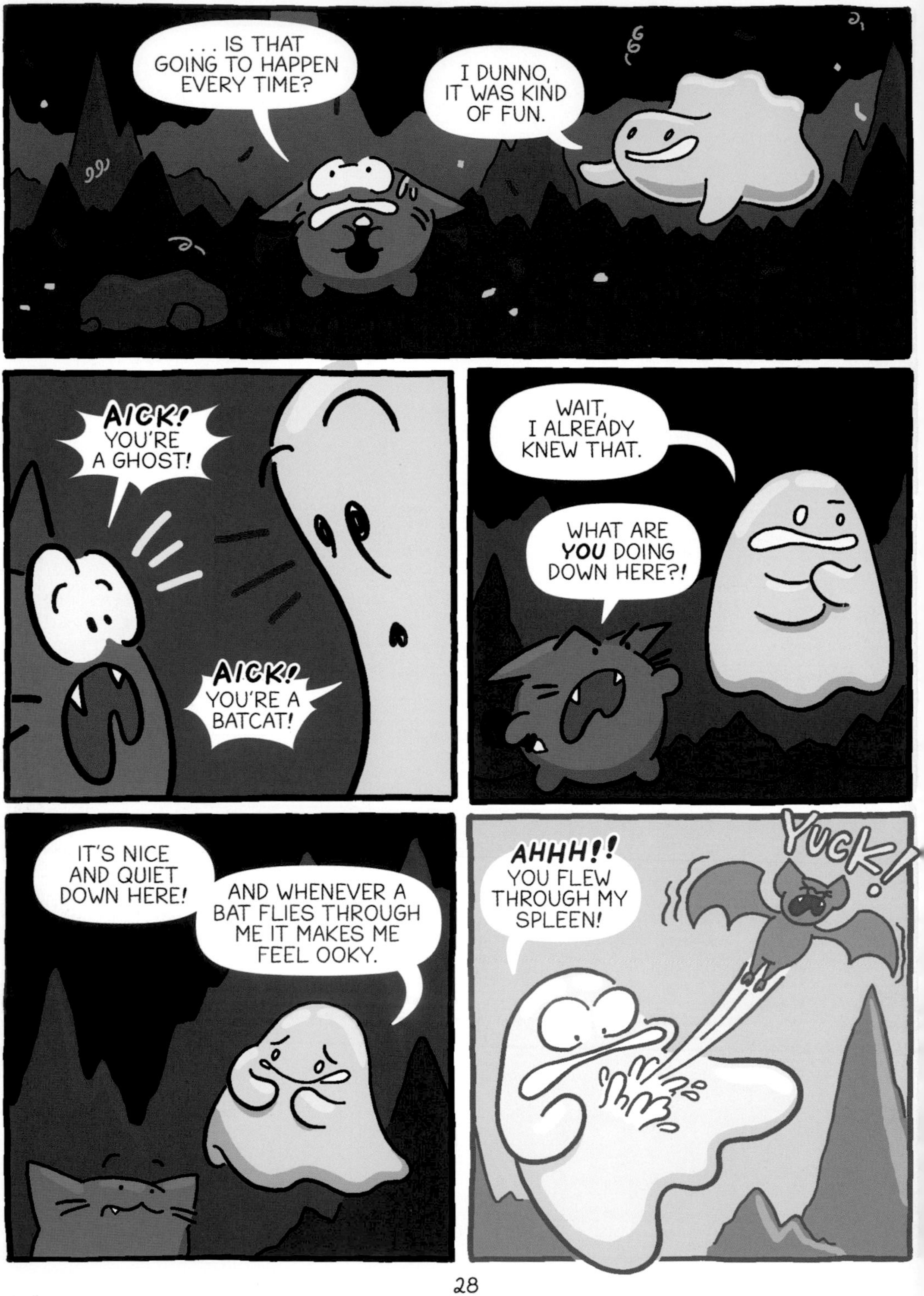

. . . IS THAT GOING TO HAPPEN EVERY TIME?
I DUNNO, IT WAS KIND OF FUN.
AICK! YOU'RE A GHOST!
AICK! YOU'RE A BATCAT!
WAIT, I ALREADY KNEW THAT.
WHAT ARE **YOU** DOING DOWN HERE?!
IT'S NICE AND QUIET DOWN HERE!
AND WHENEVER A BAT FLIES THROUGH ME IT MAKES ME FEEL OOKY.
AHHH!! YOU FLEW THROUGH MY SPLEEN!
YUCK!

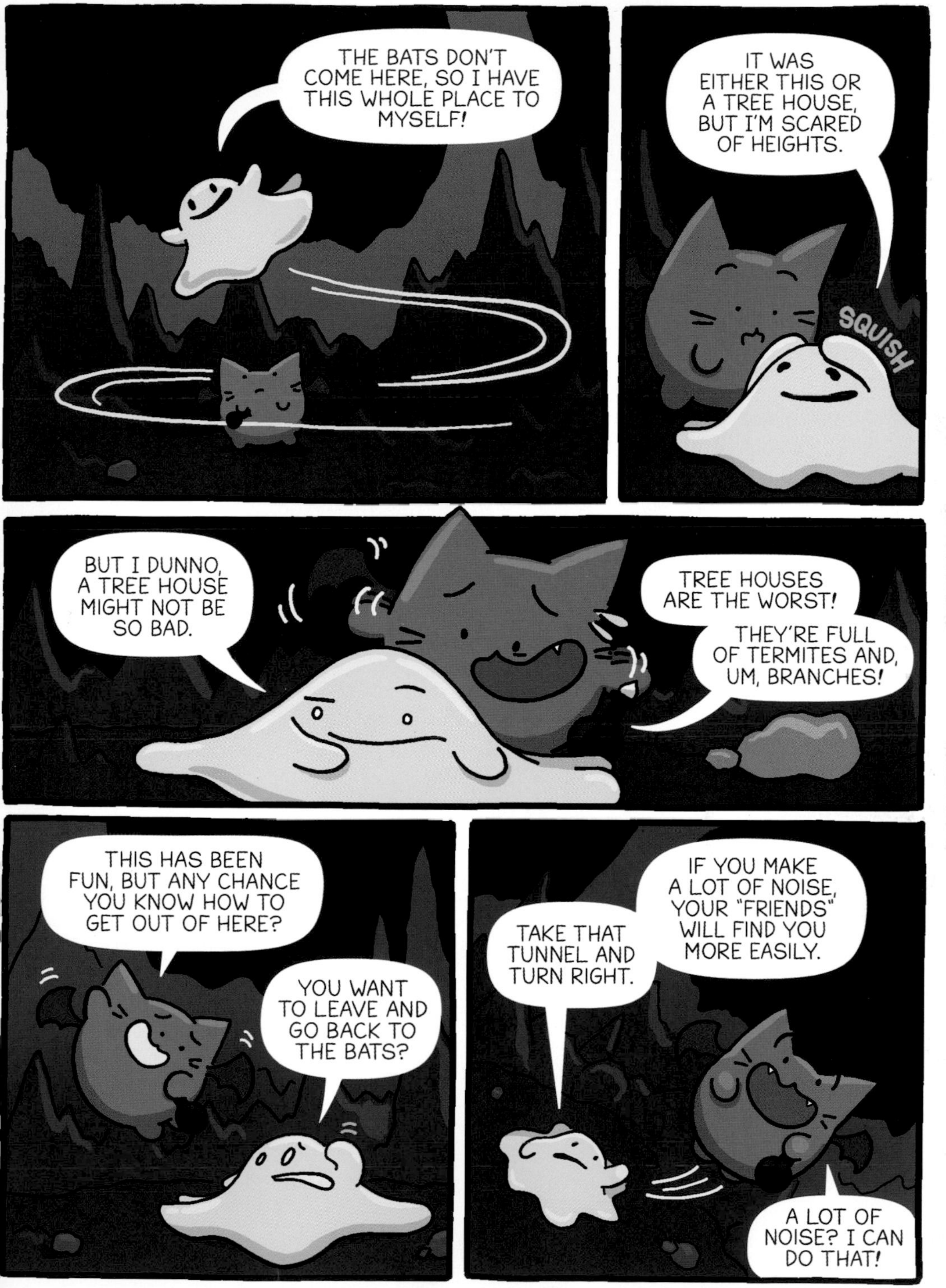
THE BATS DON'T COME HERE, SO I HAVE THIS WHOLE PLACE TO MYSELF!
IT WAS EITHER THIS OR A TREE HOUSE, BUT I'M SCARED OF HEIGHTS.
SQUISH
BUT I DUNNO, A TREE HOUSE MIGHT NOT BE SO BAD.
TREE HOUSES ARE THE WORST!
THEY'RE FULL OF TERMITES AND, UM, BRANCHES!
THIS HAS BEEN FUN, BUT ANY CHANCE YOU KNOW HOW TO GET OUT OF HERE?
YOU WANT TO LEAVE AND GO BACK TO THE BATS?
TAKE THAT TUNNEL AND TURN RIGHT.
IF YOU MAKE A LOT OF NOISE, YOUR "FRIENDS" WILL FIND YOU MORE EASILY.
A LOT OF NOISE? I CAN DO THAT!

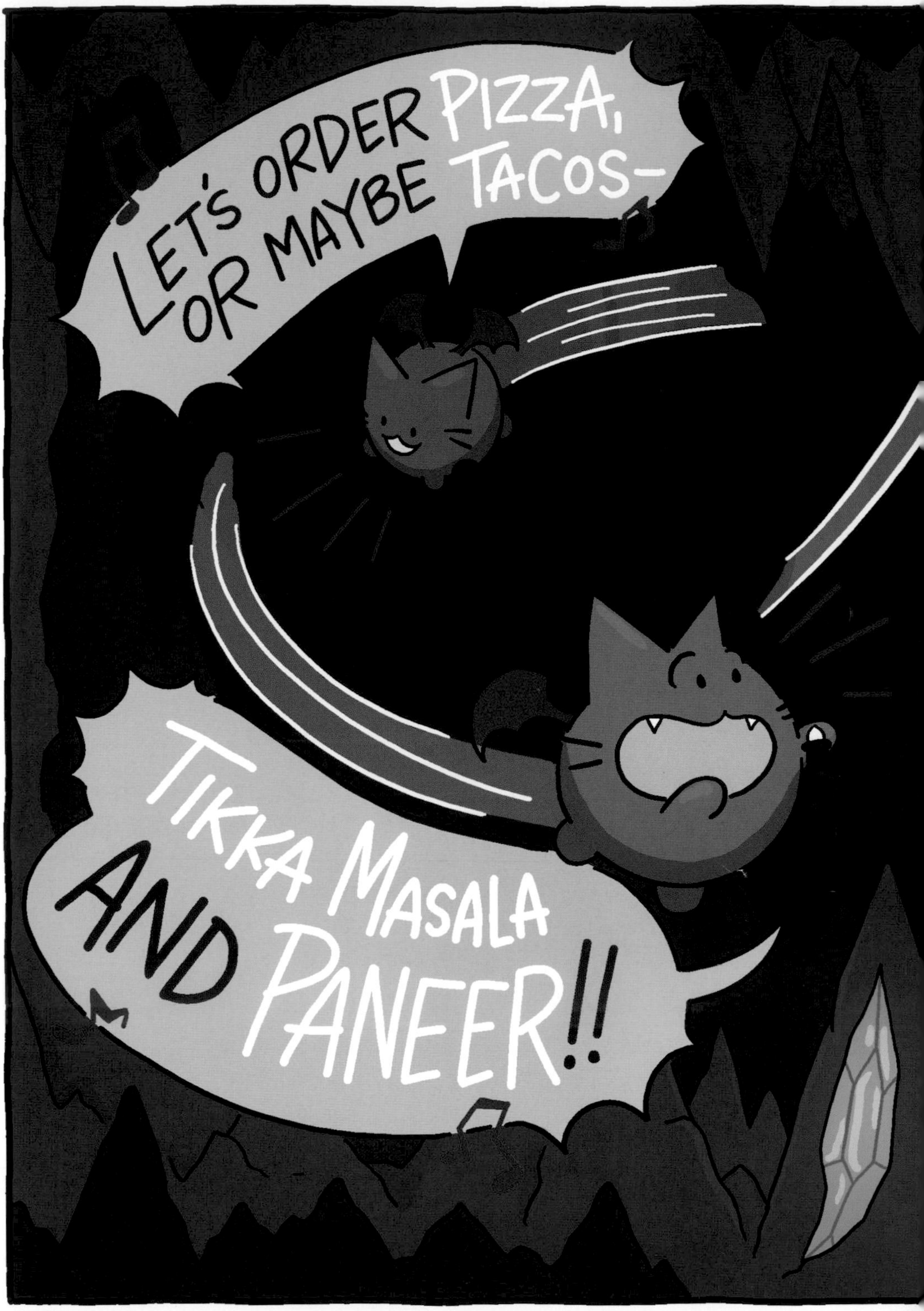
LET'S ORDER PIZZA, OR MAYBE TACOS-
TIKKA MASALA AND PANEER!!

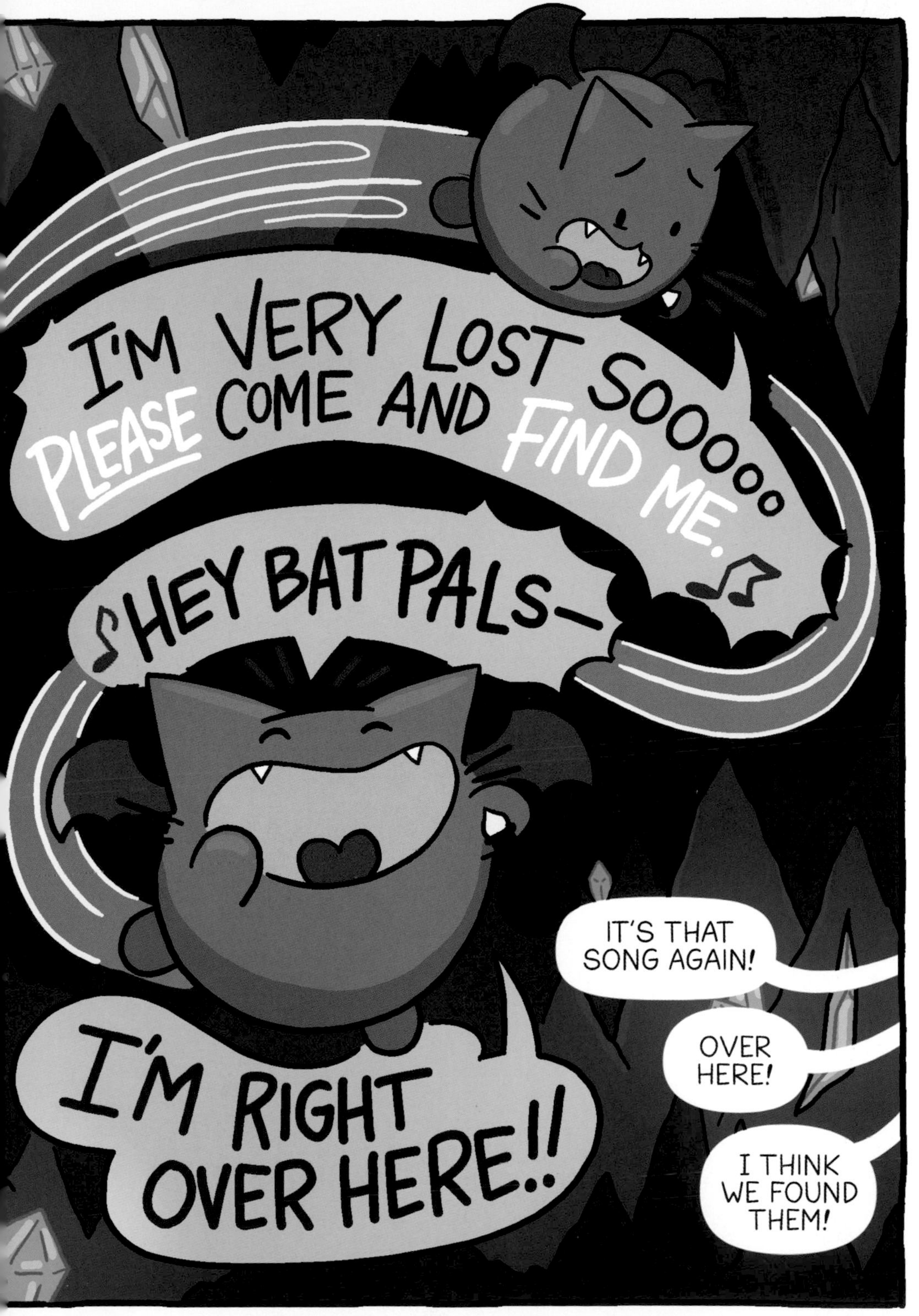
I'M VERY LOST SOOOOOO
PLEASE COME AND FIND ME.
HEY BAT PALS—
I'M RIGHT OVER HERE!!
IT'S THAT SONG AGAIN!
OVER HERE!
I THINK WE FOUND THEM!

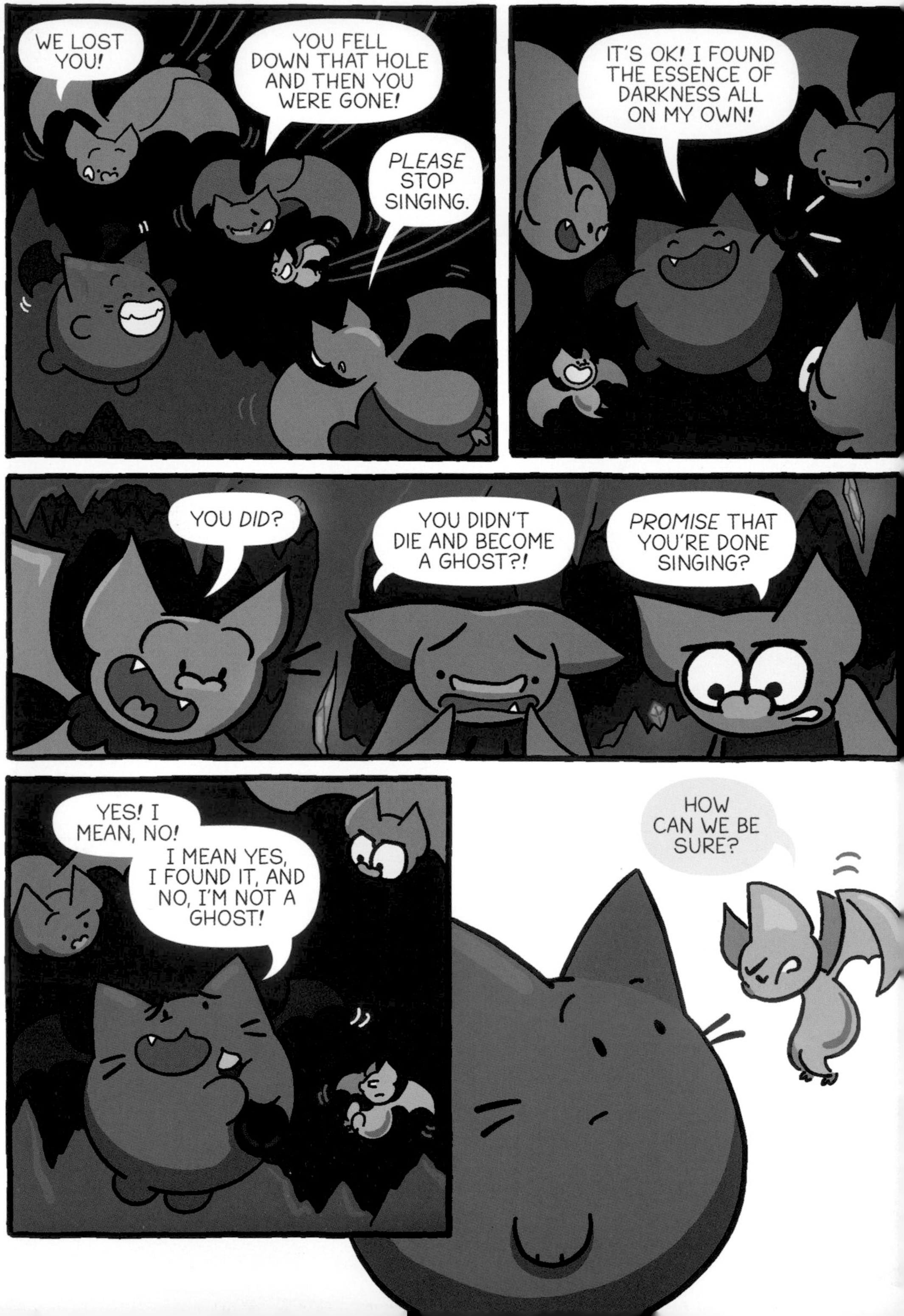
WE LOST YOU!
YOU FELL DOWN THAT HOLE AND THEN YOU WERE GONE!
PLEASE STOP SINGING.
IT'S OK! I FOUND THE ESSENCE OF DARKNESS ALL ON MY OWN!
YOU *DID*?
YOU DIDN'T DIE AND BECOME A GHOST?!
PROMISE THAT YOU'RE DONE SINGING?
YES! I MEAN, NO!
I MEAN YES, I FOUND IT, AND NO, I'M NOT A GHOST!
HOW CAN WE BE SURE?

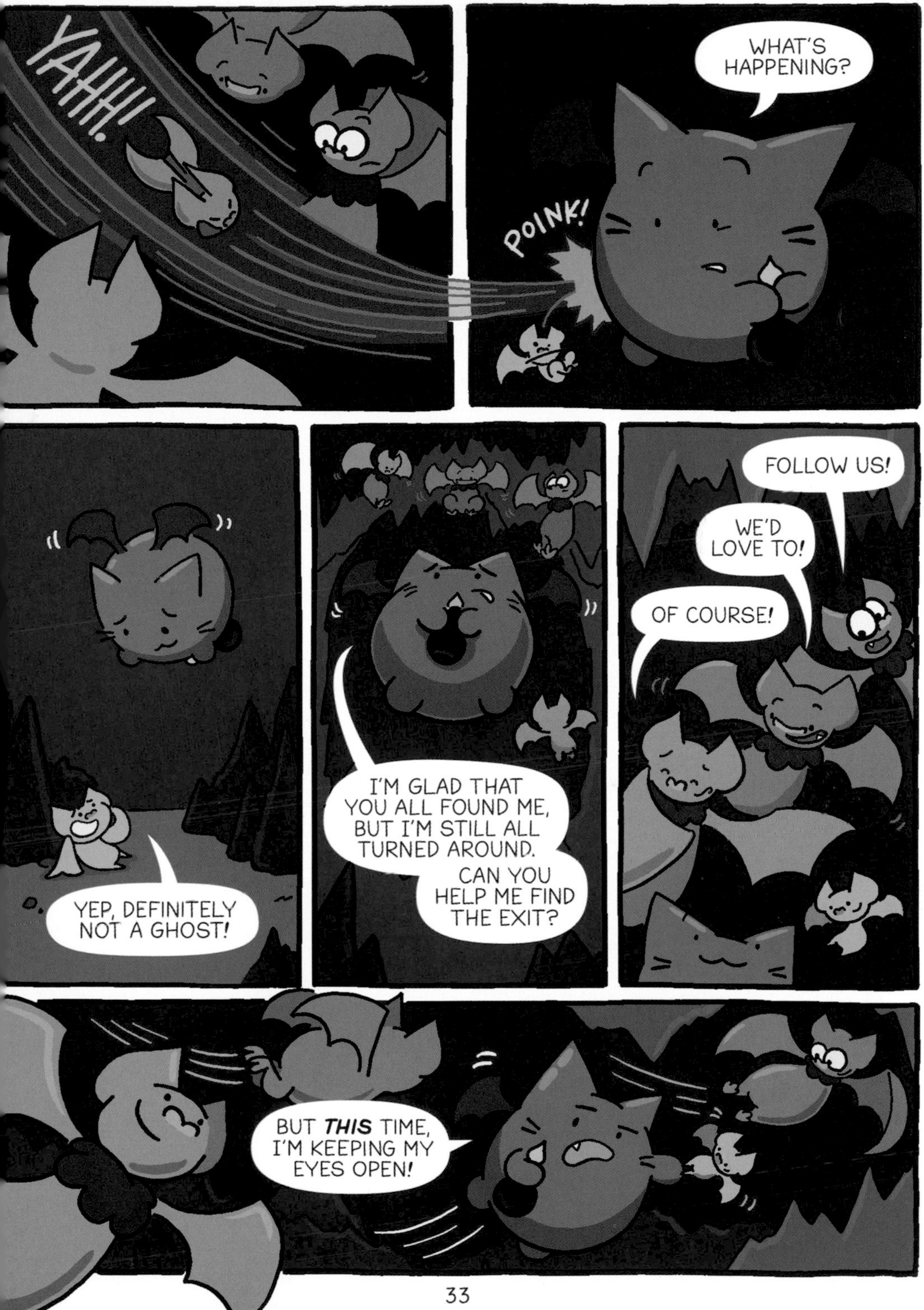

YAHH!
WHAT'S HAPPENING?
POINK!
YEP, DEFINITELY NOT A GHOST!
I'M GLAD THAT YOU ALL FOUND ME, BUT I'M STILL ALL TURNED AROUND.
CAN YOU HELP ME FIND THE EXIT?
FOLLOW US!
WE'D LOVE TO!
OF COURSE!
BUT ***THIS*** TIME, I'M KEEPING MY EYES OPEN!

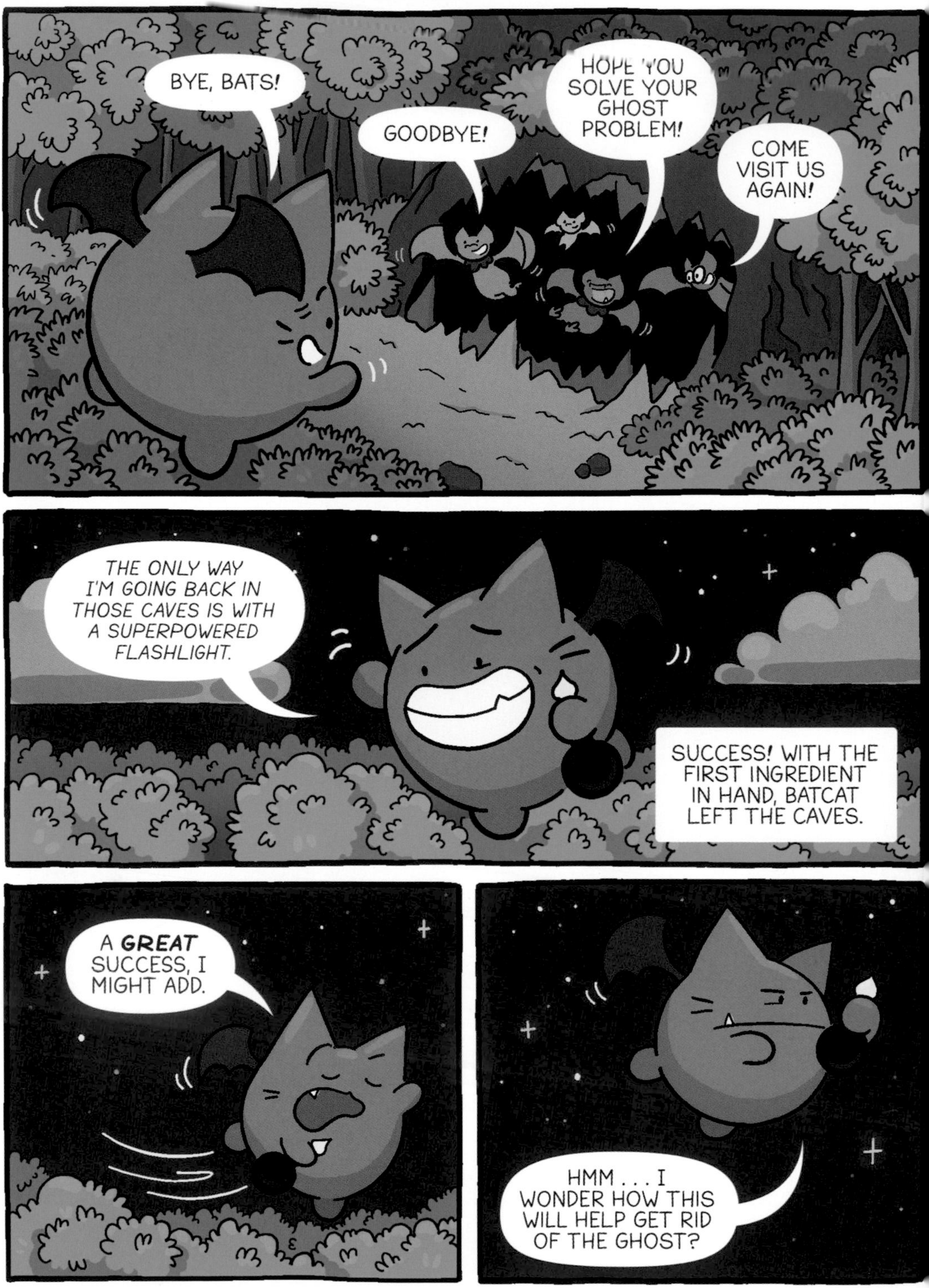
BYE, BATS!
GOODBYE!
HOPE YOU SOLVE YOUR GHOST PROBLEM!
COME VISIT US AGAIN!
THE ONLY WAY I'M GOING BACK IN THOSE CAVES IS WITH A SUPERPOWERED FLASHLIGHT.
SUCCESS! WITH THE FIRST INGREDIENT IN HAND, BATCAT LEFT THE CAVES.
A **GREAT** SUCCESS, I MIGHT ADD.
HMM . . . I WONDER HOW THIS WILL HELP GET RID OF THE GHOST?

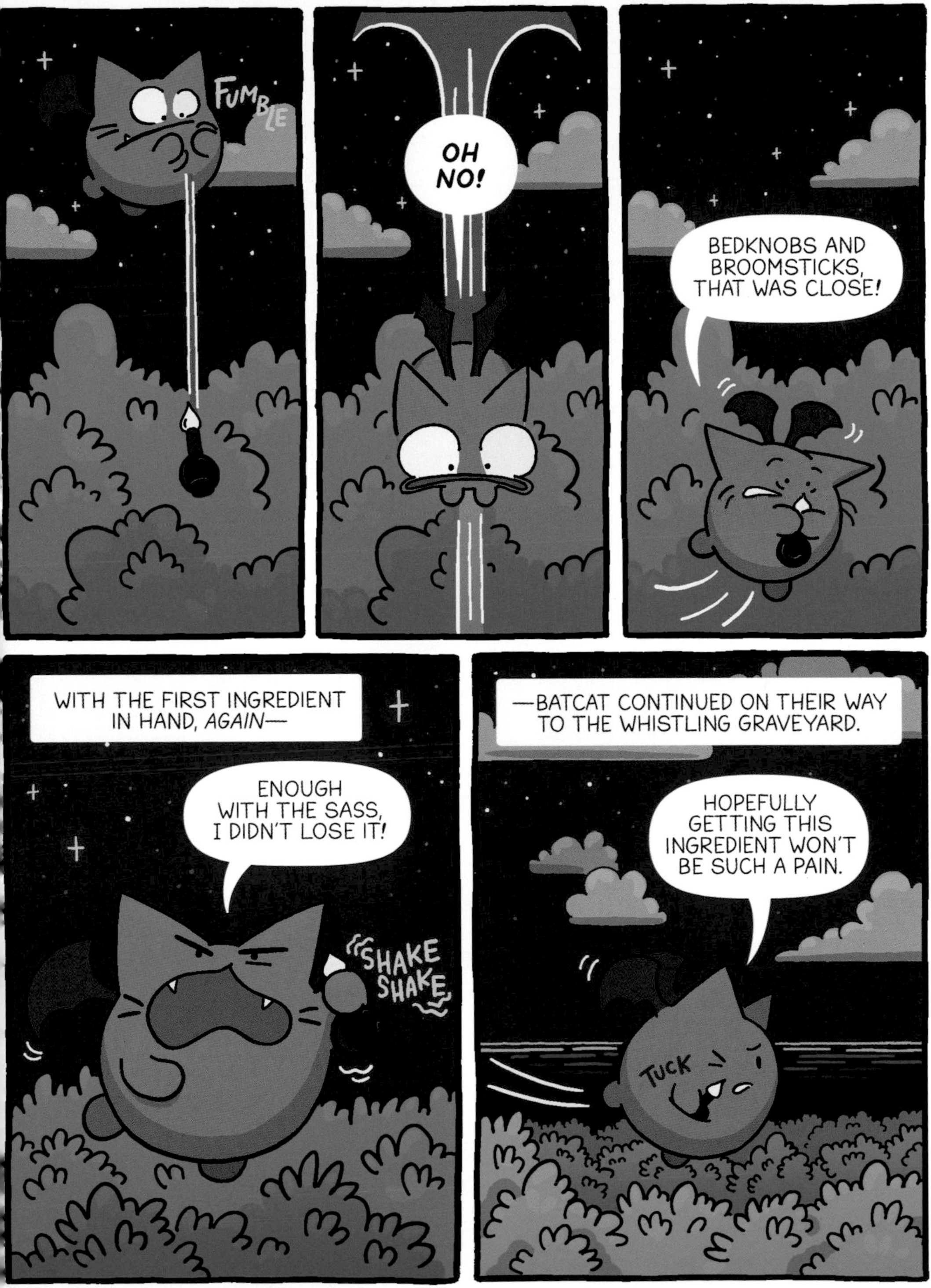
FUMBLE
OH NO!
BEDKNOBS AND BROOMSTICKS, THAT WAS CLOSE!
WITH THE FIRST INGREDIENT IN HAND, *AGAIN*—
ENOUGH WITH THE SASS, I DIDN'T LOSE IT!
SHAKE SHAKE
—BATCAT CONTINUED ON THEIR WAY TO THE WHISTLING GRAVEYARD.
HOPEFULLY GETTING THIS INGREDIENT WON'T BE SUCH A PAIN.
TUCK

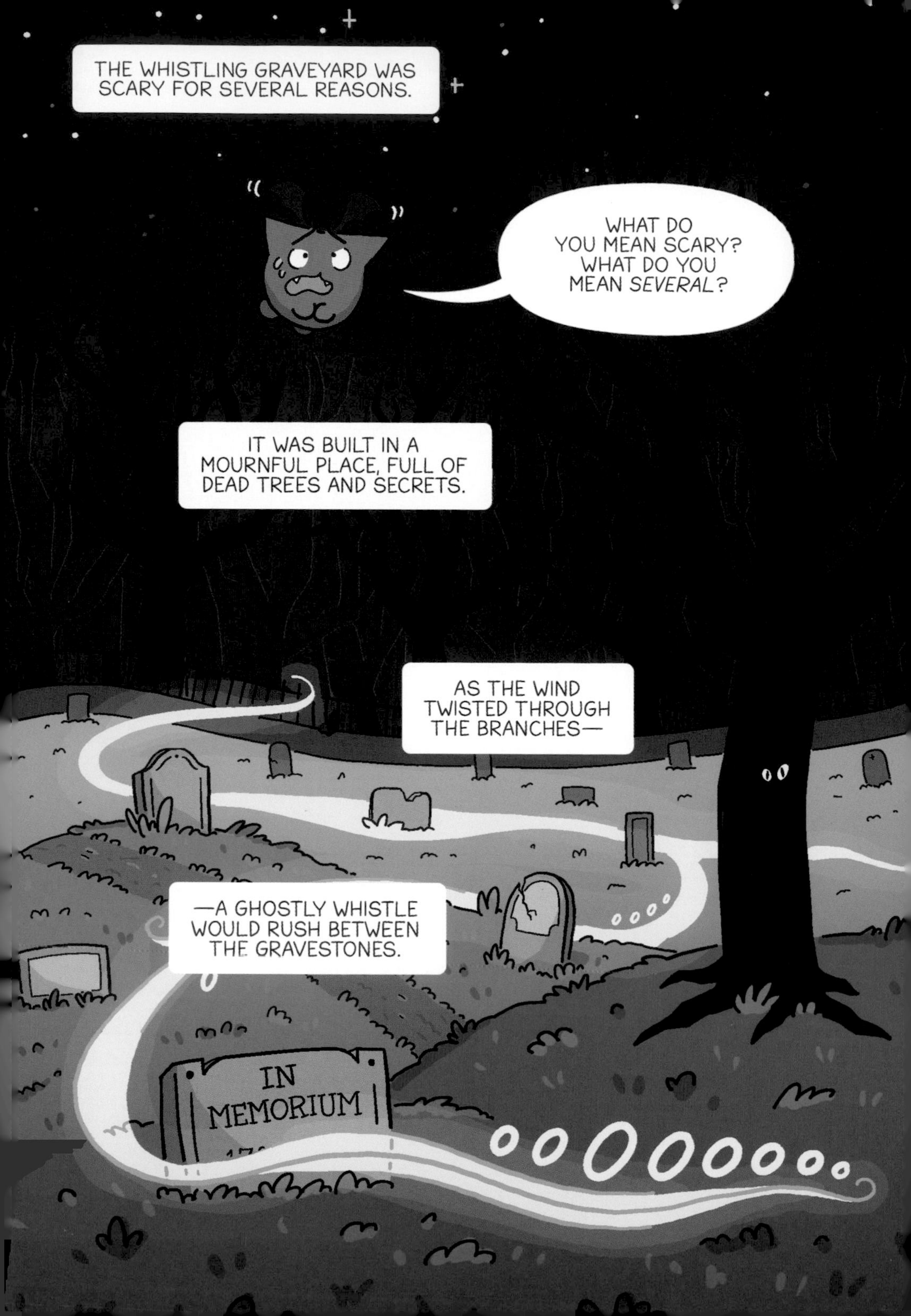
THE WHISTLING GRAVEYARD WAS SCARY FOR SEVERAL REASONS.
WHAT DO YOU MEAN SCARY? WHAT DO YOU MEAN *SEVERAL*?
IT WAS BUILT IN A MOURNFUL PLACE, FULL OF DEAD TREES AND SECRETS.
AS THE WIND TWISTED THROUGH THE BRANCHES—
—A GHOSTLY WHISTLE WOULD RUSH BETWEEN THE GRAVESTONES.
oooo
IN MEMORIUM
ooOOOOOoo

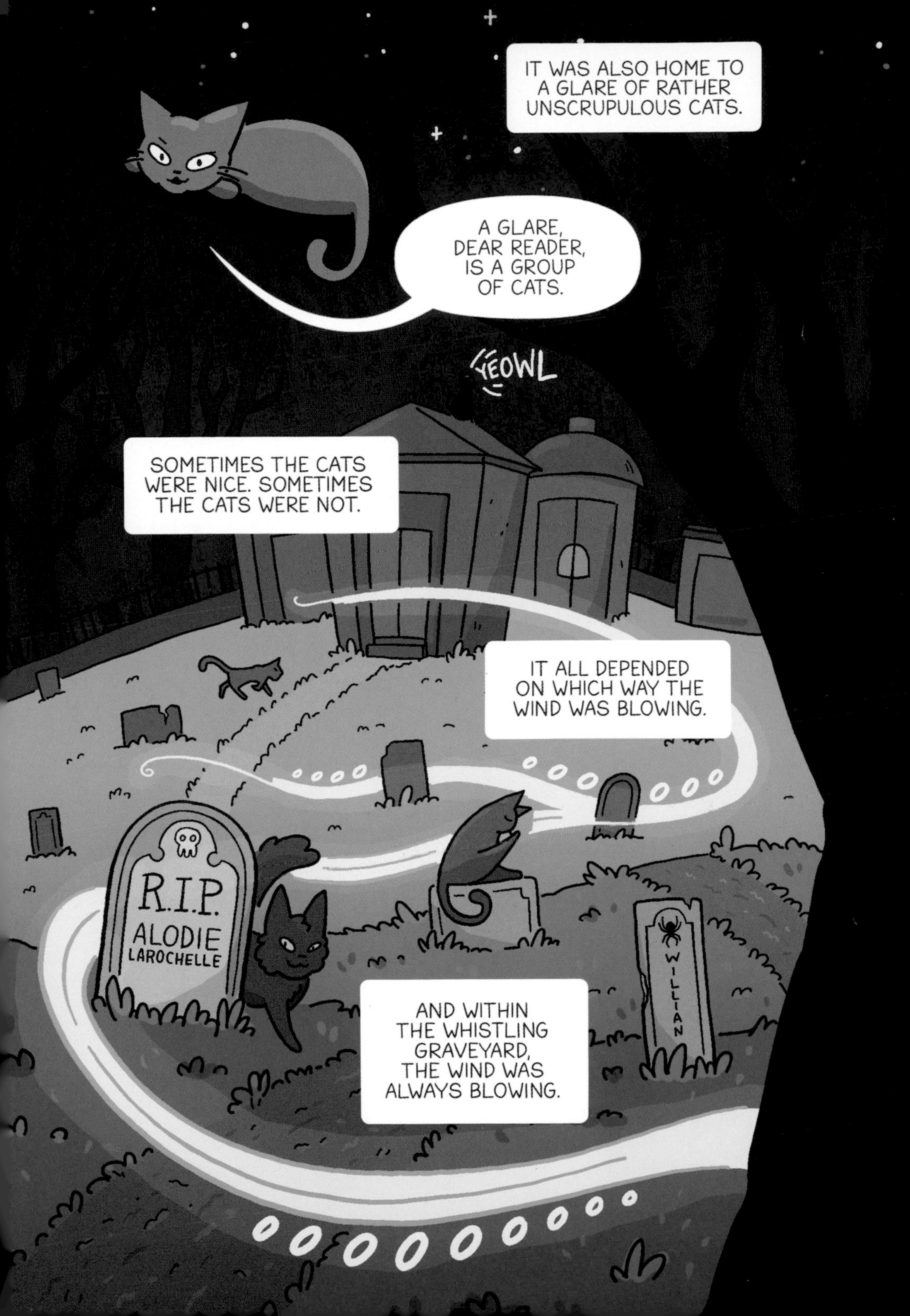
IT WAS ALSO HOME TO A GLARE OF RATHER UNSCRUPULOUS CATS.
A GLARE, DEAR READER, IS A GROUP OF CATS.
YEOWL
SOMETIMES THE CATS WERE NICE. SOMETIMES THE CATS WERE NOT.
IT ALL DEPENDED ON WHICH WAY THE WIND WAS BLOWING.
R.I.P.
ALODIE
LAROCHELLE
WILLIAN
AND WITHIN THE WHISTLING GRAVEYARD, THE WIND WAS ALWAYS BLOWING.

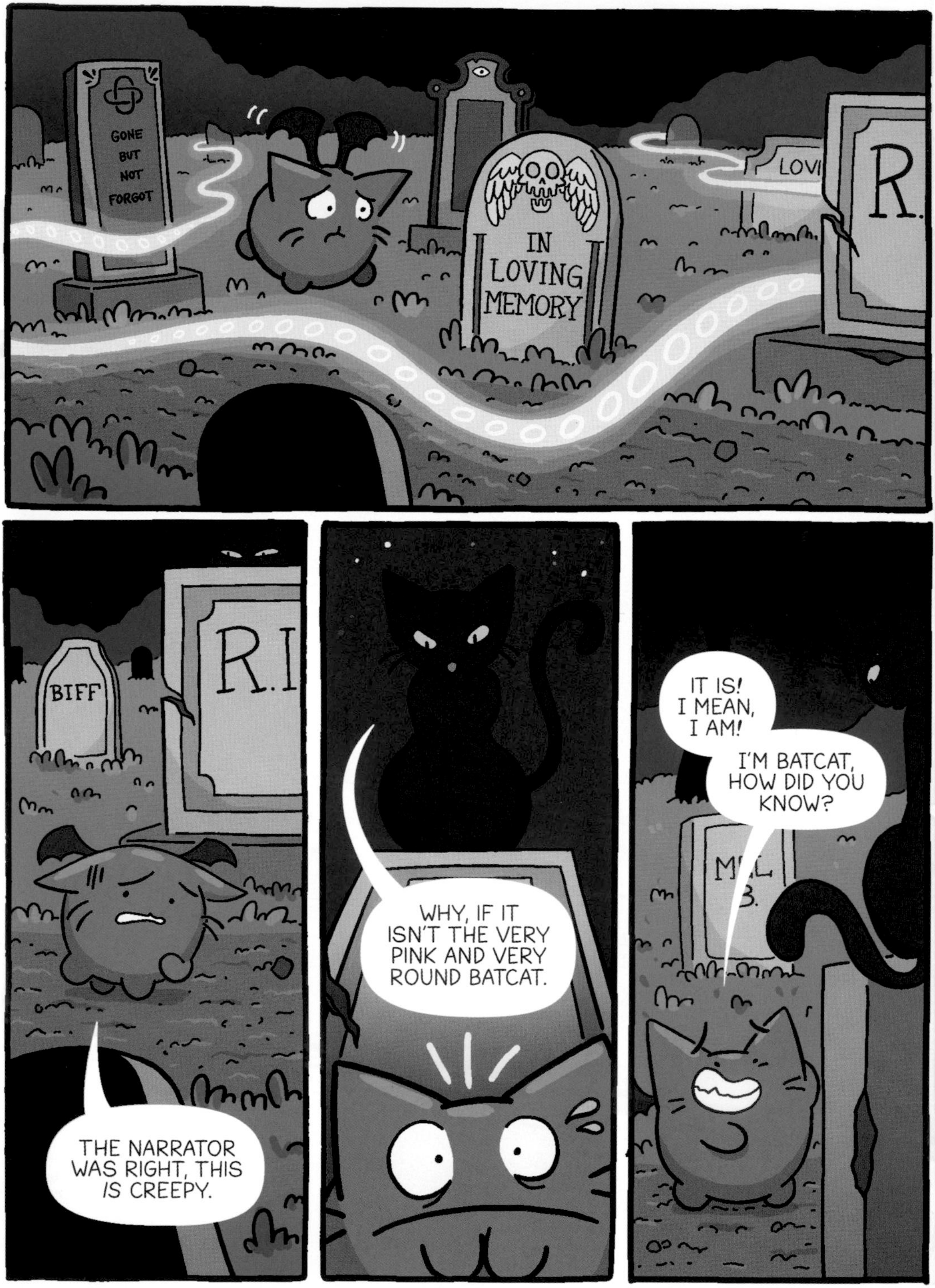
GONE BUT NOT FORGOT
IN LOVING MEMORY
BIFF
THE NARRATOR WAS RIGHT, THIS *IS* CREEPY.
WHY, IF IT ISN'T THE VERY PINK AND VERY ROUND BATCAT.
IT IS! I MEAN, I AM!
I'M BATCAT, HOW DID YOU KNOW?

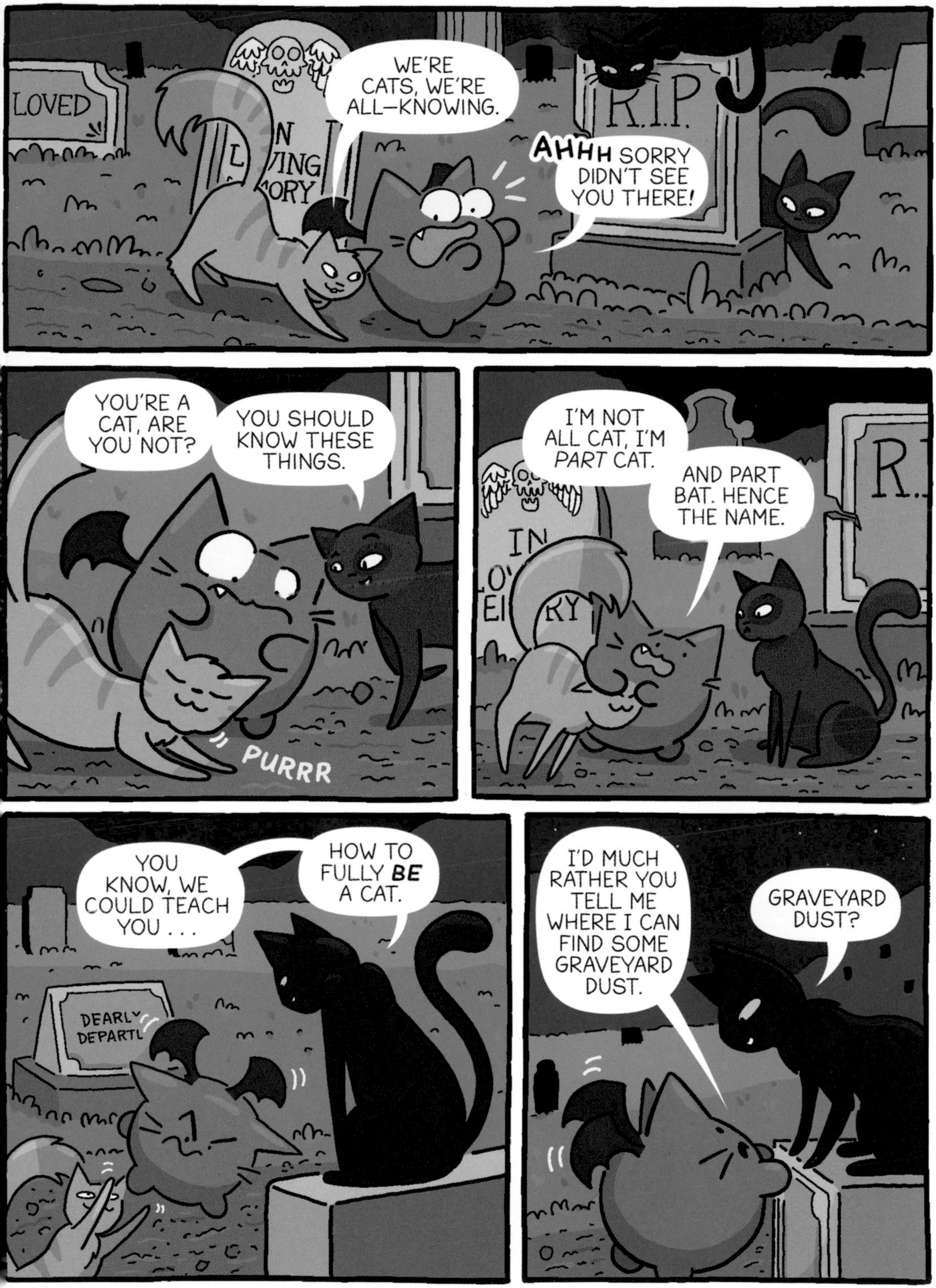

LOVED
IN LOVING MEMORY
R.I.P.
WE'RE CATS, WE'RE ALL—KNOWING.
AHHH SORRY DIDN'T SEE YOU THERE!
YOU'RE A CAT, ARE YOU NOT?
YOU SHOULD KNOW THESE THINGS.
PURRR
I'M NOT ALL CAT, I'M *PART* CAT.
AND PART BAT. HENCE THE NAME.
YOU KNOW, WE COULD TEACH YOU . . .
HOW TO FULLY **BE** A CAT.
DEARLY DEPARTE
I'D MUCH RATHER YOU TELL ME WHERE I CAN FIND SOME GRAVEYARD DUST.
GRAVEYARD DUST?

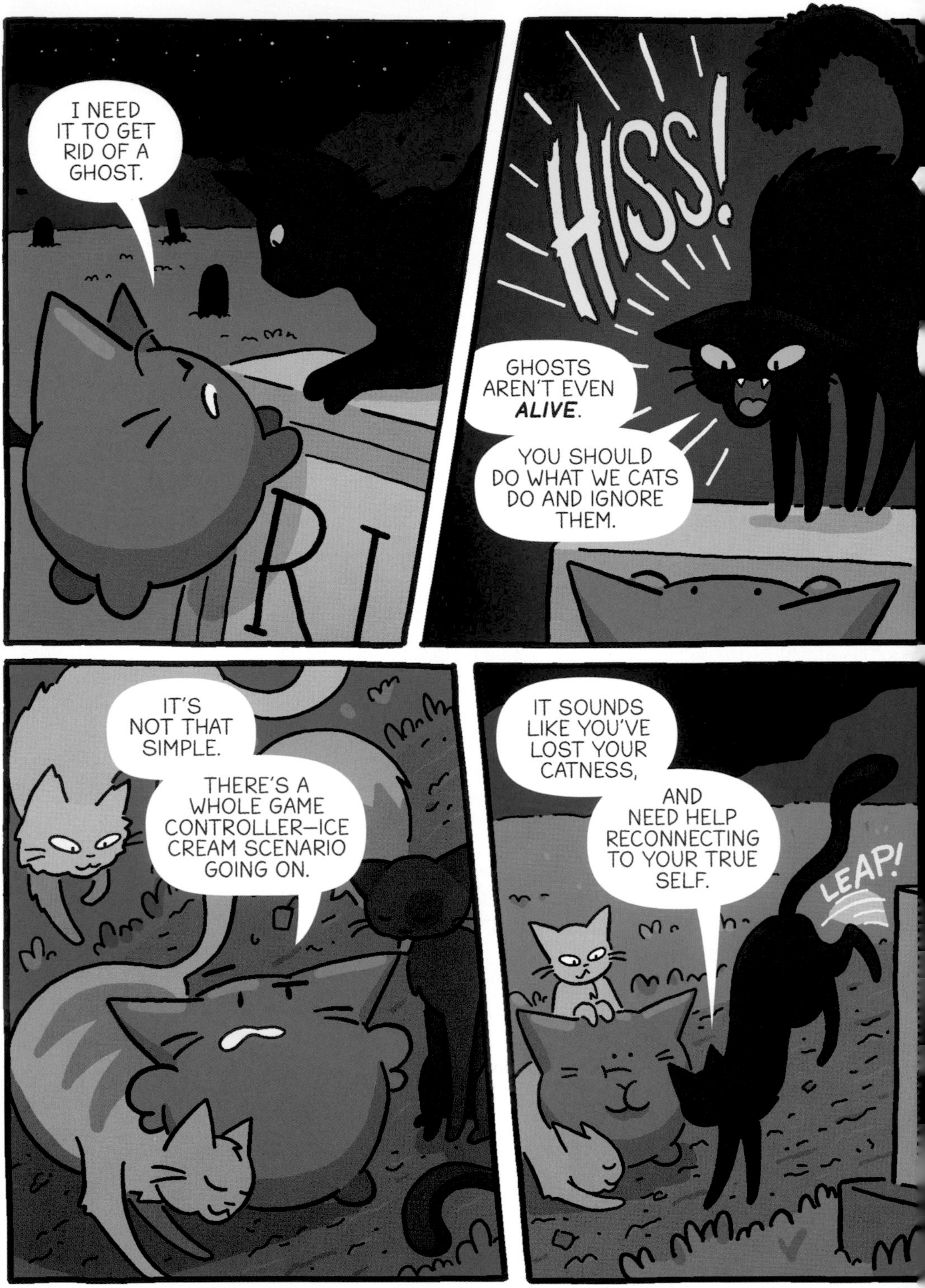
I NEED IT TO GET RID OF A GHOST.
HISS!
GHOSTS AREN'T EVEN ***ALIVE***.
YOU SHOULD DO WHAT WE CATS DO AND IGNORE THEM.
IT'S NOT THAT SIMPLE.
THERE'S A WHOLE GAME CONTROLLER–ICE CREAM SCENARIO GOING ON.
IT SOUNDS LIKE YOU'VE LOST YOUR CATNESS,
AND NEED HELP RECONNECTING TO YOUR TRUE SELF.
LEAP!

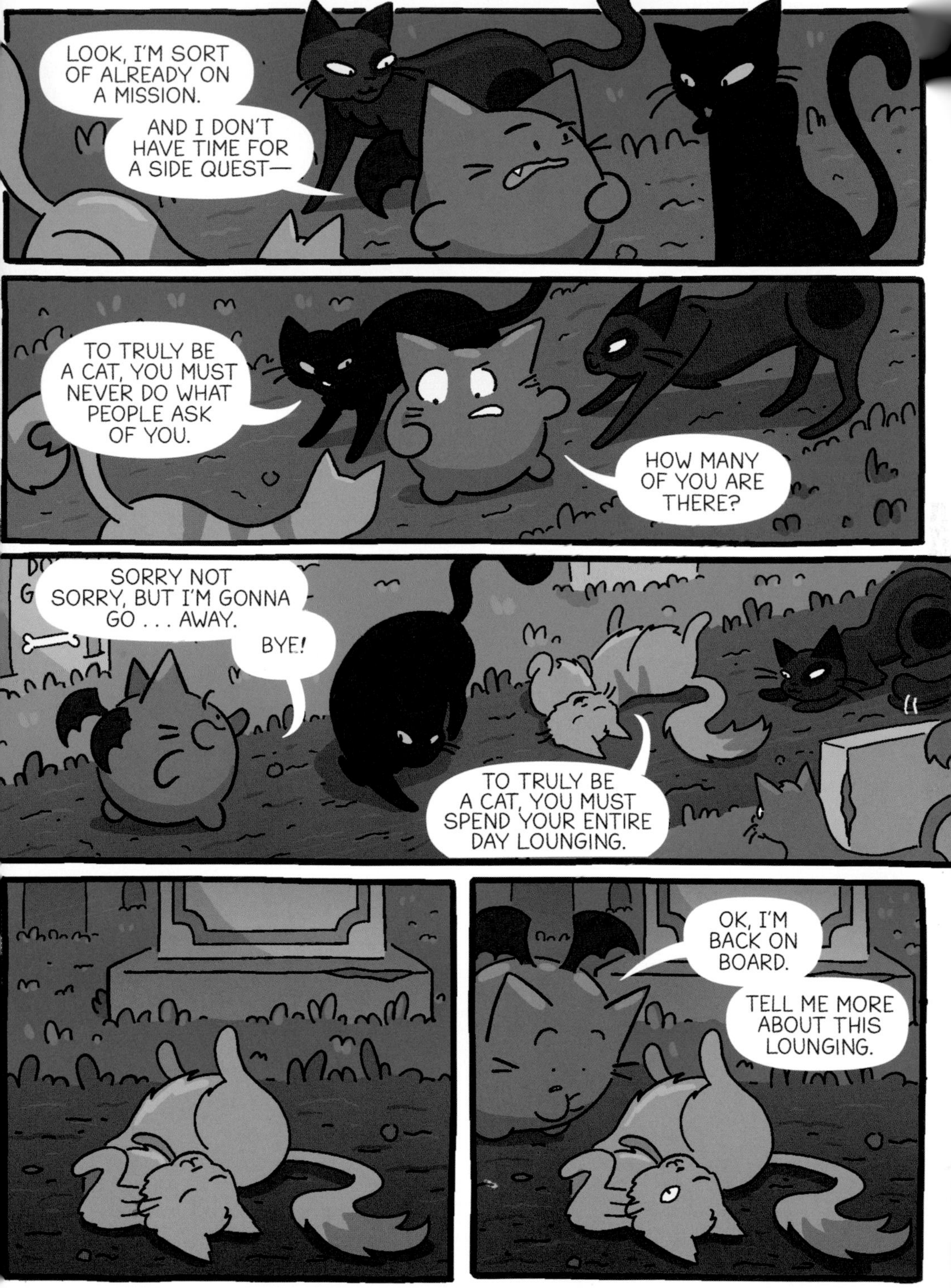
LOOK, I'M SORT OF ALREADY ON A MISSION.
AND I DON'T HAVE TIME FOR A SIDE QUEST—
TO TRULY BE A CAT, YOU MUST NEVER DO WHAT PEOPLE ASK OF YOU.
HOW MANY OF YOU ARE THERE?
SORRY NOT SORRY, BUT I'M GONNA GO . . . AWAY.
BYE!
TO TRULY BE A CAT, YOU MUST SPEND YOUR ENTIRE DAY LOUNGING.
OK, I'M BACK ON BOARD.
TELL ME MORE ABOUT THIS LOUNGING.

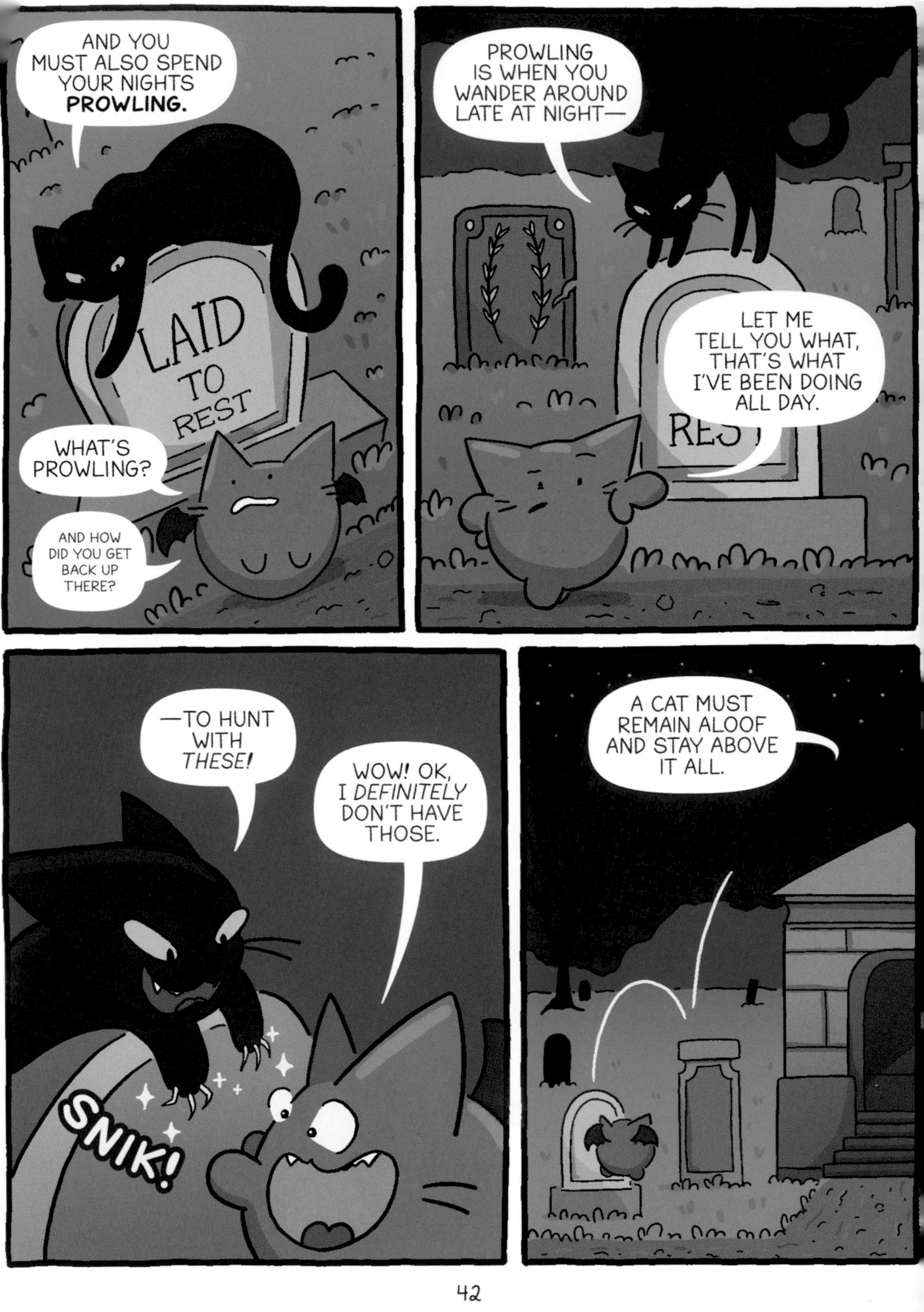
AND YOU MUST ALSO SPEND YOUR NIGHTS **PROWLING.**
LAID TO REST
WHAT'S PROWLING?
AND HOW DID YOU GET BACK UP THERE?
PROWLING IS WHEN YOU WANDER AROUND LATE AT NIGHT—
LET ME TELL YOU WHAT, THAT'S WHAT I'VE BEEN DOING ALL DAY.
—TO HUNT WITH *THESE!*
WOW! OK, I *DEFINITELY* DON'T HAVE THOSE.
SNIK!
A CAT MUST REMAIN ALOOF AND STAY ABOVE IT ALL.

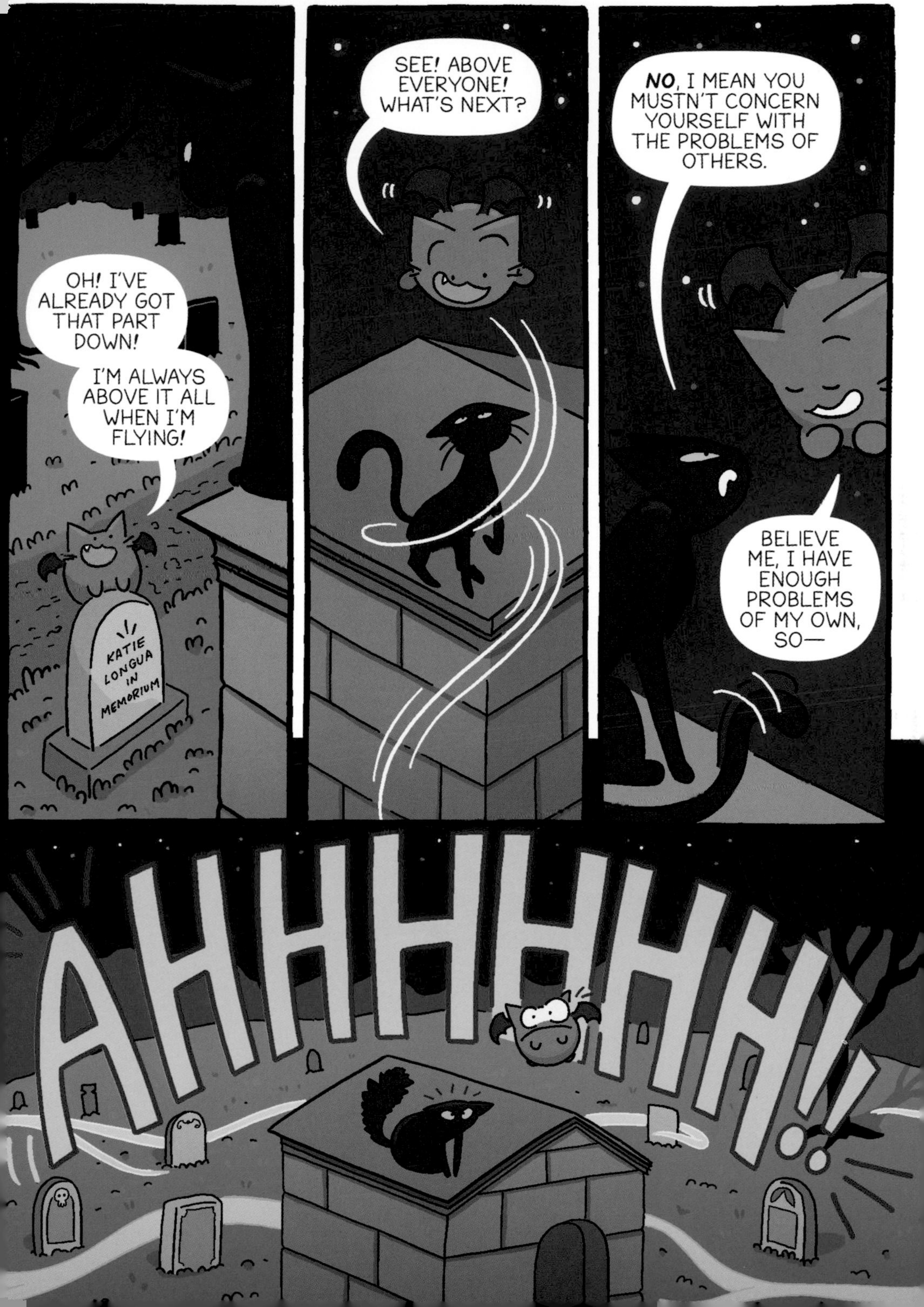

OH! I'VE ALREADY GOT THAT PART DOWN!
I'M ALWAYS ABOVE IT ALL WHEN I'M FLYING!
KATIE LONGUA IN MEMORIUM
SEE! ABOVE EVERYONE! WHAT'S NEXT?
NO, I MEAN YOU MUSTN'T CONCERN YOURSELF WITH THE PROBLEMS OF OTHERS.
BELIEVE ME, I HAVE ENOUGH PROBLEMS OF MY OWN, SO—
AHHHHHH!!

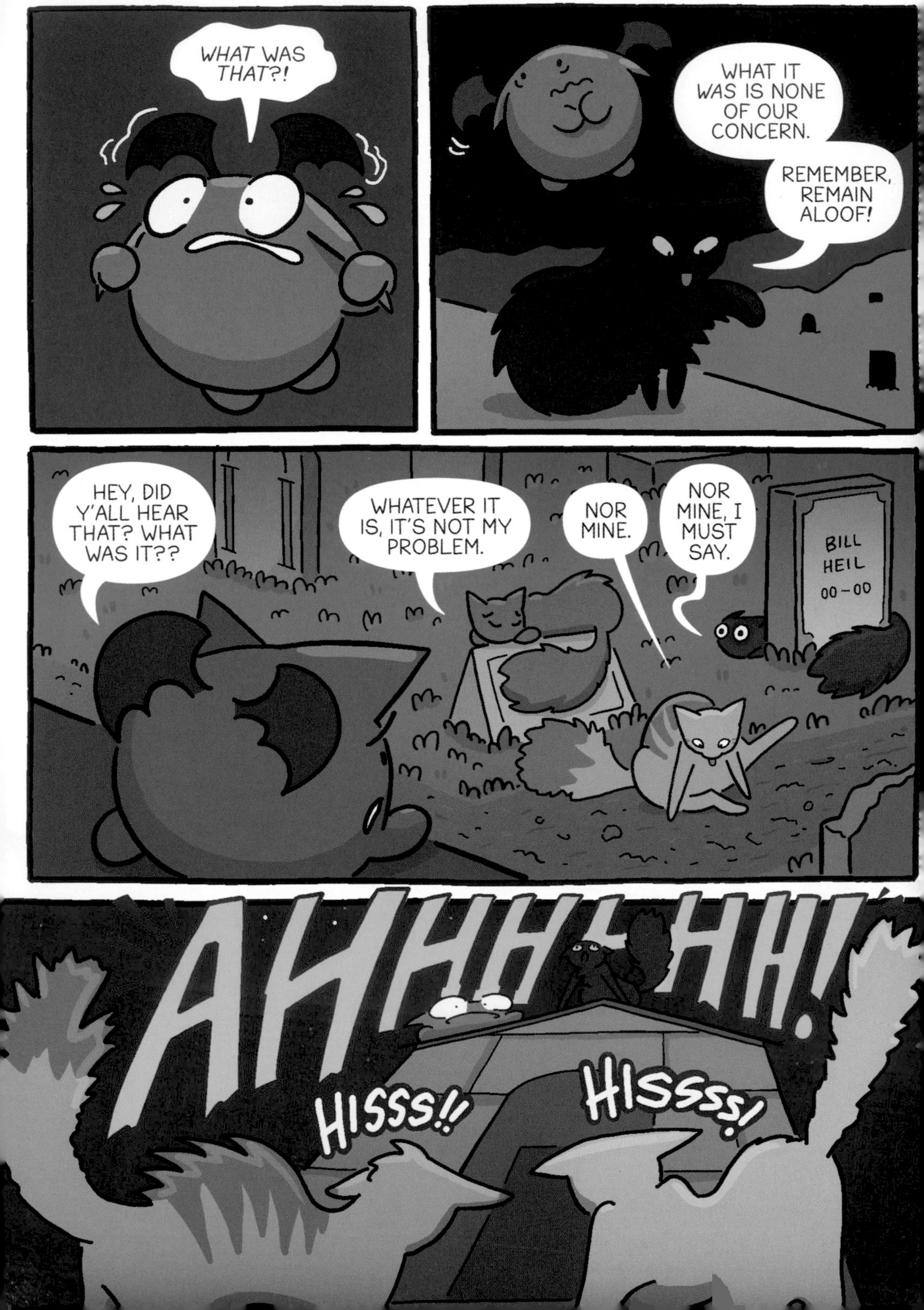
WHAT WAS THAT?!
WHAT IT WAS IS NONE OF OUR CONCERN.
REMEMBER, REMAIN ALOOF!
HEY, DID Y'ALL HEAR THAT? WHAT WAS IT??
WHATEVER IT IS, IT'S NOT MY PROBLEM.
NOR MINE.
NOR MINE, I MUST SAY.
BILL HEIL 00-00
HISSS!!
HISSSS!

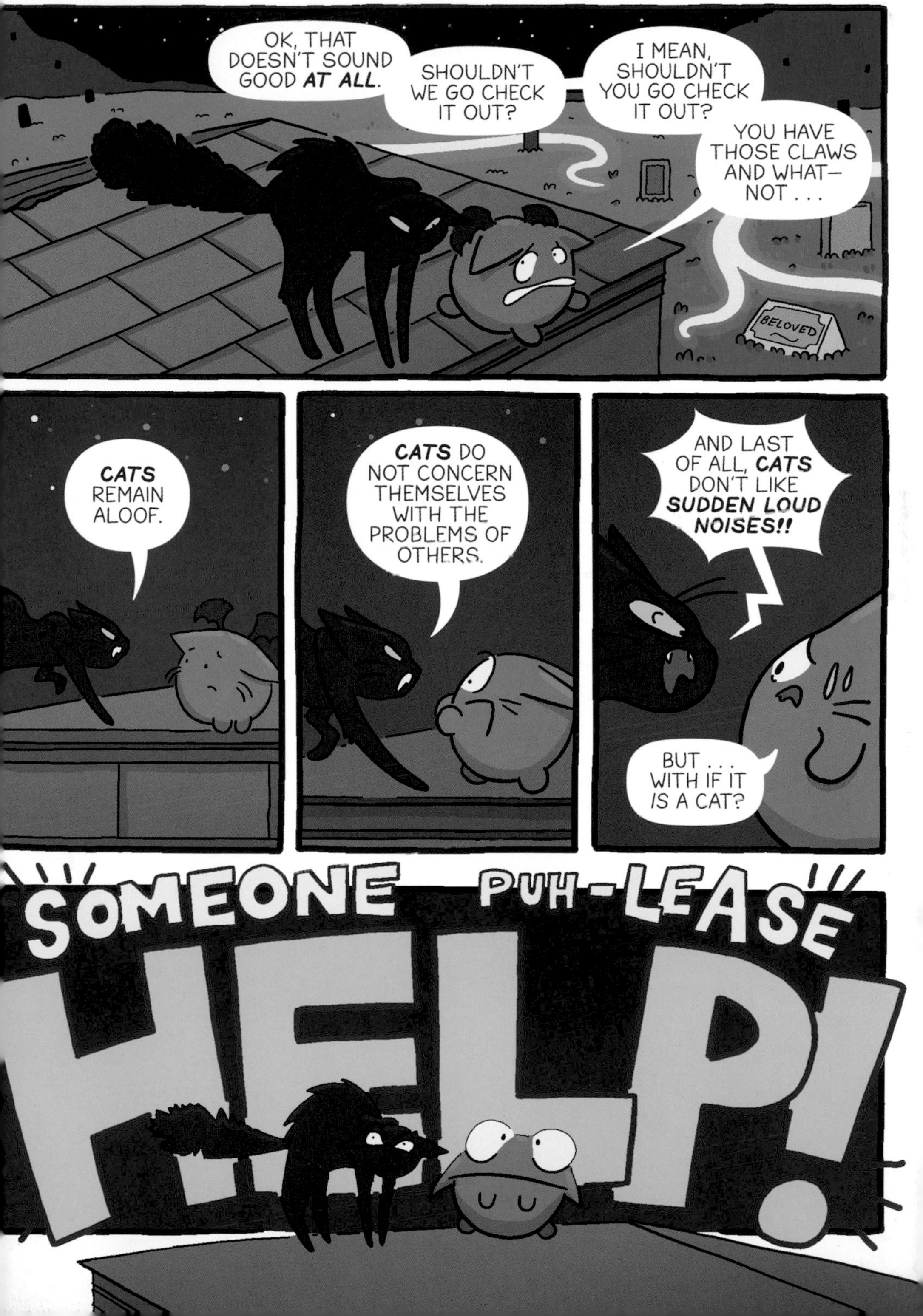

OK, THAT DOESN'T SOUND GOOD **AT ALL**.
SHOULDN'T WE GO CHECK IT OUT?
I MEAN, SHOULDN'T YOU GO CHECK IT OUT?
YOU HAVE THOSE CLAWS AND WHAT— NOT . . .
BELOVED
CATS REMAIN ALOOF.
CATS DO NOT CONCERN THEMSELVES WITH THE PROBLEMS OF OTHERS.
AND LAST OF ALL, **CATS** DON'T LIKE **SUDDEN LOUD NOISES!!**
BUT . . . WITH IF IT IS A CAT?
SOMEONE PUH-LEASE HELP!

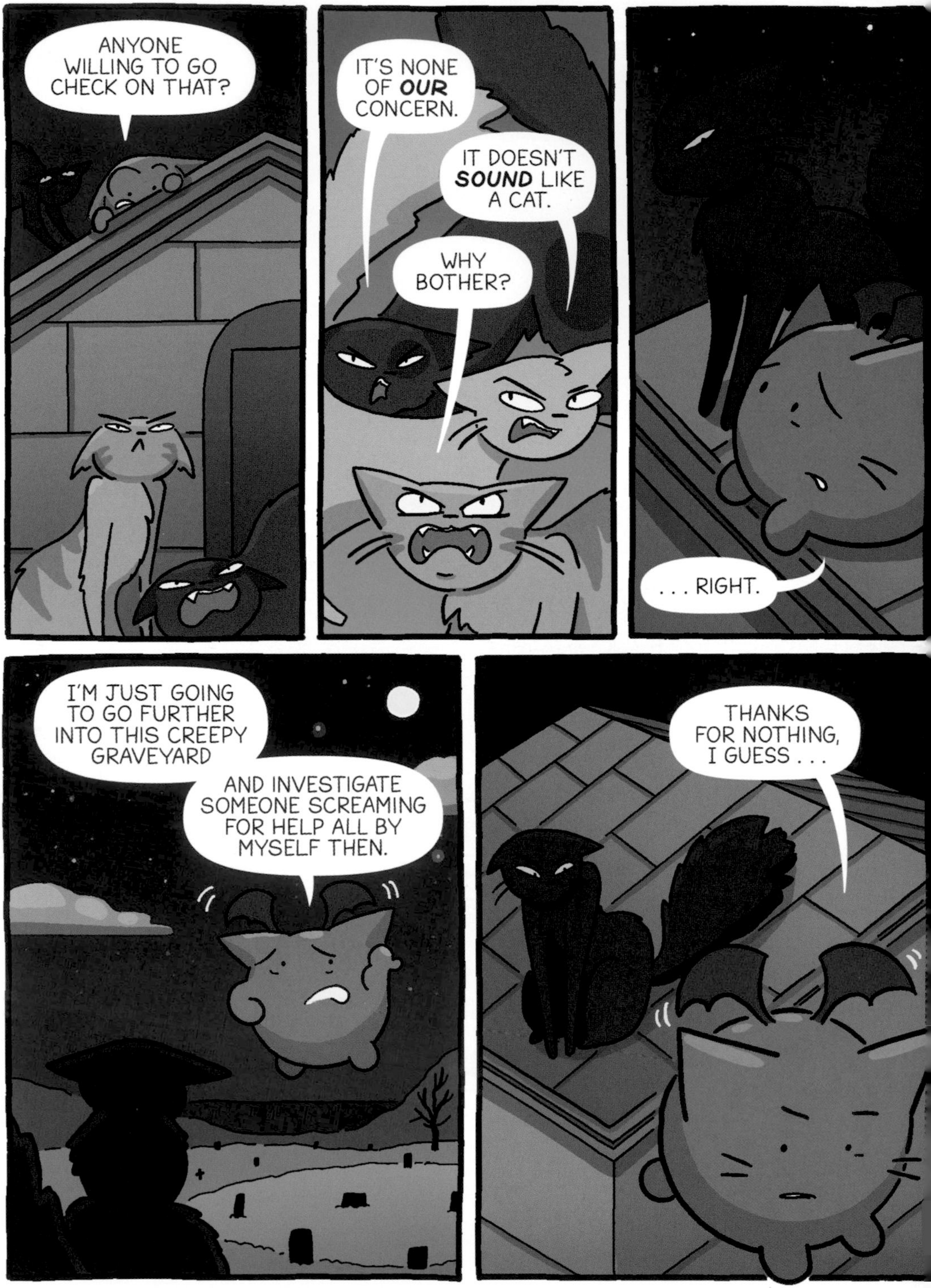

ANYONE WILLING TO GO CHECK ON THAT?
IT'S NONE OF **OUR** CONCERN.
IT DOESN'T **SOUND** LIKE A CAT.
WHY BOTHER?
. . . RIGHT.
I'M JUST GOING TO GO FURTHER INTO THIS CREEPY GRAVEYARD
AND INVESTIGATE SOMEONE SCREAMING FOR HELP ALL BY MYSELF THEN.
THANKS FOR NOTHING, I GUESS . . .

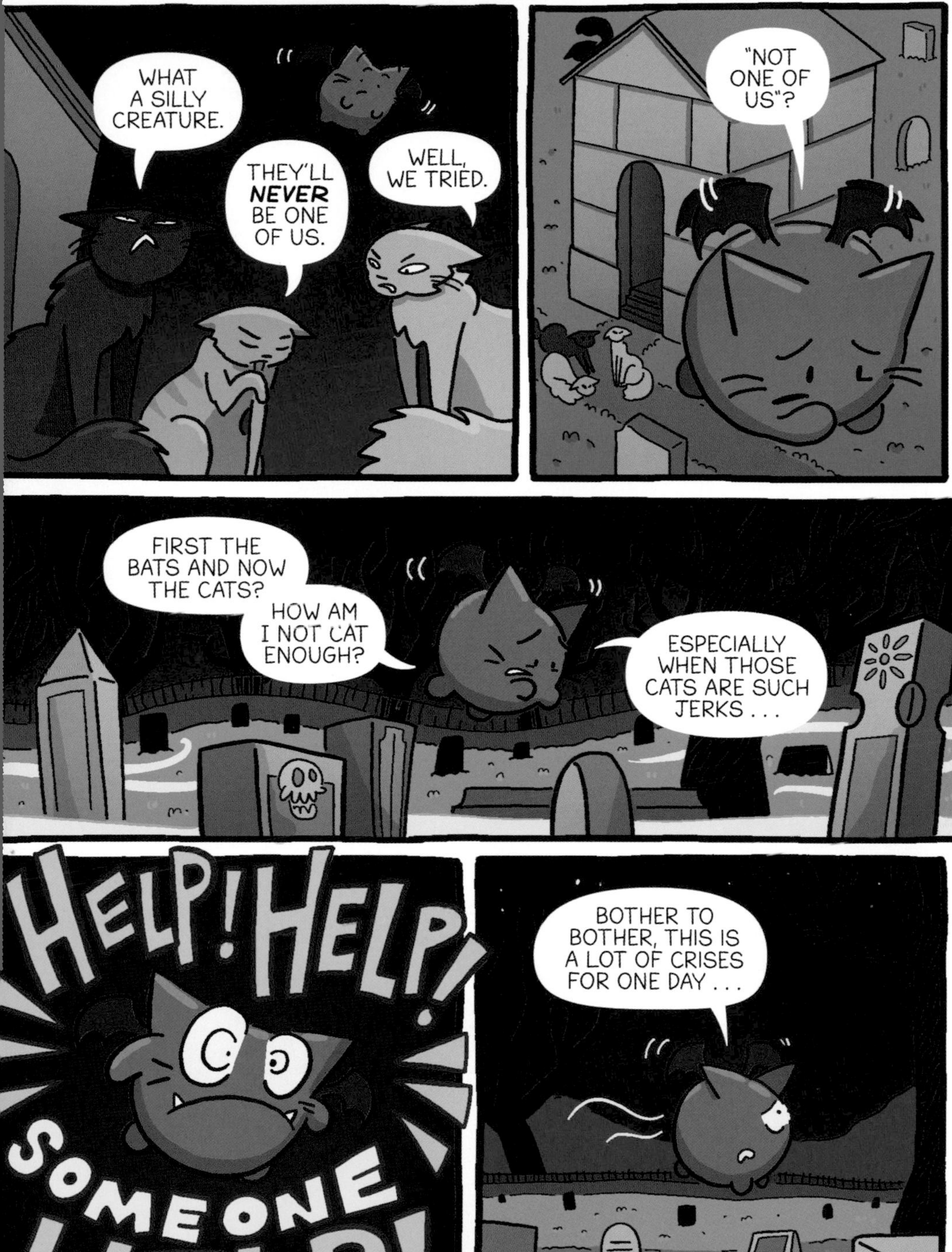

WHAT A SILLY CREATURE.
THEY'LL **NEVER** BE ONE OF US.
WELL, WE TRIED.
"NOT ONE OF US"?
FIRST THE BATS AND NOW THE CATS?
HOW AM I NOT CAT ENOUGH?
ESPECIALLY WHEN THOSE CATS ARE SUCH JERKS . . .
HELP! HELP!
SOMEONE HELP!
BOTHER TO BOTHER, THIS IS A LOT OF CRISES FOR ONE DAY . . .

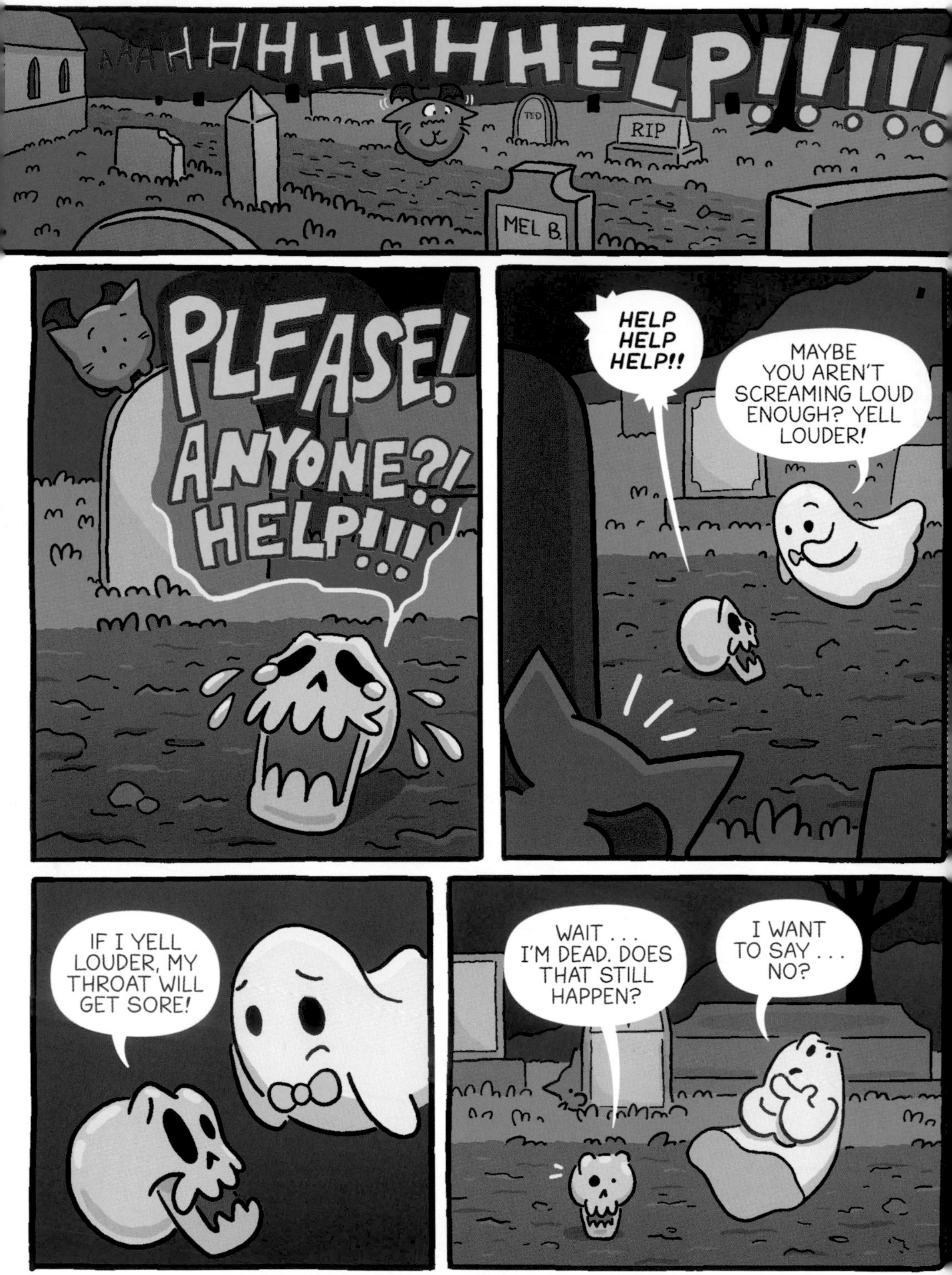

AAAHHHHHHHHELP!!!!!
TED
RIP
MEL B.
PLEASE! ANYONE?! HELP!!!
HELP HELP HELP!!
MAYBE YOU AREN'T SCREAMING LOUD ENOUGH? YELL LOUDER!
IF I YELL LOUDER, MY THROAT WILL GET SORE!
WAIT . . . I'M DEAD. DOES THAT STILL HAPPEN?
I WANT TO SAY . . . NO?

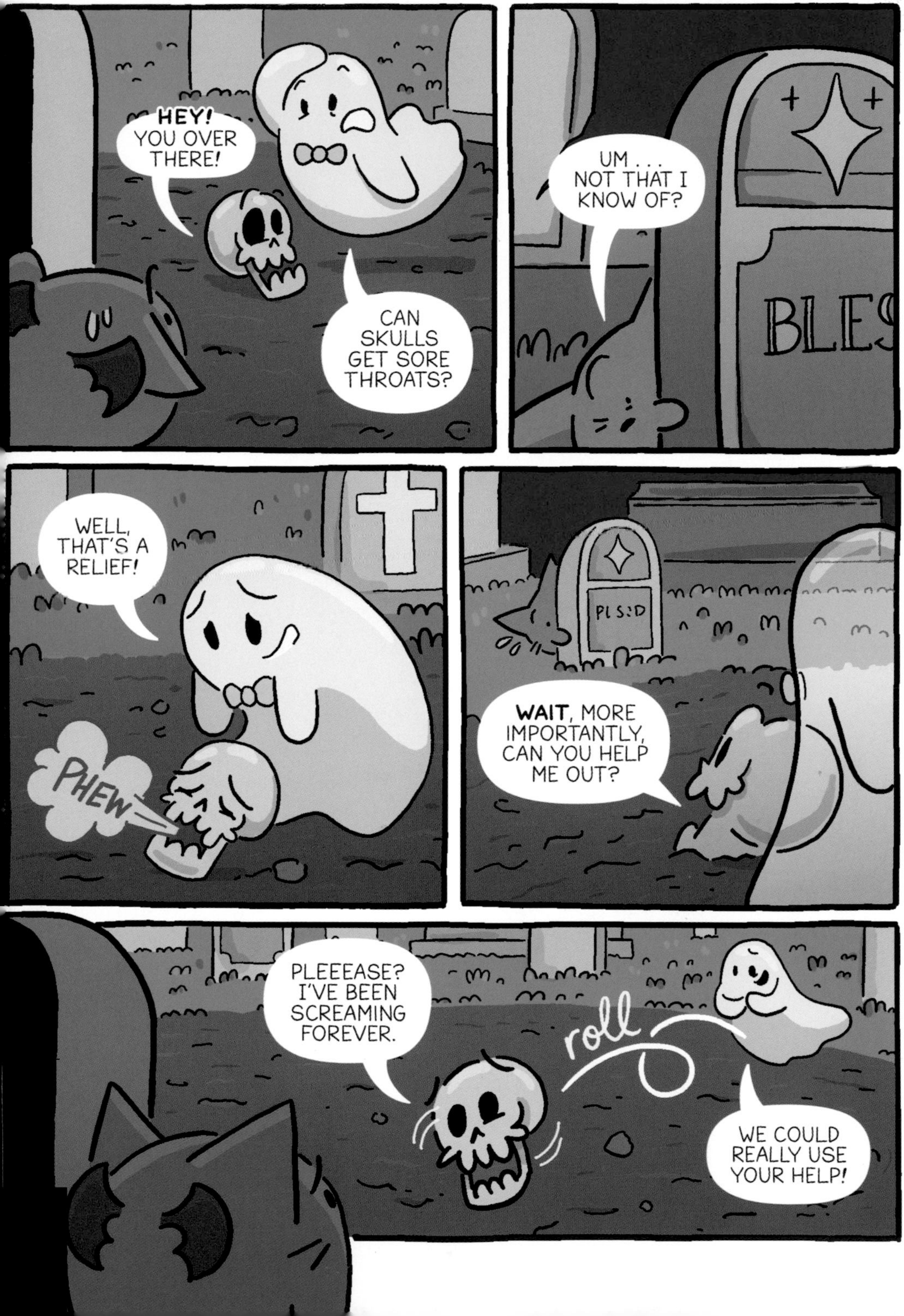
HEY! YOU OVER THERE!
CAN SKULLS GET SORE THROATS?
UM . . . NOT THAT I KNOW OF?
BLES
WELL, THAT'S A RELIEF!
PHEW
PLS:D
WAIT, MORE IMPORTANTLY, CAN YOU HELP ME OUT?
PLEEEASE? I'VE BEEN SCREAMING FOREVER.
roll
WE COULD REALLY USE YOUR HELP!

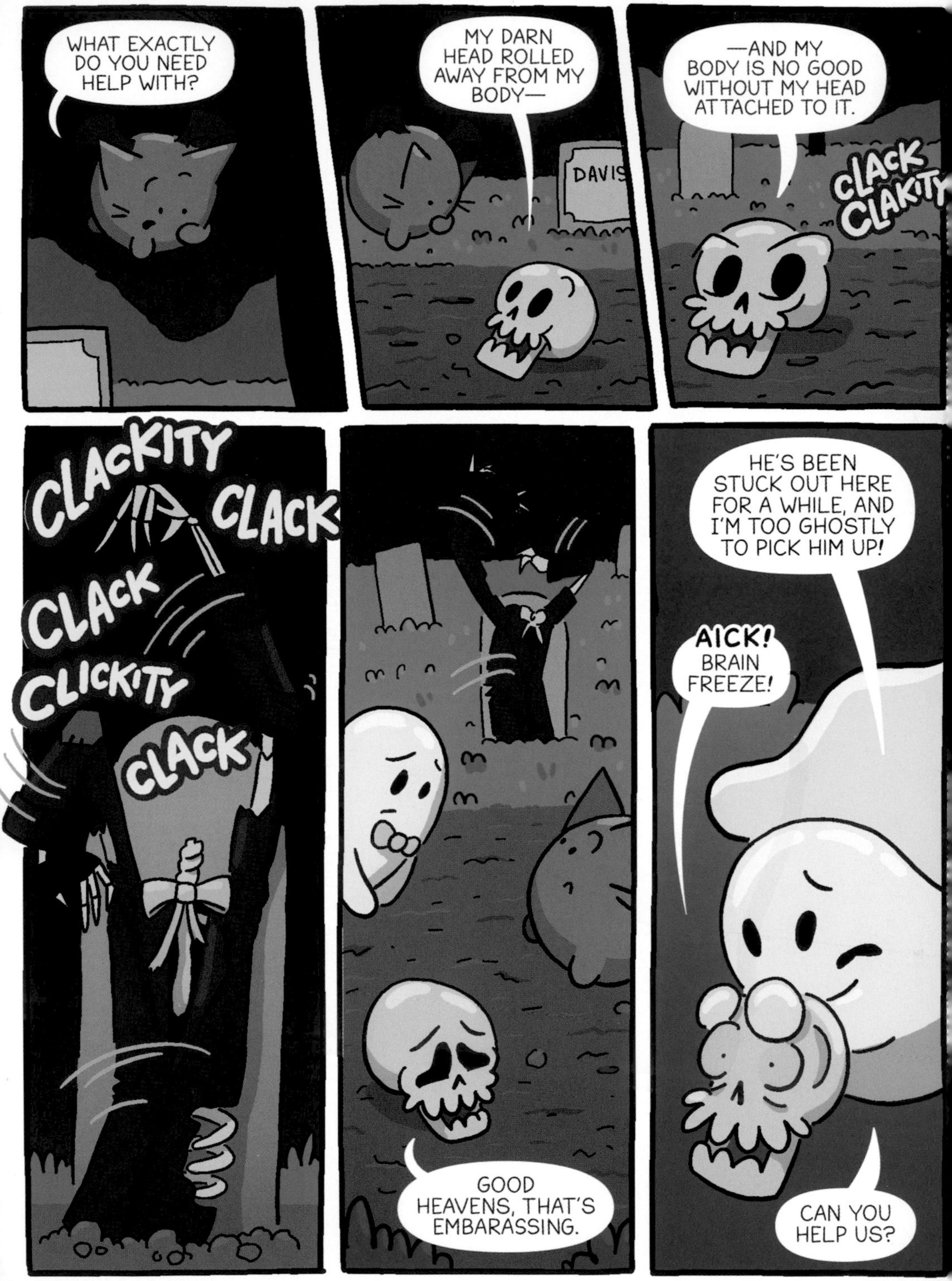
WHAT EXACTLY DO YOU NEED HELP WITH?
MY DARN HEAD ROLLED AWAY FROM MY BODY—
DAVIS
—AND MY BODY IS NO GOOD WITHOUT MY HEAD ATTACHED TO IT.
CLACK CLAKITY
CLACKITY
CLACK
CLACK
CLICKITY
CLACK
GOOD HEAVENS, THAT'S EMBARASSING.
HE'S BEEN STUCK OUT HERE FOR A WHILE, AND I'M TOO GHOSTLY TO PICK HIM UP!
AICK! BRAIN FREEZE!
CAN YOU HELP US?

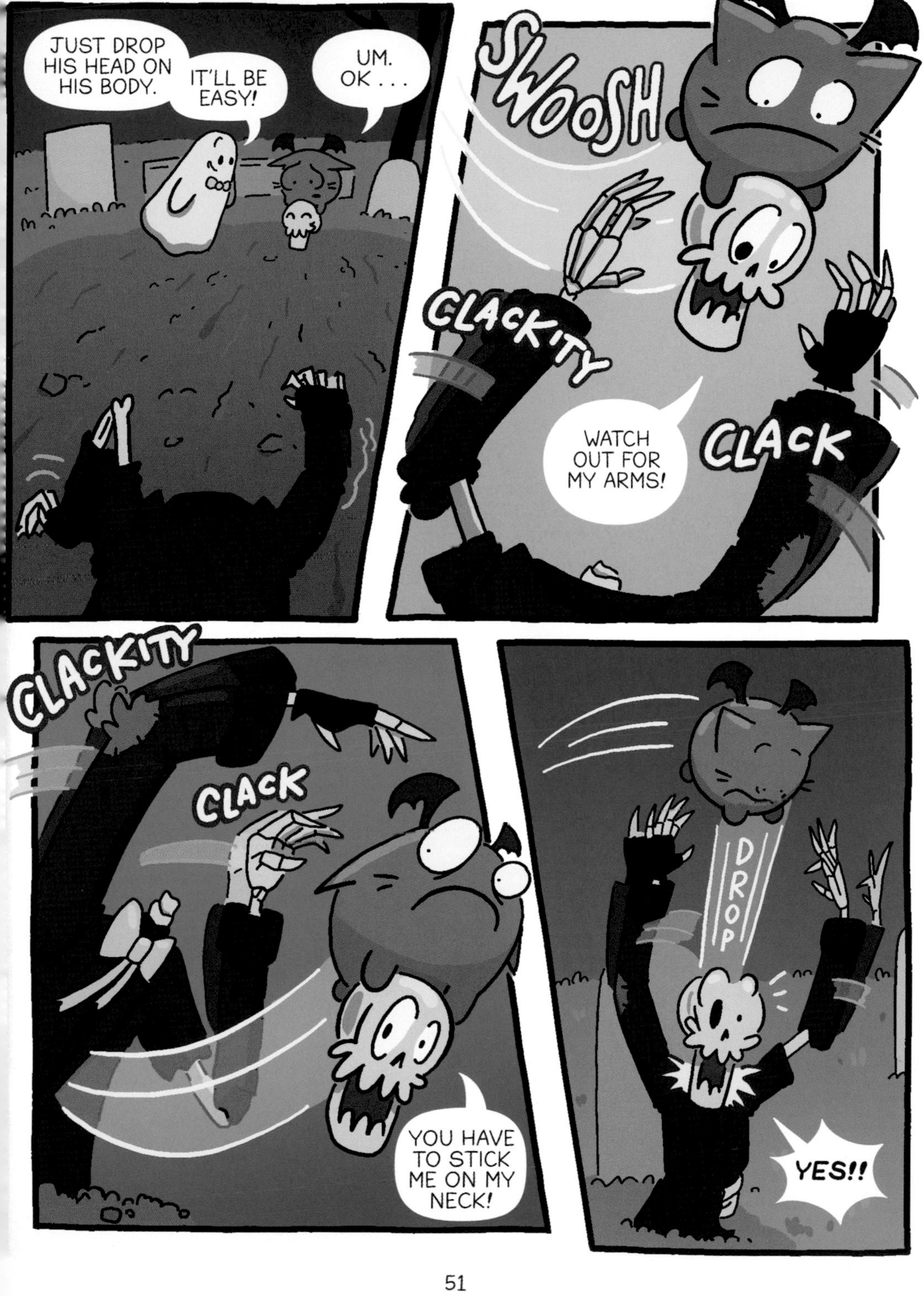

JUST DROP HIS HEAD ON HIS BODY.
IT'LL BE EASY!
UM. OK . . .
SWOOSH
CLACKITY
WATCH OUT FOR MY ARMS!
CLACK
CLACKITY
CLACK
YOU HAVE TO STICK ME ON MY NECK!
DROP
YES!!

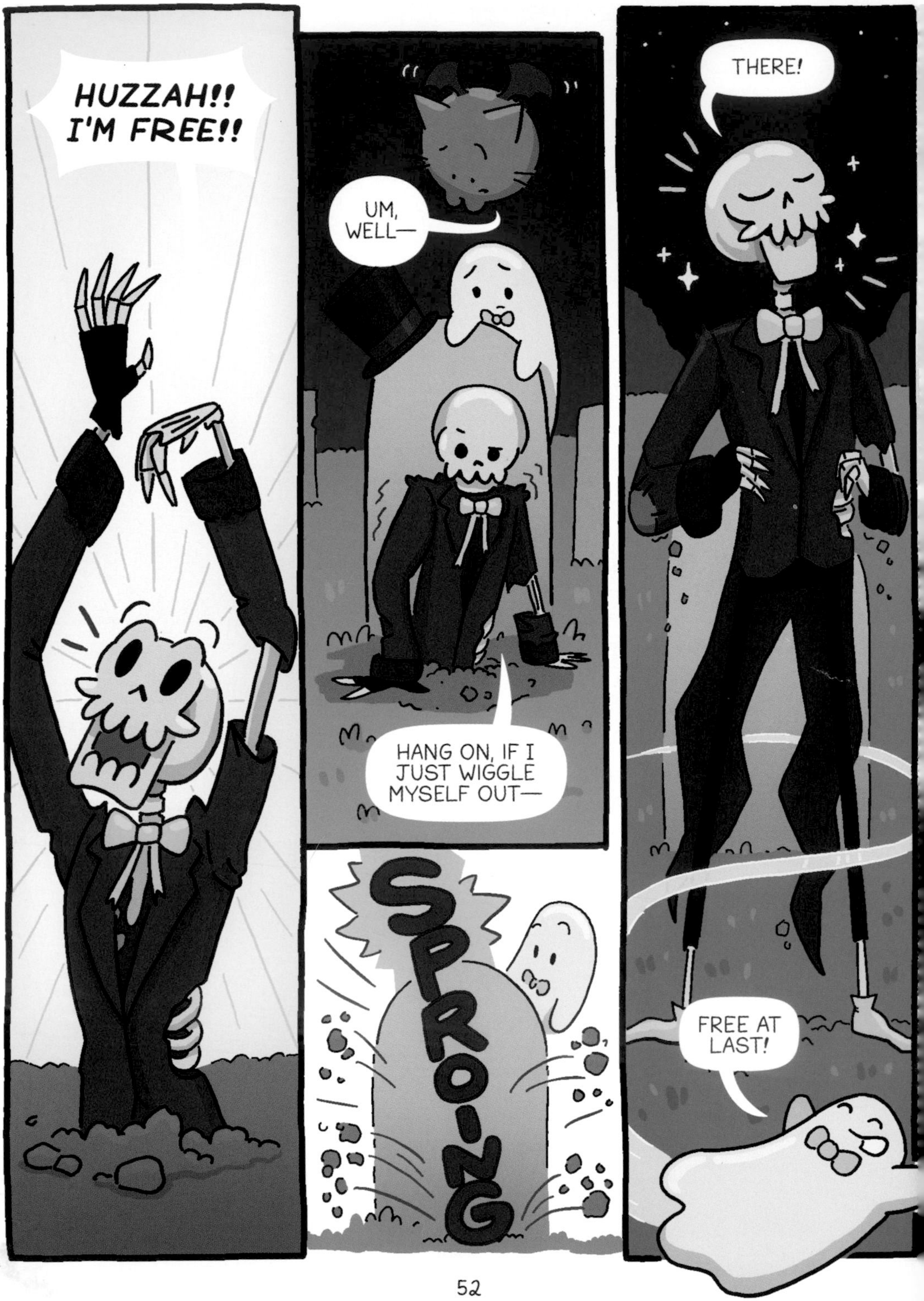

HUZZAH!! I'M FREE!!
UM, WELL—
HANG ON, IF I JUST WIGGLE MYSELF OUT—
SPROING
THERE!
FREE AT LAST!

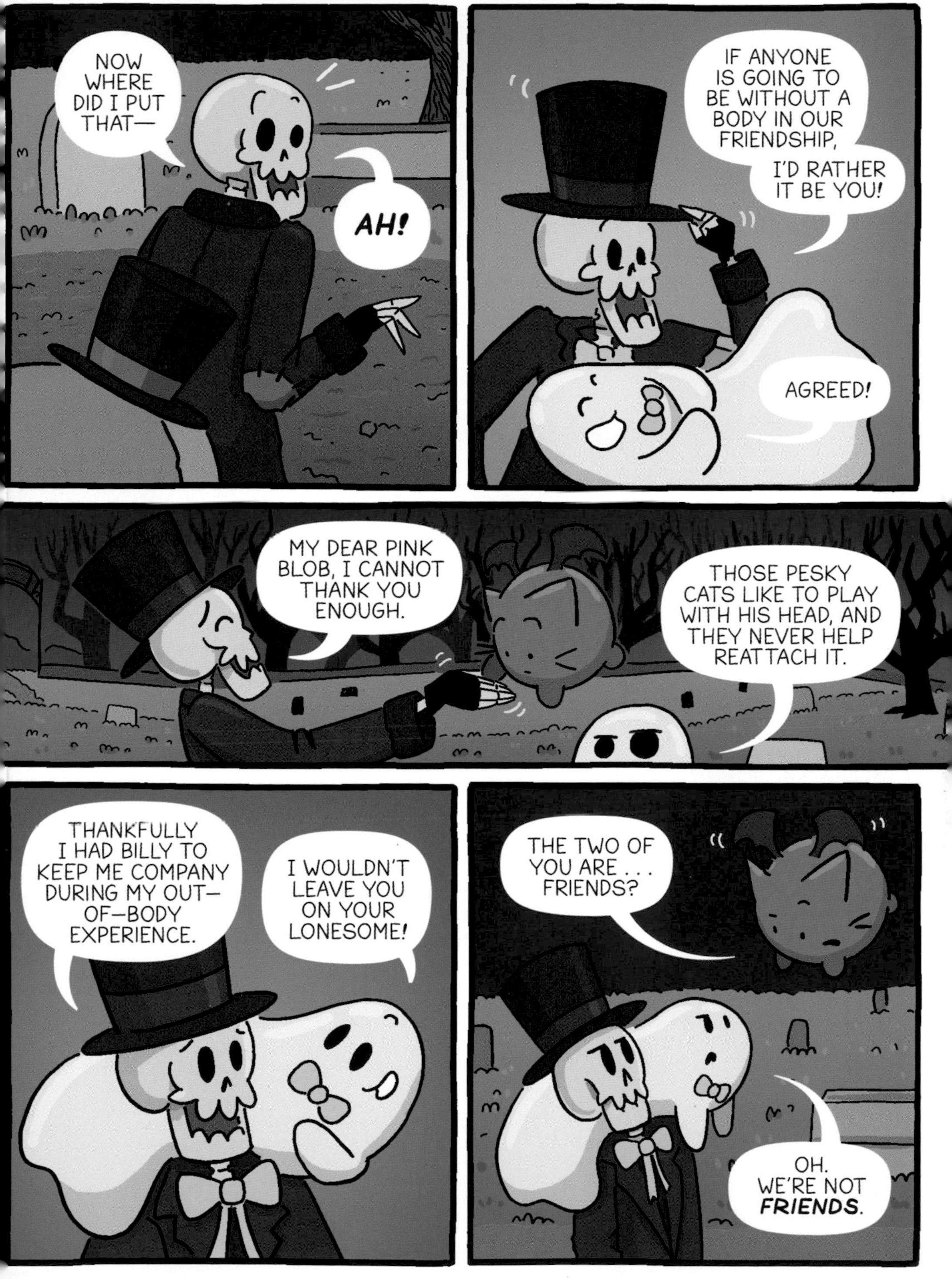

NOW WHERE DID I PUT THAT—
AH!
IF ANYONE IS GOING TO BE WITHOUT A BODY IN OUR FRIENDSHIP,
I'D RATHER IT BE YOU!
AGREED!
MY DEAR PINK BLOB, I CANNOT THANK YOU ENOUGH.
THOSE PESKY CATS LIKE TO PLAY WITH HIS HEAD, AND THEY NEVER HELP REATTACH IT.
THANKFULLY I HAD BILLY TO KEEP ME COMPANY DURING MY OUT-OF-BODY EXPERIENCE.
I WOULDN'T LEAVE YOU ON YOUR LONESOME!
THE TWO OF YOU ARE . . . FRIENDS?
OH. WE'RE NOT **FRIENDS**.

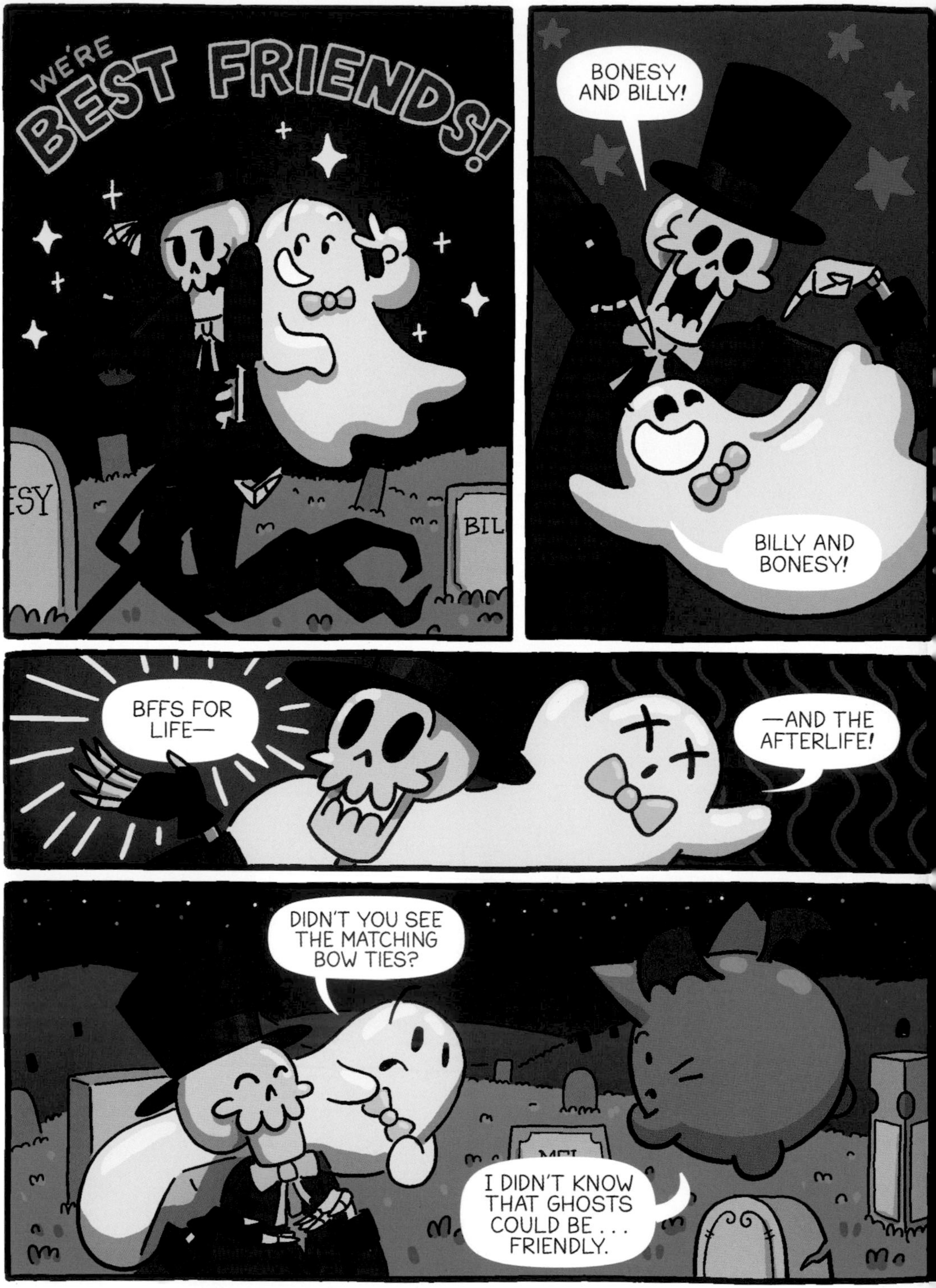
WE'RE BEST FRIENDS!
ESY
BIL
BONESY AND BILLY!
BILLY AND BONESY!
BFFS FOR LIFE—
—AND THE AFTERLIFE!
DIDN'T YOU SEE THE MATCHING BOW TIES?
I DIDN'T KNOW THAT GHOSTS COULD BE . . . FRIENDLY.

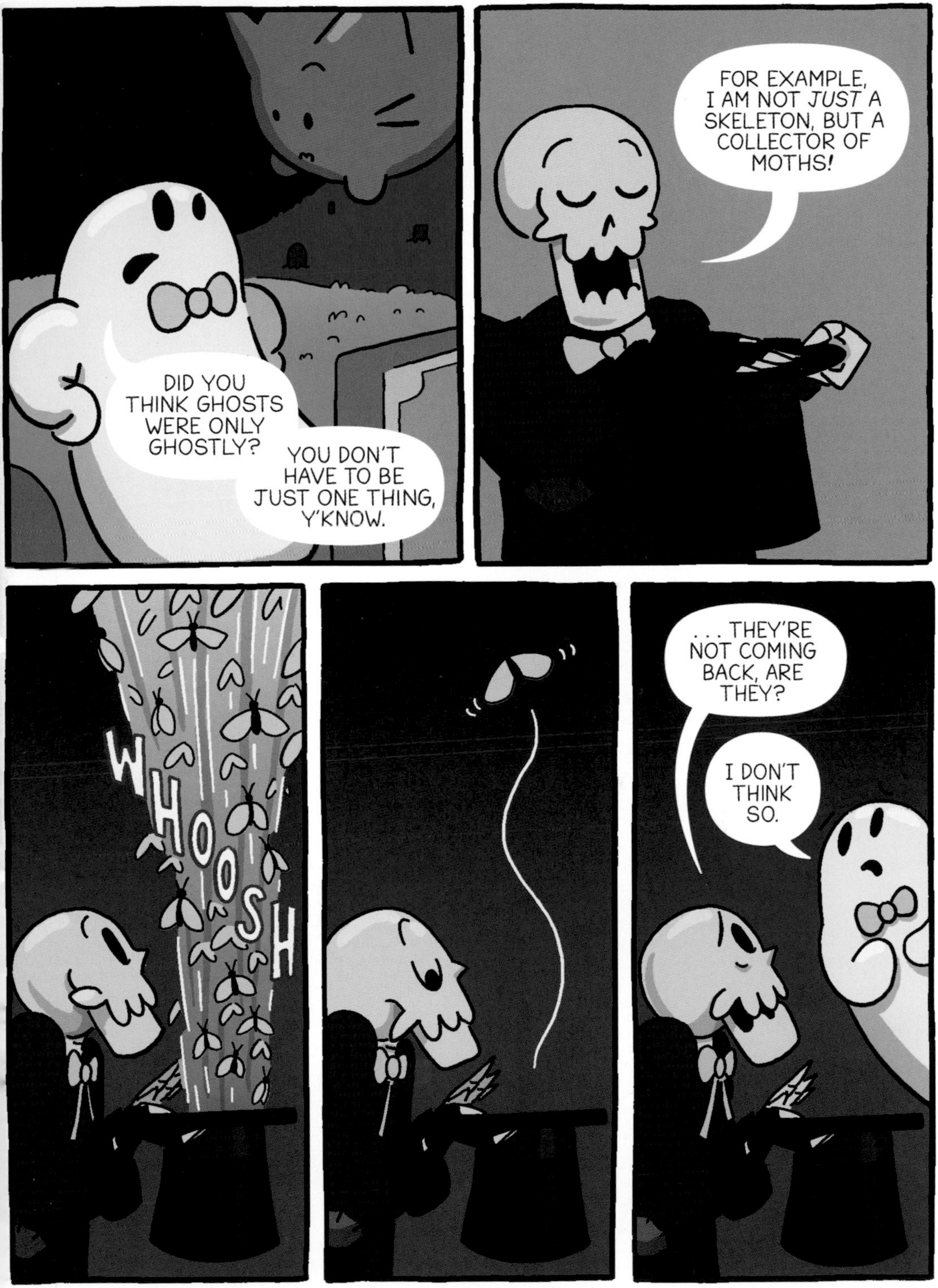
DID YOU THINK GHOSTS WERE ONLY GHOSTLY?
YOU DON'T HAVE TO BE JUST ONE THING, Y'KNOW.
FOR EXAMPLE, I AM NOT *JUST* A SKELETON, BUT A COLLECTOR OF MOTHS!
WHOOSH
. . . THEY'RE NOT COMING BACK, ARE THEY?
I DON'T THINK SO.

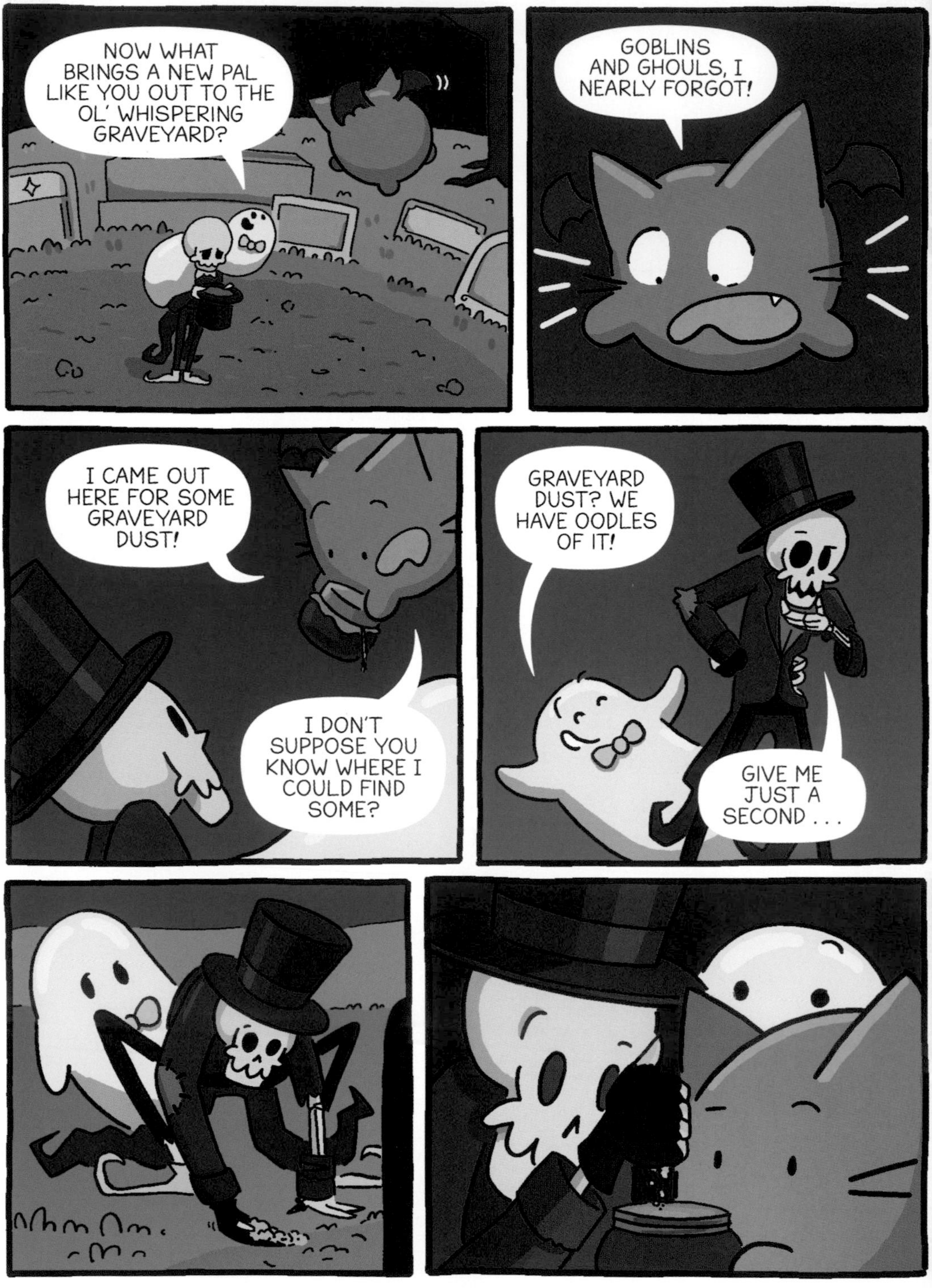
NOW WHAT BRINGS A NEW PAL LIKE YOU OUT TO THE OL' WHISPERING GRAVEYARD?
GOBLINS AND GHOULS, I NEARLY FORGOT!
I CAME OUT HERE FOR SOME GRAVEYARD DUST!
I DON'T SUPPOSE YOU KNOW WHERE I COULD FIND SOME?
GRAVEYARD DUST? WE HAVE OODLES OF IT!
GIVE ME JUST A SECOND . . .

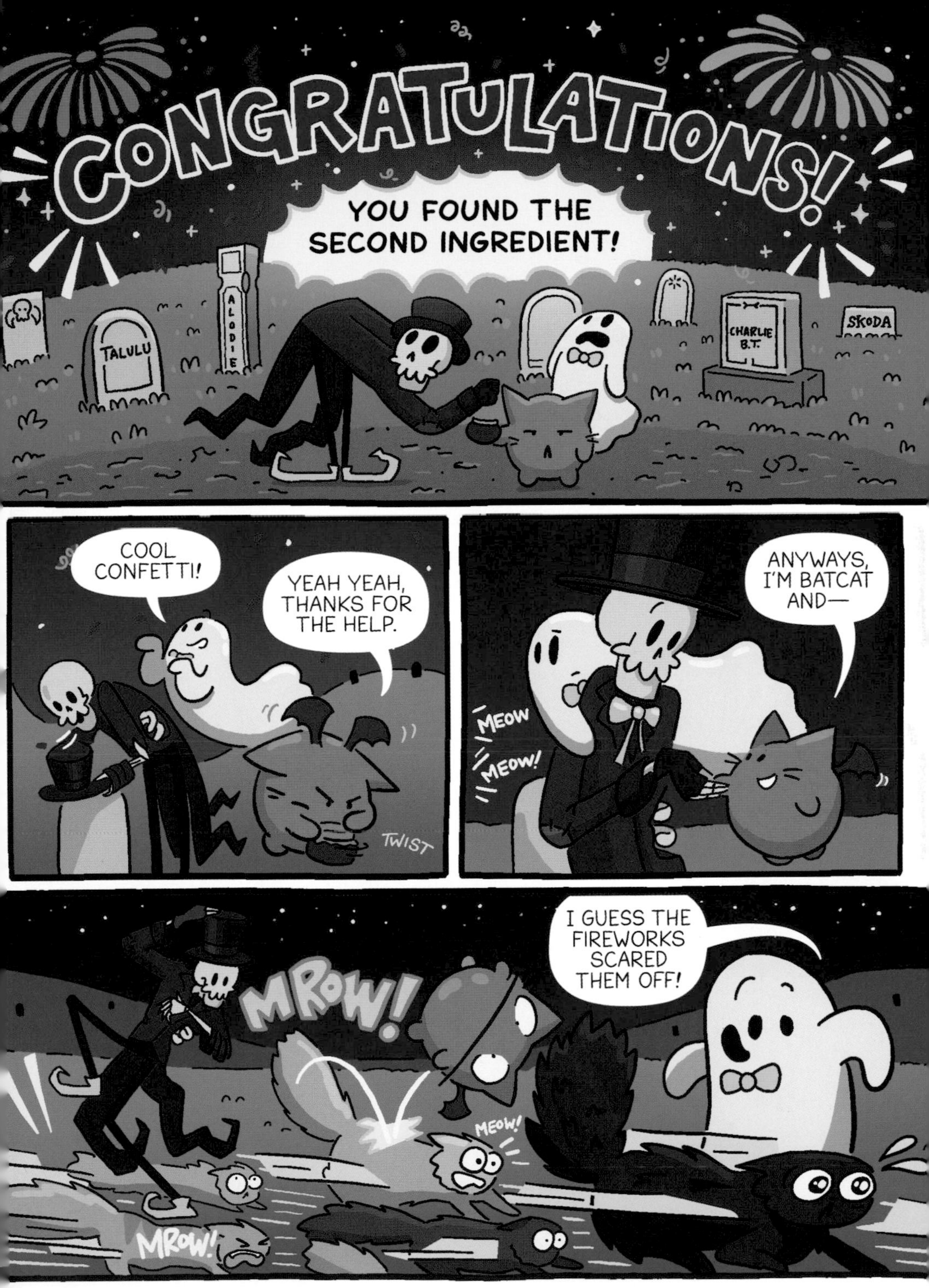
CONGRATULATIONS!
YOU FOUND THE SECOND INGREDIENT!
TALULU
ALODIE
CHARLIE B.T.
SKODA
COOL CONFETTI!
YEAH YEAH, THANKS FOR THE HELP.
TWIST
ANYWAYS, I'M BATCAT AND—
MEOW
MEOW!
MROW!
I GUESS THE FIREWORKS SCARED THEM OFF!
MEOW!
MROW!

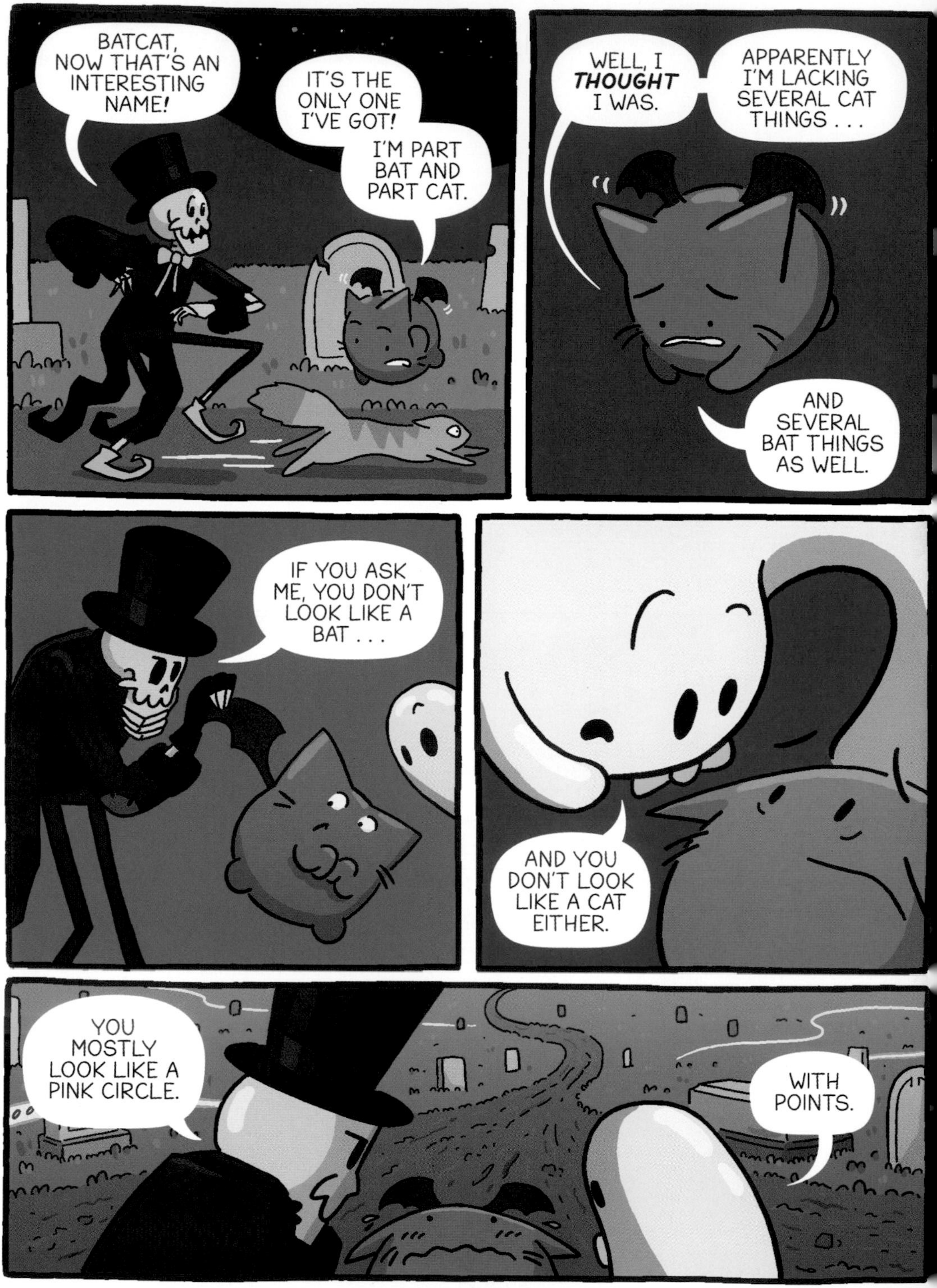

BATCAT, NOW THAT'S AN INTERESTING NAME!
IT'S THE ONLY ONE I'VE GOT!
I'M PART BAT AND PART CAT.
WELL, I **THOUGHT** I WAS.
APPARENTLY I'M LACKING SEVERAL CAT THINGS . . .
AND SEVERAL BAT THINGS AS WELL.
IF YOU ASK ME, YOU DON'T LOOK LIKE A BAT . . .
AND YOU DON'T LOOK LIKE A CAT EITHER.
YOU MOSTLY LOOK LIKE A PINK CIRCLE.
WITH POINTS.

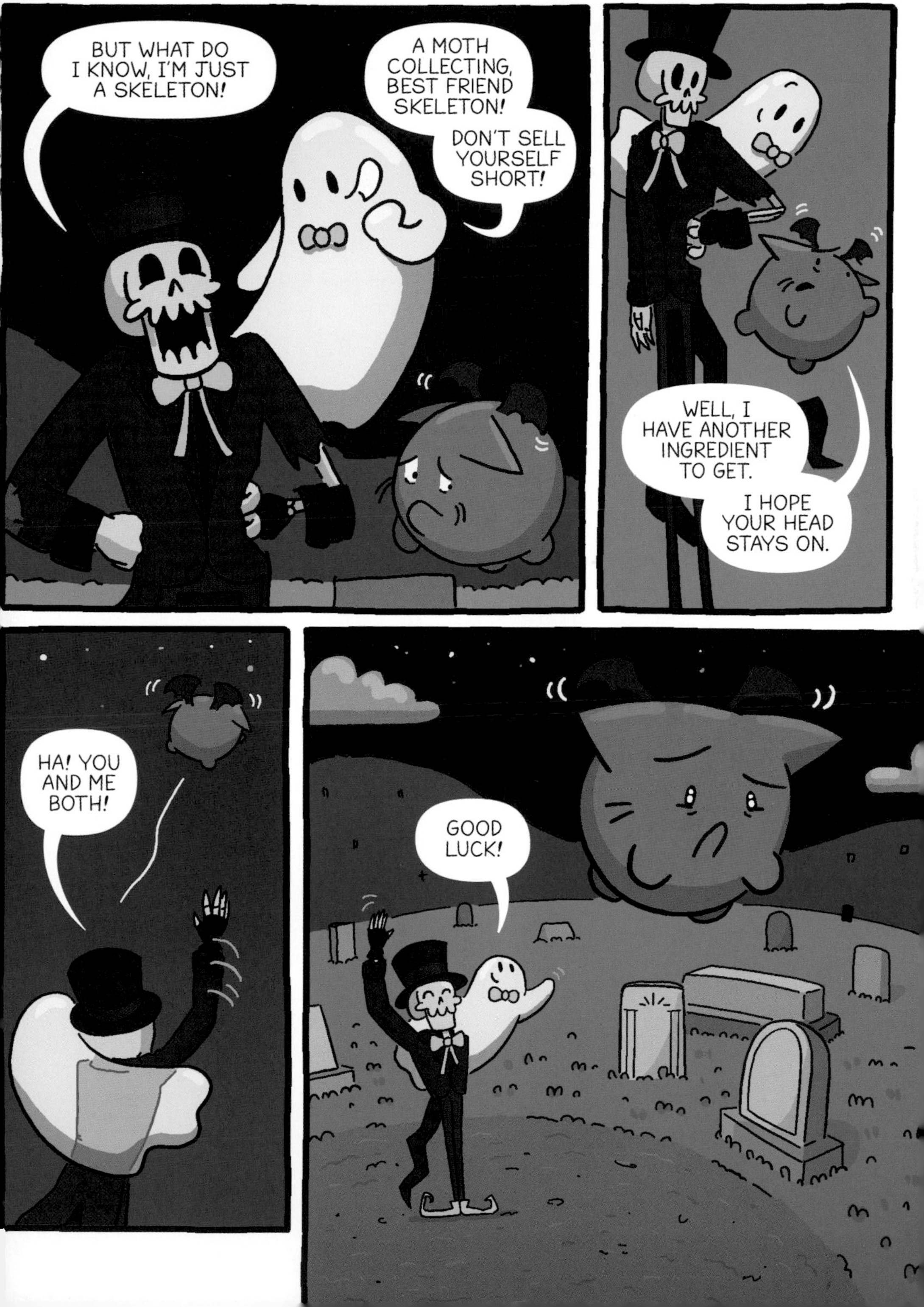
BUT WHAT DO I KNOW, I'M JUST A SKELETON!
A MOTH COLLECTING, BEST FRIEND SKELETON!
DON'T SELL YOURSELF SHORT!
WELL, I HAVE ANOTHER INGREDIENT TO GET.
I HOPE YOUR HEAD STAYS ON.
HA! YOU AND ME BOTH!
GOOD LUCK!

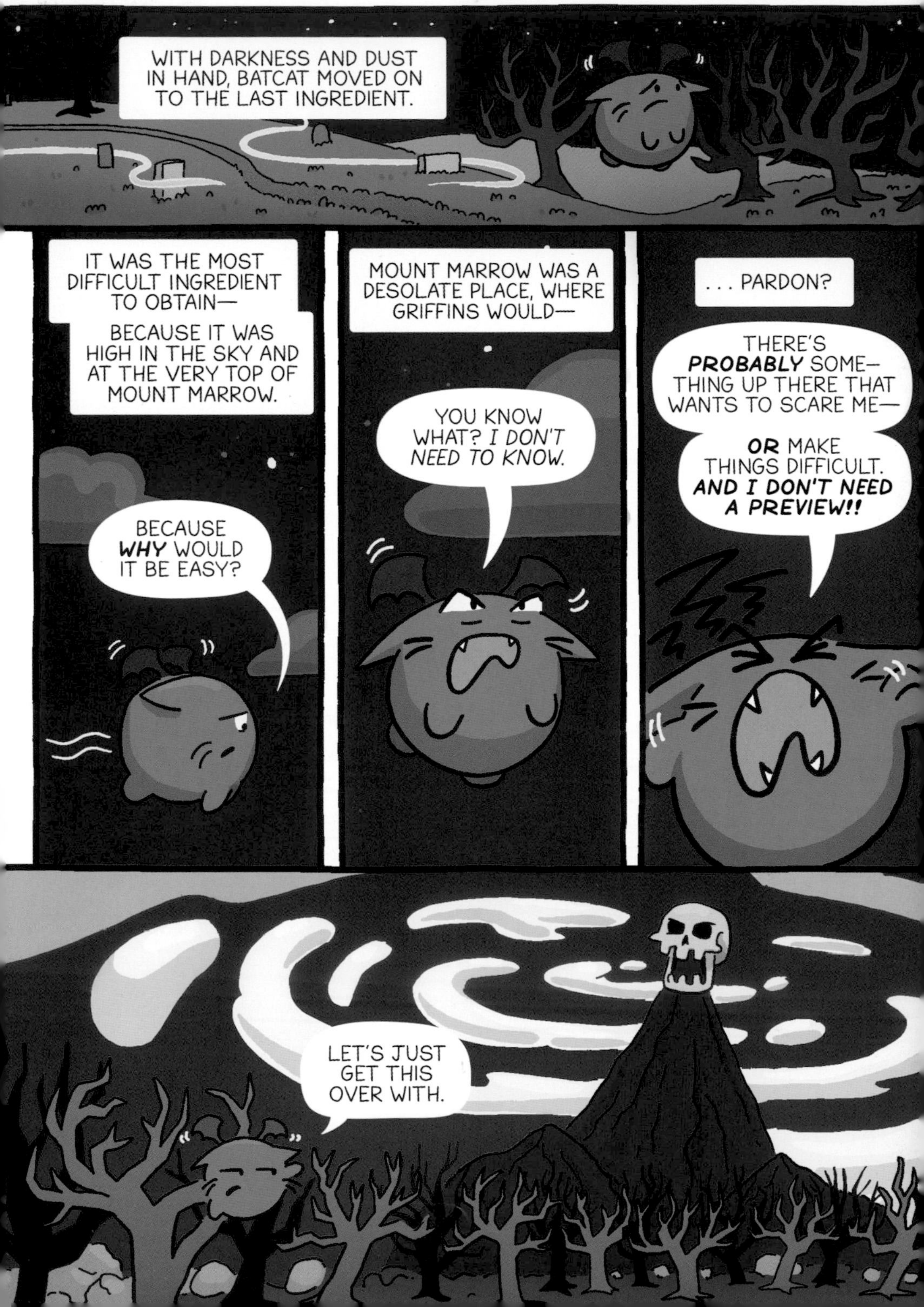

WITH DARKNESS AND DUST IN HAND, BATCAT MOVED ON TO THE LAST INGREDIENT.
IT WAS THE MOST DIFFICULT INGREDIENT TO OBTAIN—
BECAUSE IT WAS HIGH IN THE SKY AND AT THE VERY TOP OF MOUNT MARROW.
BECAUSE **WHY** WOULD IT BE EASY?
MOUNT MARROW WAS A DESOLATE PLACE, WHERE GRIFFINS WOULD—
YOU KNOW WHAT? *I DON'T NEED TO KNOW.*
. . . PARDON?
THERE'S ***PROBABLY*** SOME-THING UP THERE THAT WANTS TO SCARE ME—
OR MAKE THINGS DIFFICULT. ***AND I DON'T NEED A PREVIEW!!***
LET'S JUST GET THIS OVER WITH.

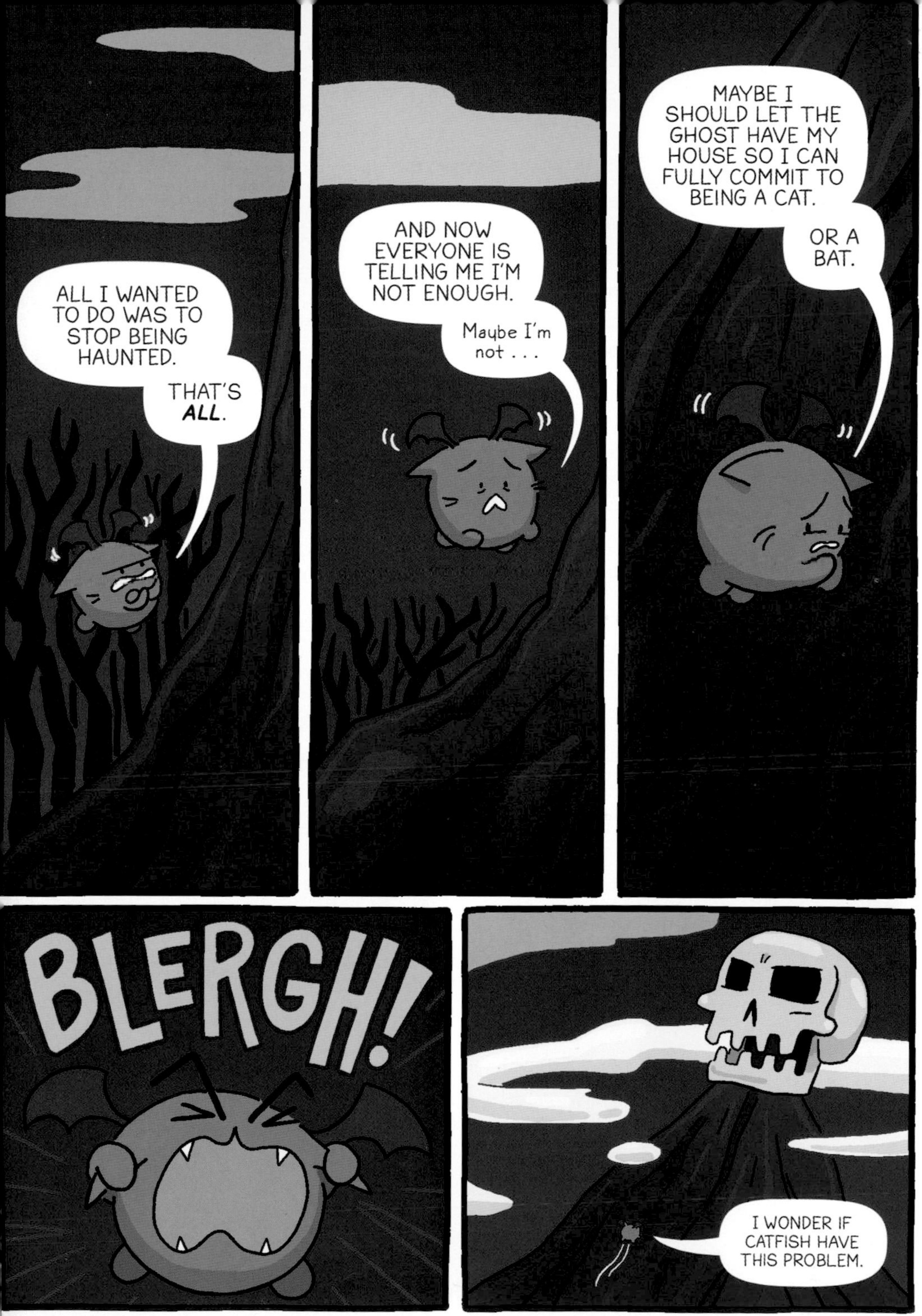
ALL I WANTED TO DO WAS TO STOP BEING HAUNTED.
THAT'S ALL.
AND NOW EVERYONE IS TELLING ME I'M NOT ENOUGH.
Maybe I'm not . . .
MAYBE I SHOULD LET THE GHOST HAVE MY HOUSE SO I CAN FULLY COMMIT TO BEING A CAT.
OR A BAT.
BLERGH!
I WONDER IF CATFISH HAVE THIS PROBLEM.

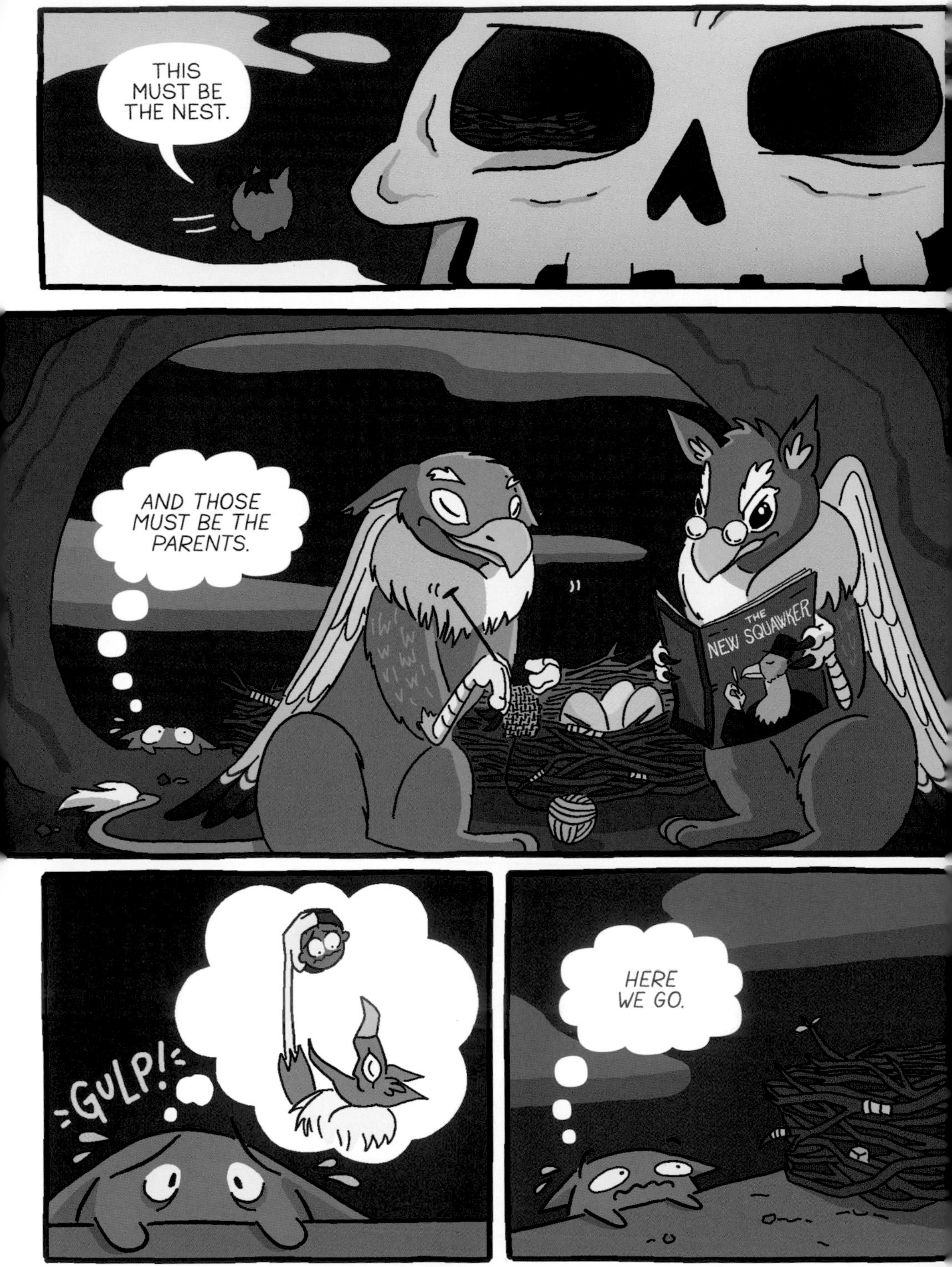
THIS MUST BE THE NEST.
AND THOSE MUST BE THE PARENTS.
THE NEW SQUAWKER
GULP!
HERE WE GO.

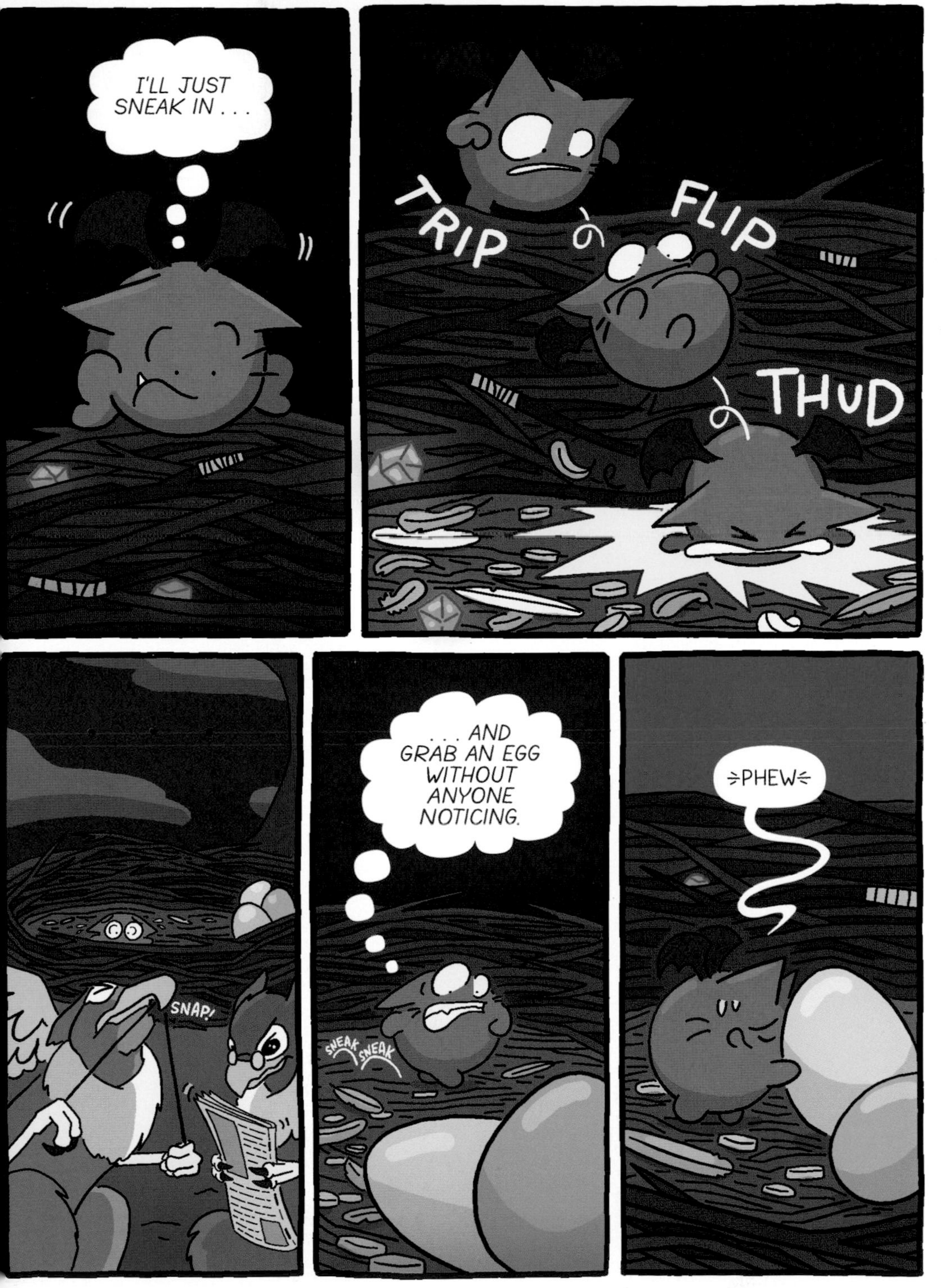
I'LL JUST SNEAK IN . . .
TRIP
FLIP
THUD
SNAP!
. . . AND GRAB AN EGG WITHOUT ANYONE NOTICING.
SNEAK SNEAK
PHEW

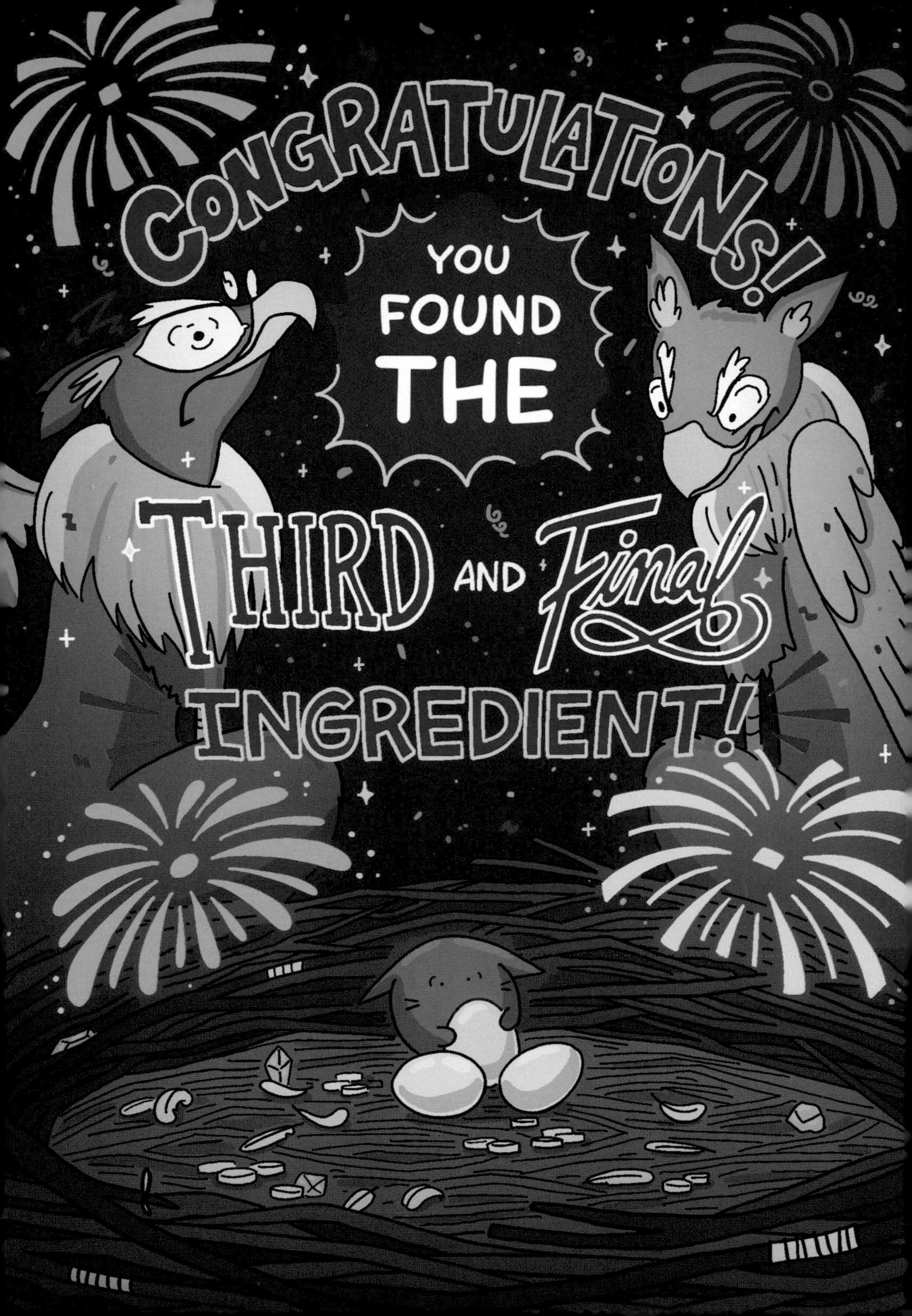
CONGRATULATIONS!
YOU FOUND THE
THIRD AND Final
INGREDIENT!

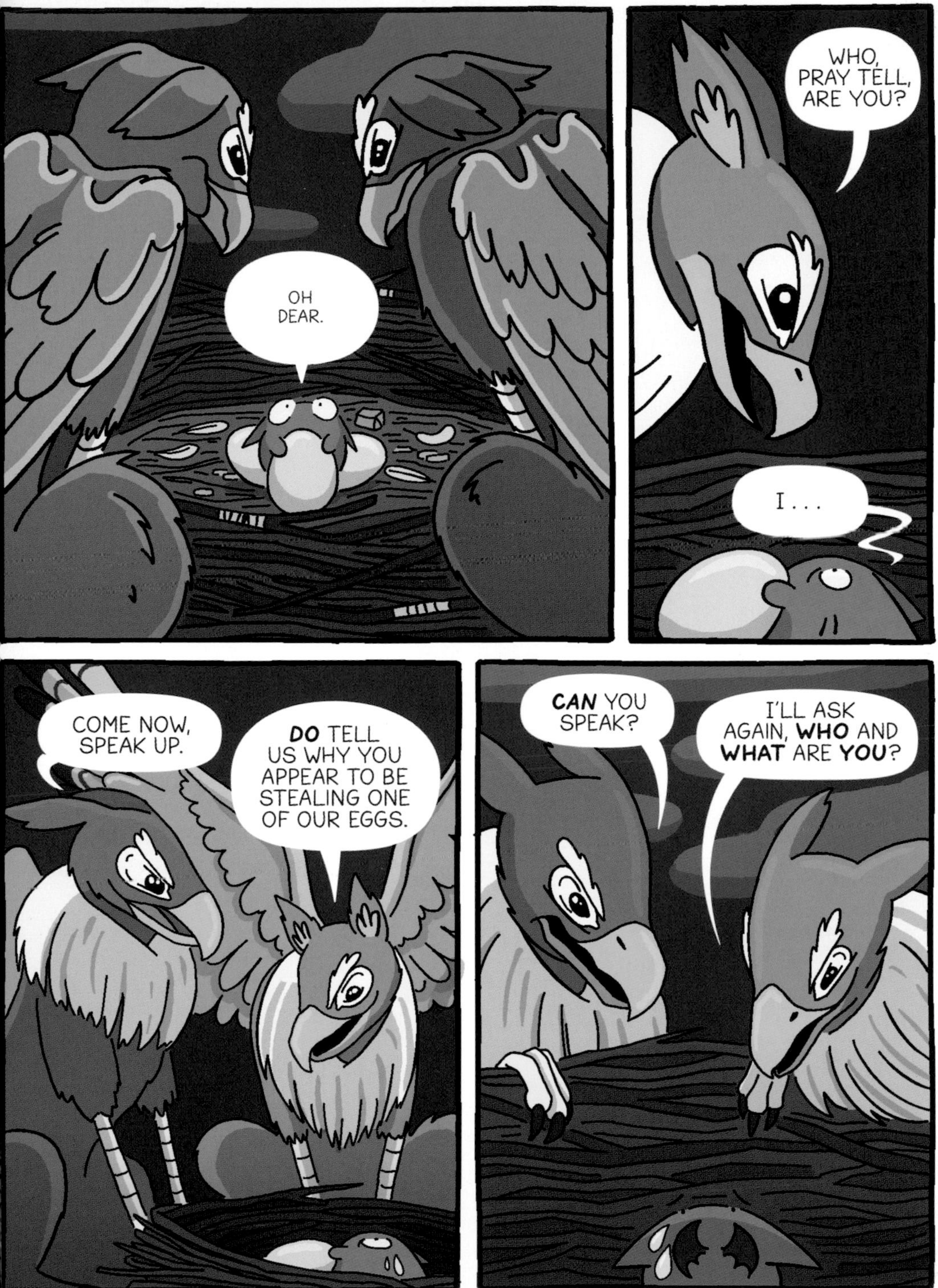
OH DEAR.
WHO, PRAY TELL, ARE YOU?
I . . .
COME NOW, SPEAK UP.
DO TELL US WHY YOU APPEAR TO BE STEALING ONE OF OUR EGGS.
CAN YOU SPEAK?
I'LL ASK AGAIN, **WHO** AND **WHAT** ARE **YOU**?

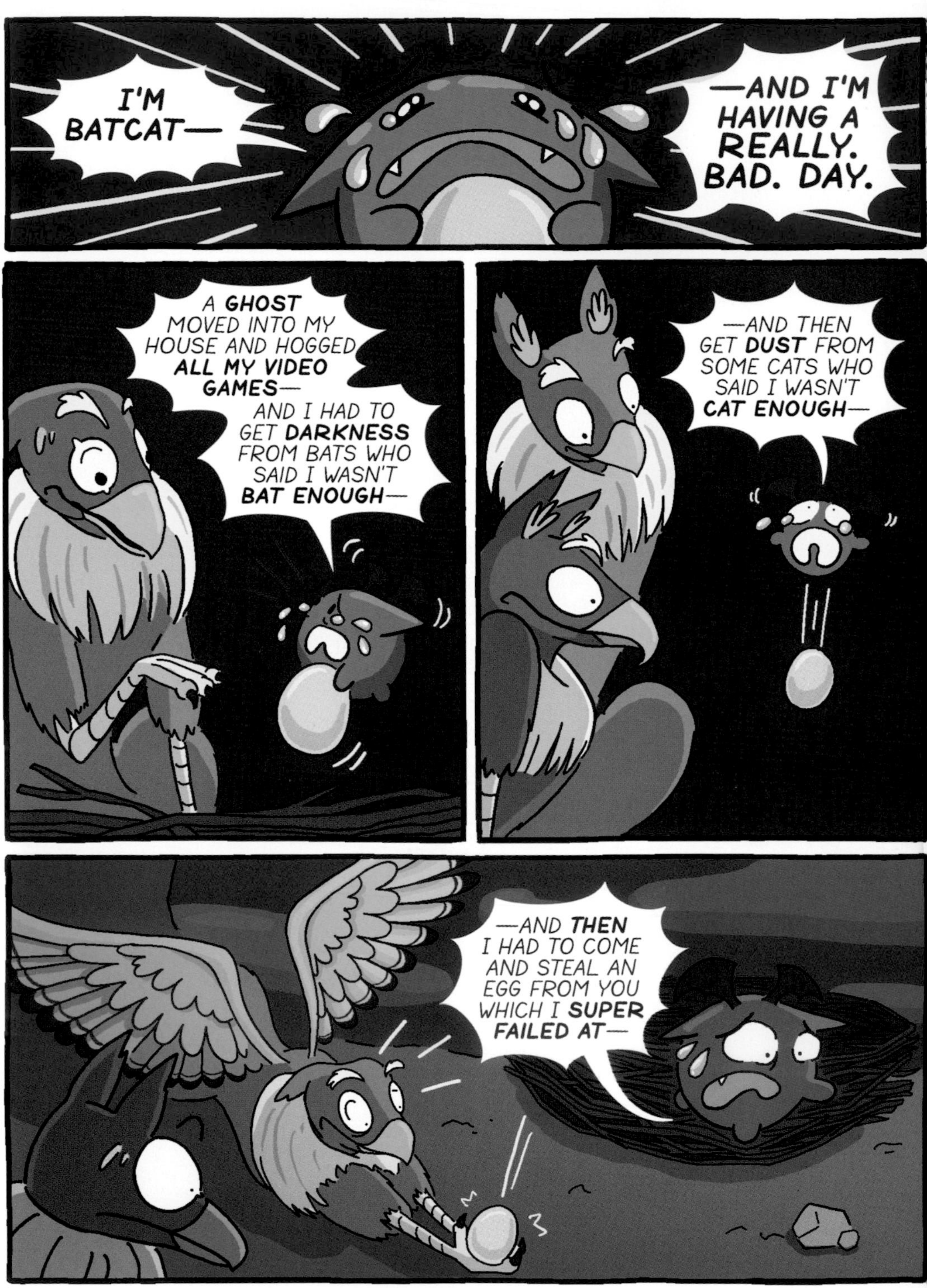
I'M BATCAT—
—AND I'M HAVING A REALLY. BAD. DAY.
A GHOST MOVED INTO MY HOUSE AND HOGGED ALL MY VIDEO GAMES—
AND I HAD TO GET DARKNESS FROM BATS WHO SAID I WASN'T BAT ENOUGH—
—AND THEN GET DUST FROM SOME CATS WHO SAID I WASN'T CAT ENOUGH—
—AND THEN I HAD TO COME AND STEAL AN EGG FROM YOU WHICH I SUPER FAILED AT—

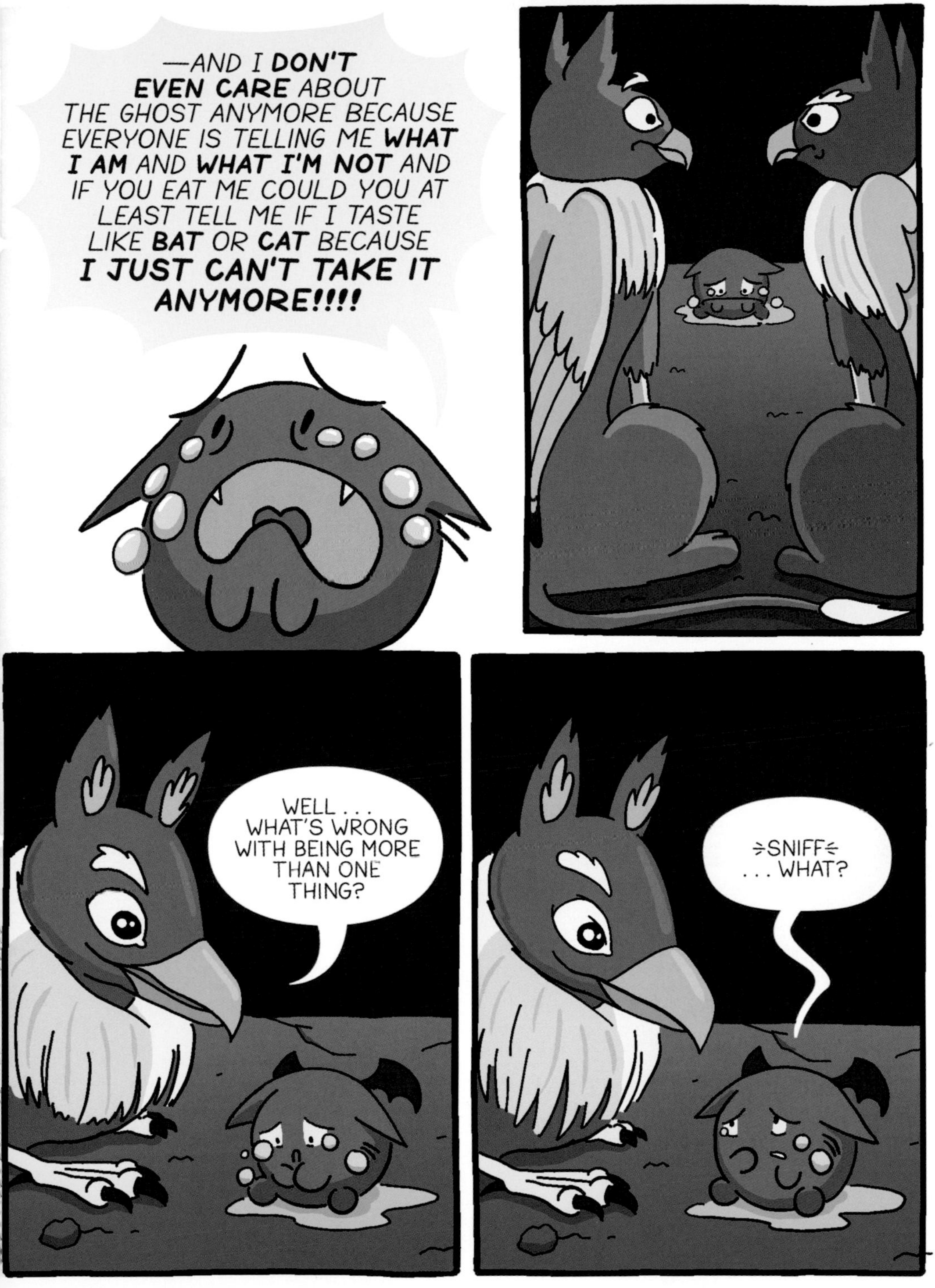
—AND I **DON'T EVEN CARE** ABOUT THE GHOST ANYMORE BECAUSE EVERYONE IS TELLING ME **WHAT I AM** AND **WHAT I'M NOT** AND IF YOU EAT ME COULD YOU AT LEAST TELL ME IF I TASTE LIKE **BAT** OR **CAT** BECAUSE **I JUST CAN'T TAKE IT ANYMORE!!!!**
WELL . . . WHAT'S WRONG WITH BEING MORE THAN ONE THING?
⇒SNIFF⇐ . . . WHAT?

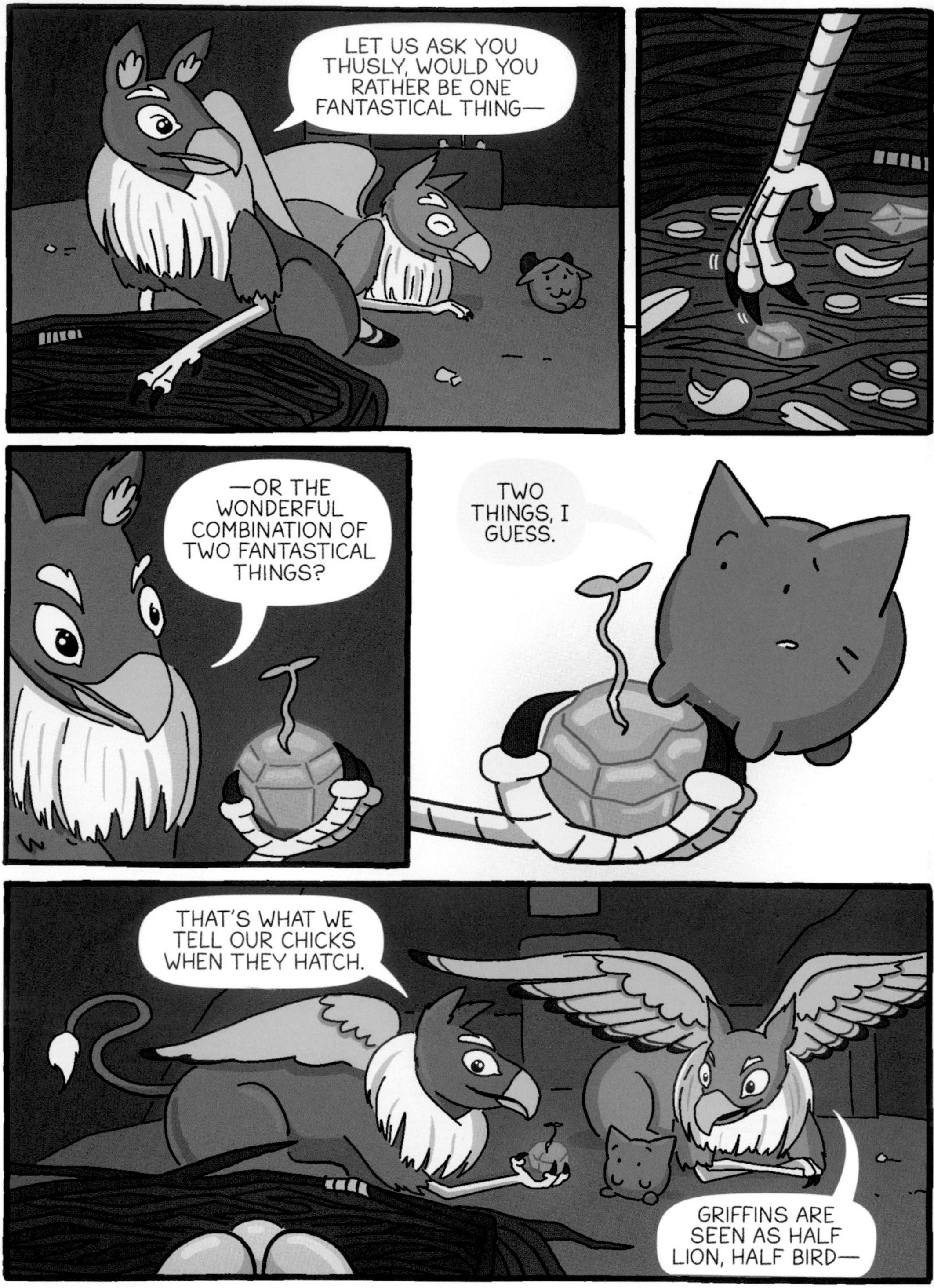
LET US ASK YOU THUSLY, WOULD YOU RATHER BE ONE FANTASTICAL THING—
—OR THE WONDERFUL COMBINATION OF TWO FANTASTICAL THINGS?
TWO THINGS, I GUESS.
THAT'S WHAT WE TELL OUR CHICKS WHEN THEY HATCH.
GRIFFINS ARE SEEN AS HALF LION, HALF BIRD—

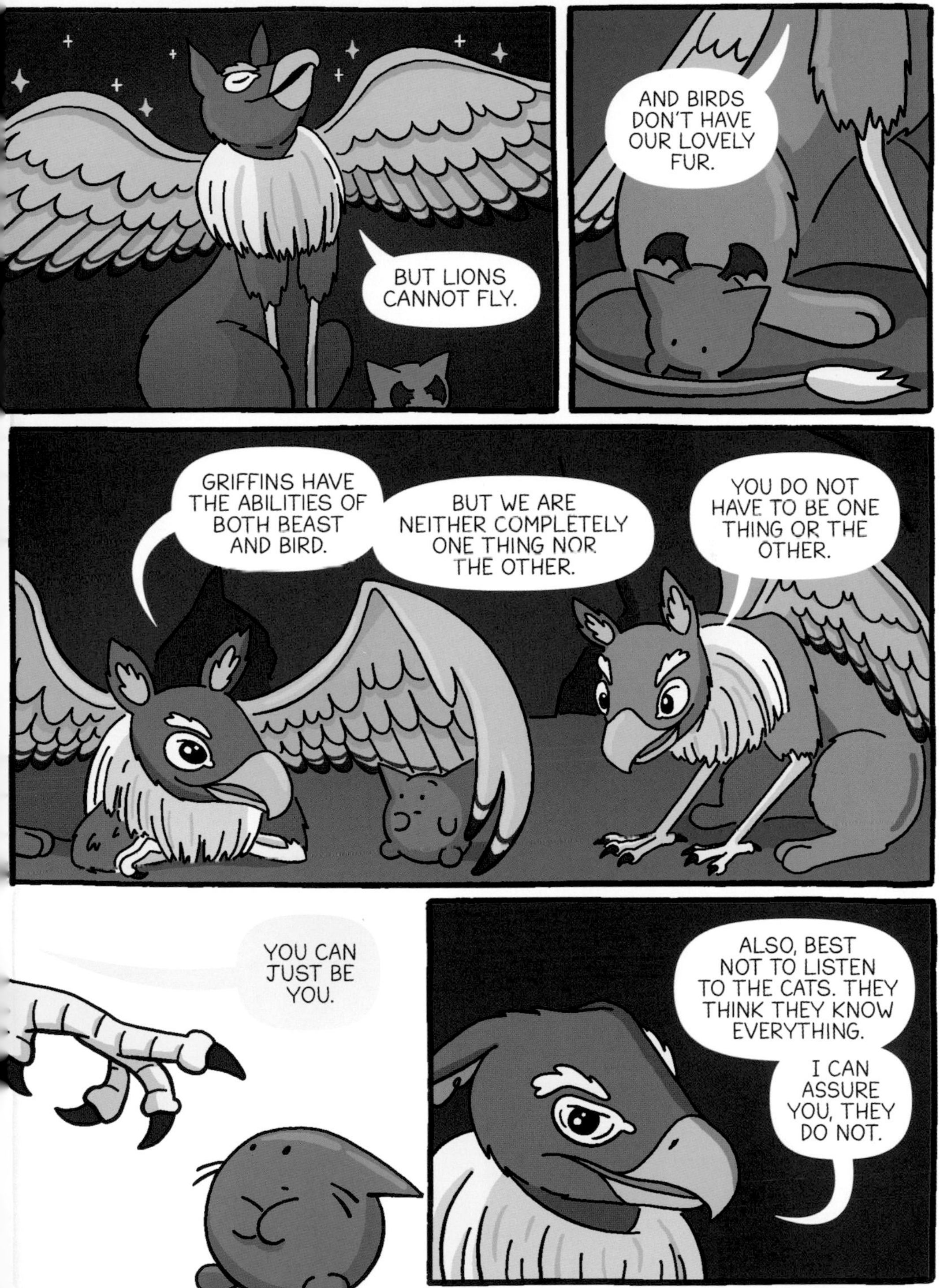
BUT LIONS CANNOT FLY.
AND BIRDS DON'T HAVE OUR LOVELY FUR.
GRIFFINS HAVE THE ABILITIES OF BOTH BEAST AND BIRD.
BUT WE ARE NEITHER COMPLETELY ONE THING NOR THE OTHER.
YOU DO NOT HAVE TO BE ONE THING OR THE OTHER.
YOU CAN JUST BE YOU.
ALSO, BEST NOT TO LISTEN TO THE CATS. THEY THINK THEY KNOW EVERYTHING.
I CAN ASSURE YOU, THEY DO NOT.

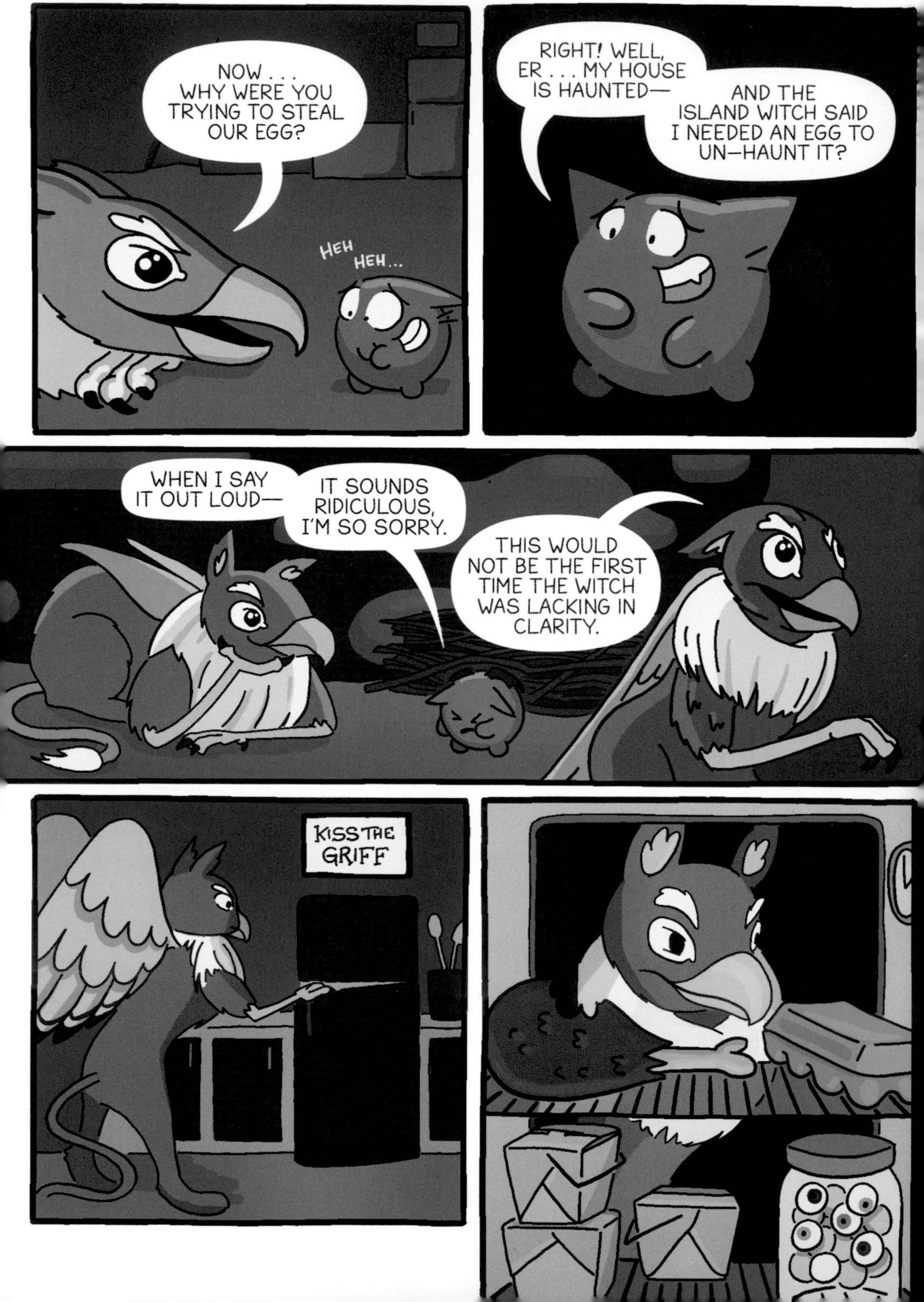
NOW . . . WHY WERE YOU TRYING TO STEAL OUR EGG?
HEH HEH...
RIGHT! WELL, ER . . . MY HOUSE IS HAUNTED—
AND THE ISLAND WITCH SAID I NEEDED AN EGG TO UN—HAUNT IT?
WHEN I SAY IT OUT LOUD—
IT SOUNDS RIDICULOUS, I'M SO SORRY.
THIS WOULD NOT BE THE FIRST TIME THE WITCH WAS LACKING IN CLARITY.
KISS THE GRIFF

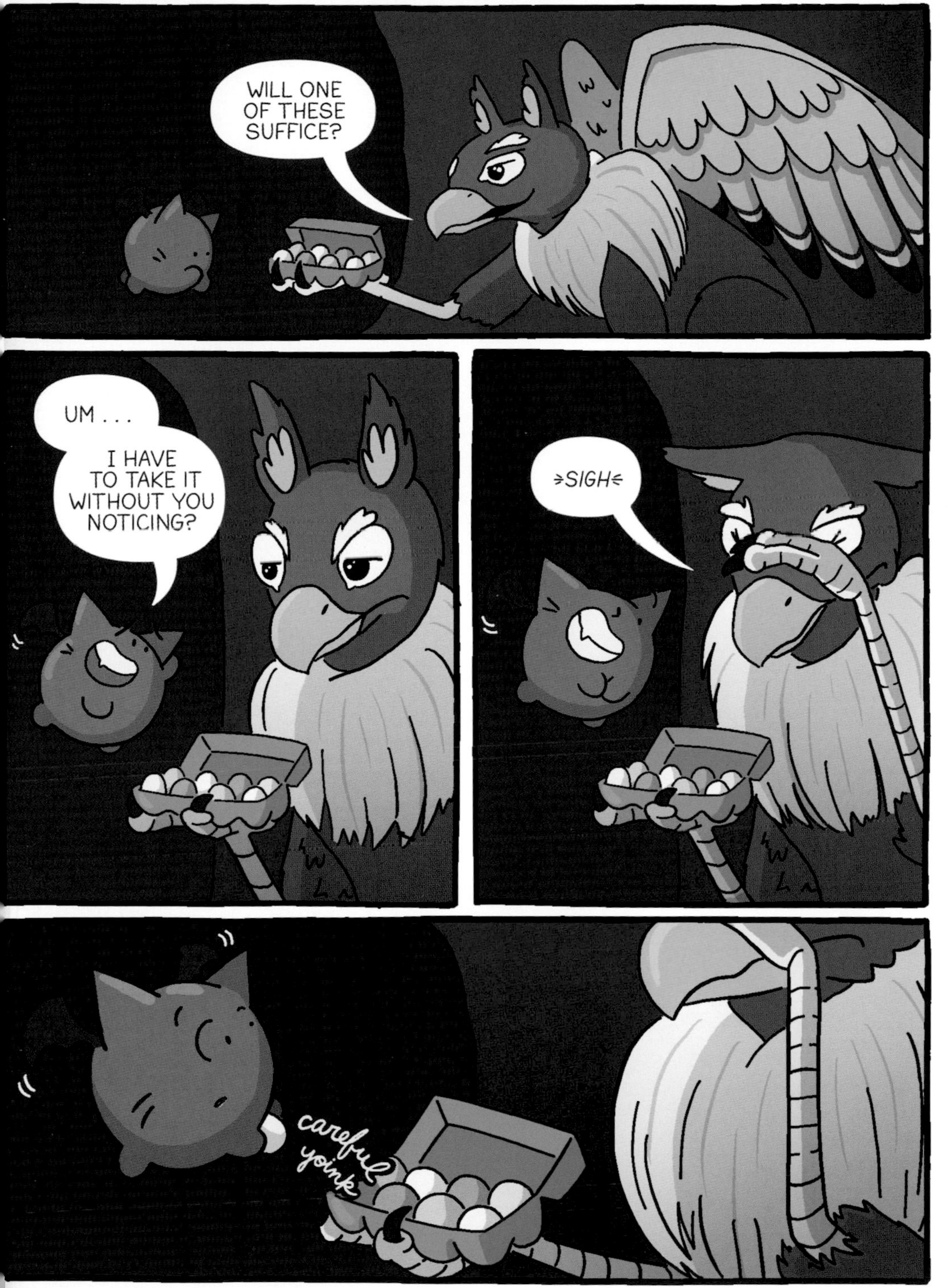
WILL ONE OF THESE SUFFICE?
UM . . .
I HAVE TO TAKE IT WITHOUT YOU NOTICING?
SIGH
careful yoink

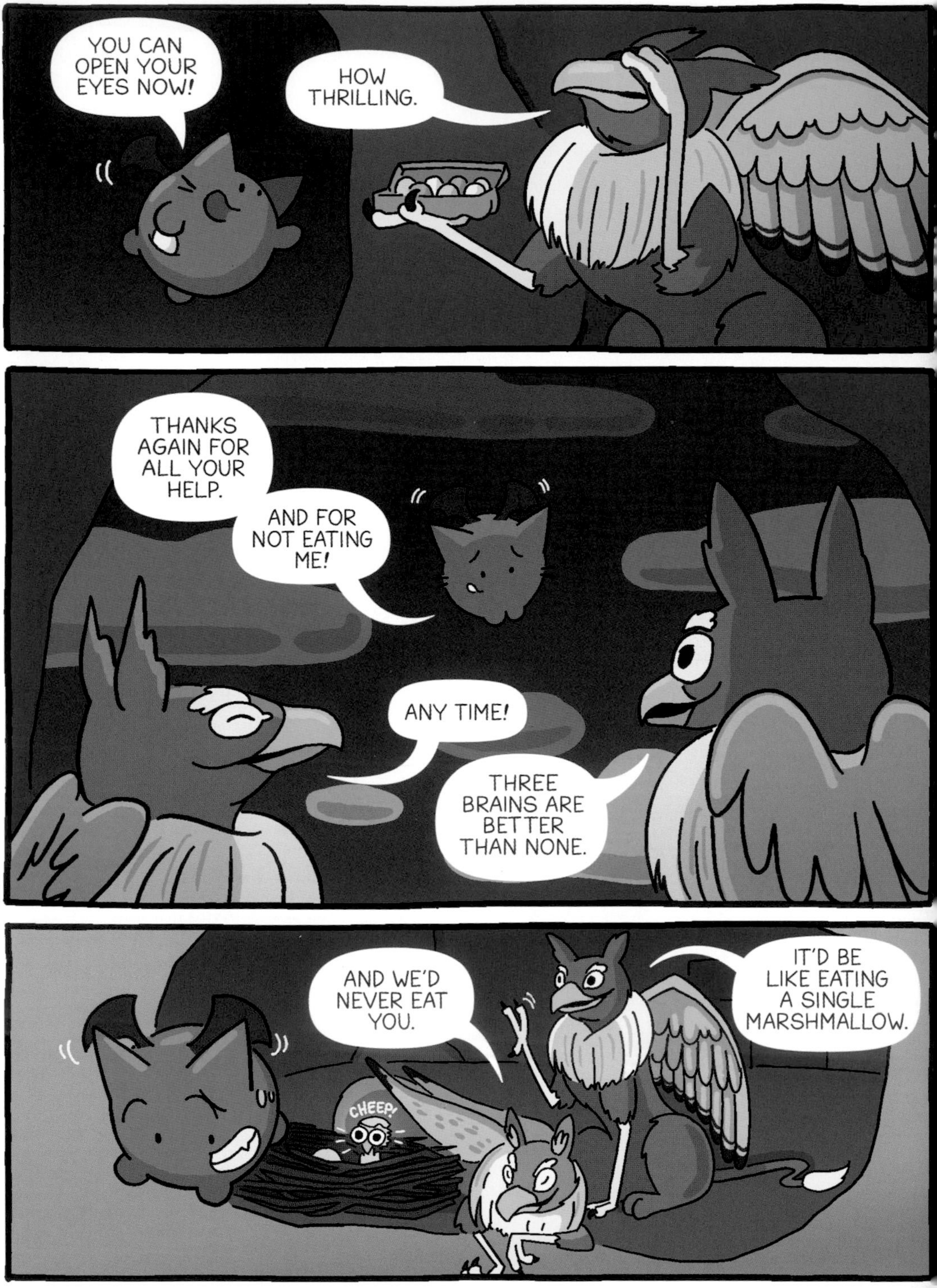
YOU CAN OPEN YOUR EYES NOW!
HOW THRILLING.
THANKS AGAIN FOR ALL YOUR HELP.
AND FOR NOT EATING ME!
ANY TIME!
THREE BRAINS ARE BETTER THAN NONE.
AND WE'D NEVER EAT YOU.
IT'D BE LIKE EATING A SINGLE MARSHMALLOW.
CHEEP!

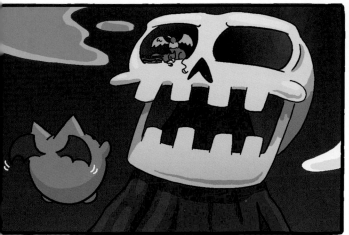

IT'S KIND OF QUIET UP HERE . . .

IF SOMEONE WANTS TO BREAK UP THE SILENCE.

REALLY?

REALLY REALLY!

TONIGHT, I'M ORDERING VICTORY TACOS!!

AND SO BATCAT, VICTORIOUSLY PINK, FLEW BACK TO THE ISLAND WITCH WITH THEIR THREE INGREDIENTS.

BACK AT THE ISLAND WITCH'S HOUSE

GUESS WHAT, GUESS WHAT!!

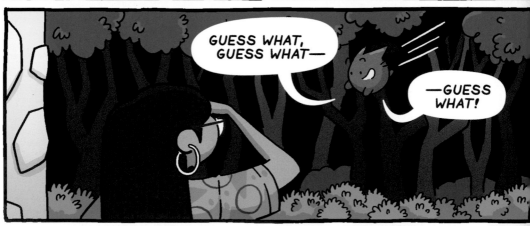

GUESS WHAT, GUESS WHAT—

—GUESS WHAT!

WHAT?

I GOT ALL OF THE INGREDIENTS!

YOU DID?

I DID! ALL THREE OF THEM!

74

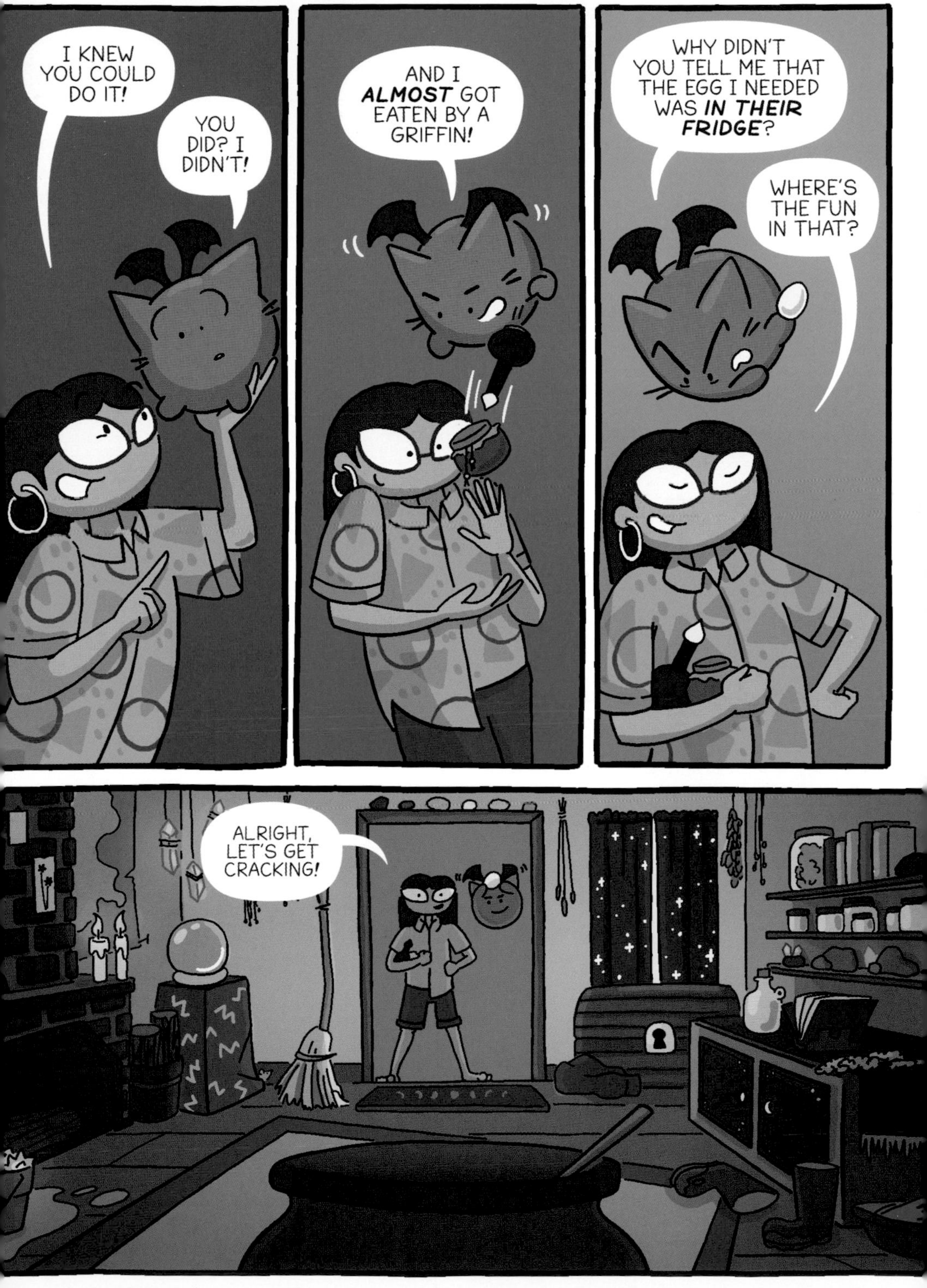
I KNEW YOU COULD DO IT!
YOU DID? I DIDN'T!
AND I **ALMOST** GOT EATEN BY A GRIFFIN!
WHY DIDN'T YOU TELL ME THAT THE EGG I NEEDED WAS ***IN THEIR FRIDGE***?
WHERE'S THE FUN IN THAT?
ALRIGHT, LET'S GET CRACKING!

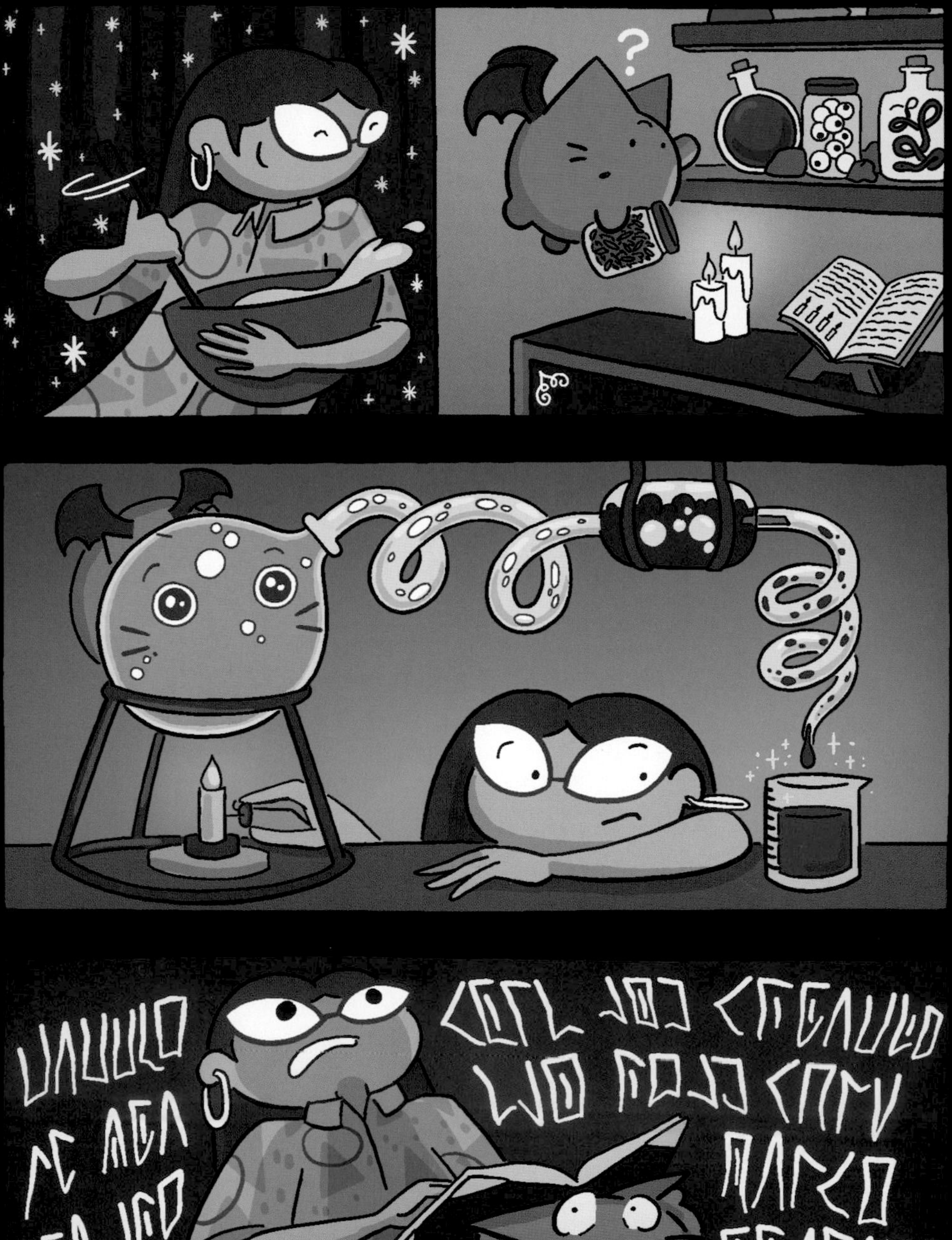

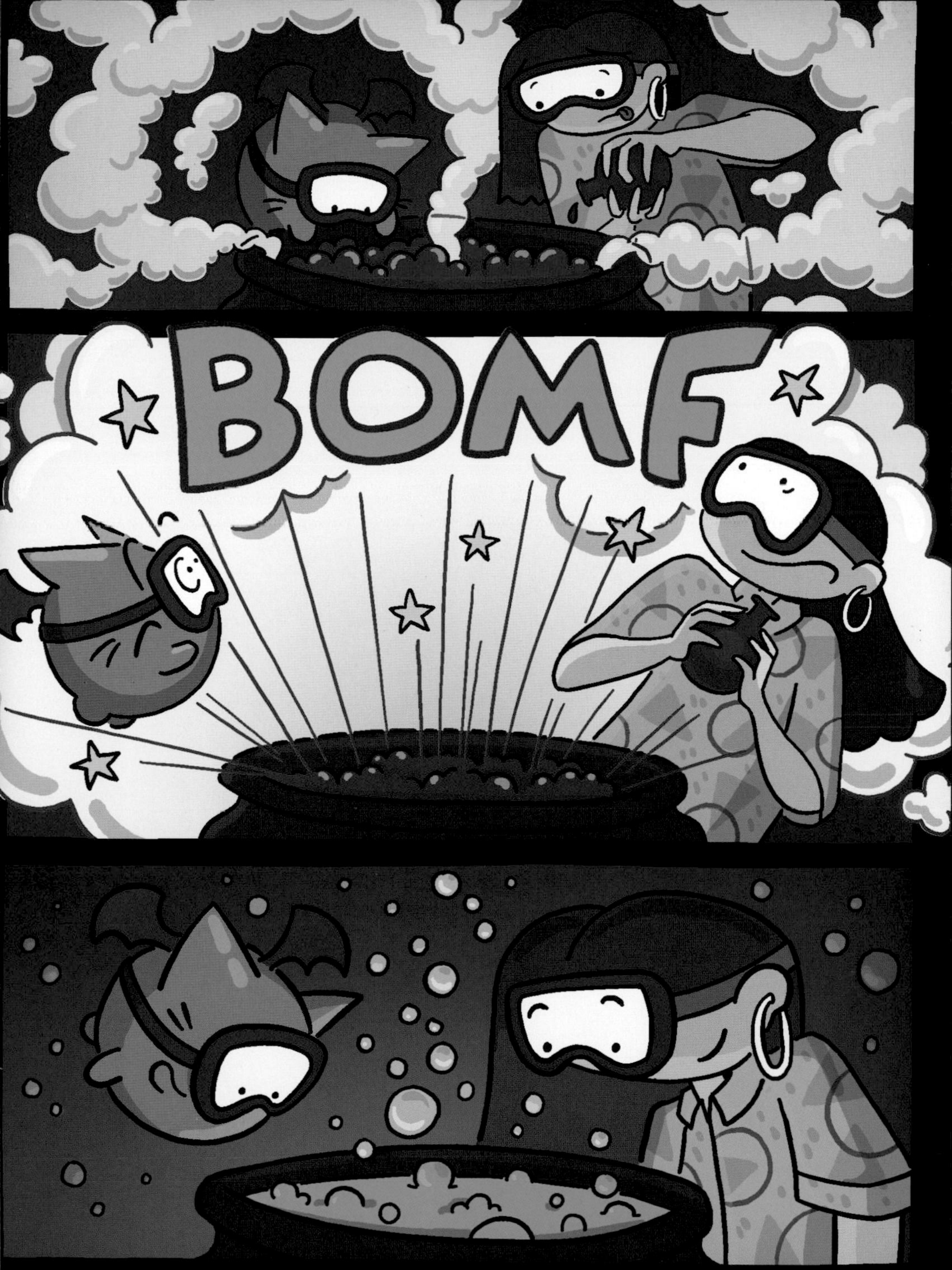
BOMF

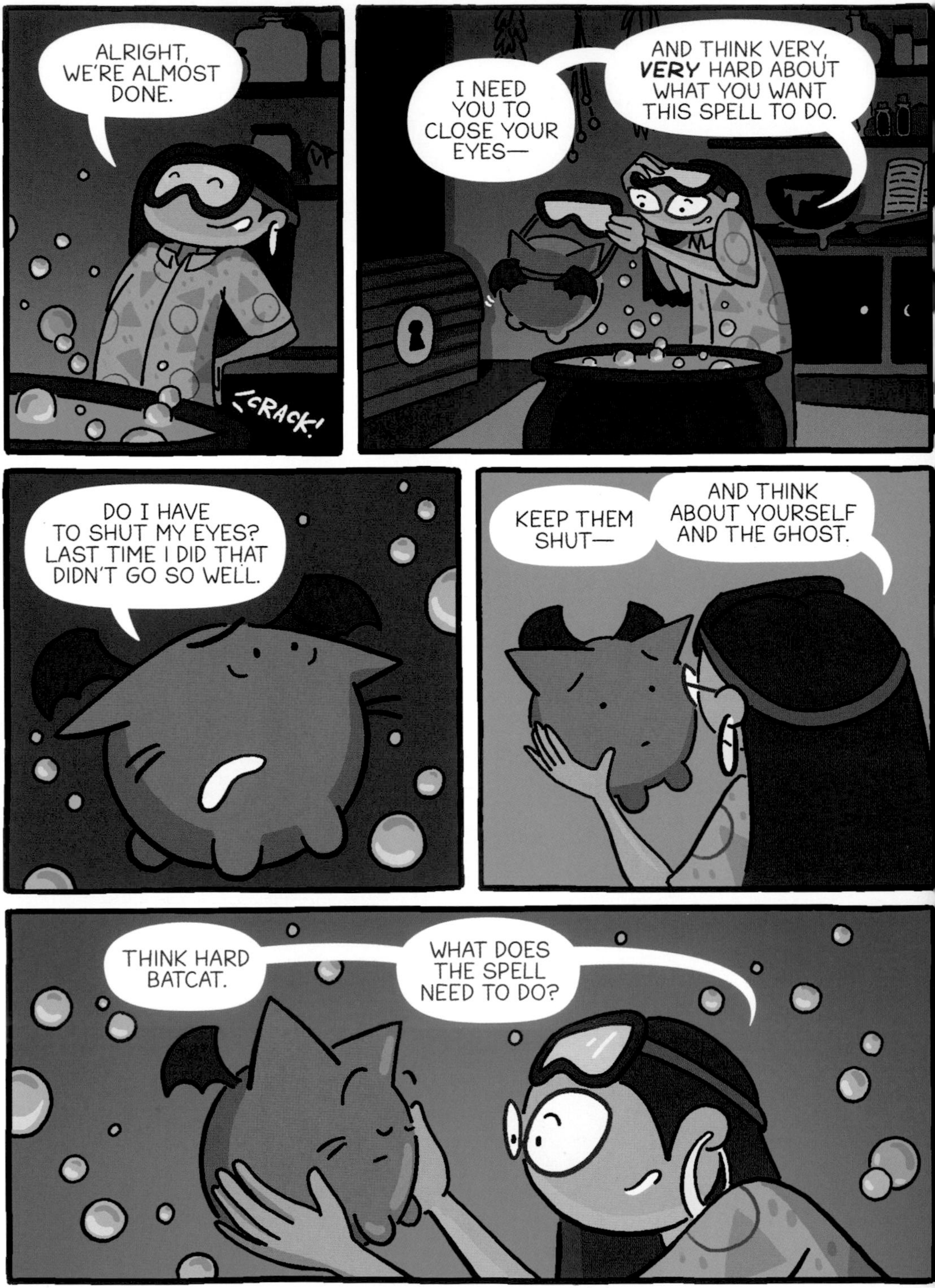
ALRIGHT, WE'RE ALMOST DONE.
¡CRACK!
I NEED YOU TO CLOSE YOUR EYES—
AND THINK VERY, **VERY** HARD ABOUT WHAT YOU WANT THIS SPELL TO DO.
DO I HAVE TO SHUT MY EYES? LAST TIME I DID THAT DIDN'T GO SO WELL.
KEEP THEM SHUT—
AND THINK ABOUT YOURSELF AND THE GHOST.
THINK HARD BATCAT.
WHAT DOES THE SPELL NEED TO DO?

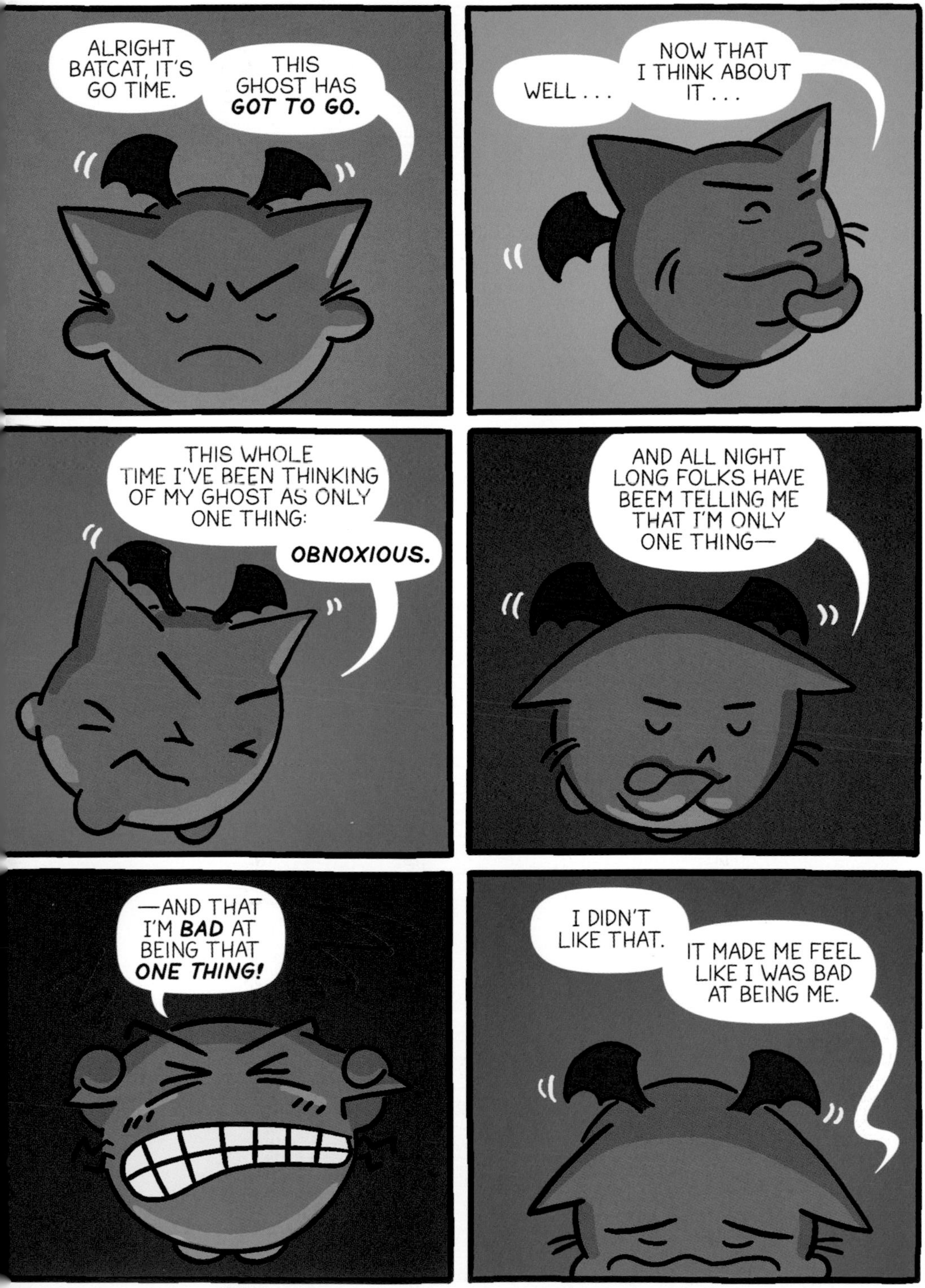

ALRIGHT BATCAT, IT'S GO TIME.
THIS GHOST HAS **GOT TO GO.**
WELL . . .
NOW THAT I THINK ABOUT IT . . .
THIS WHOLE TIME I'VE BEEN THINKING OF MY GHOST AS ONLY ONE THING:
OBNOXIOUS.
AND ALL NIGHT LONG FOLKS HAVE BEEM TELLING ME THAT I'M ONLY ONE THING—
—AND THAT I'M **BAD** AT BEING THAT ***ONE THING!***
I DIDN'T LIKE THAT.
IT MADE ME FEEL LIKE I WAS BAD AT BEING ME.

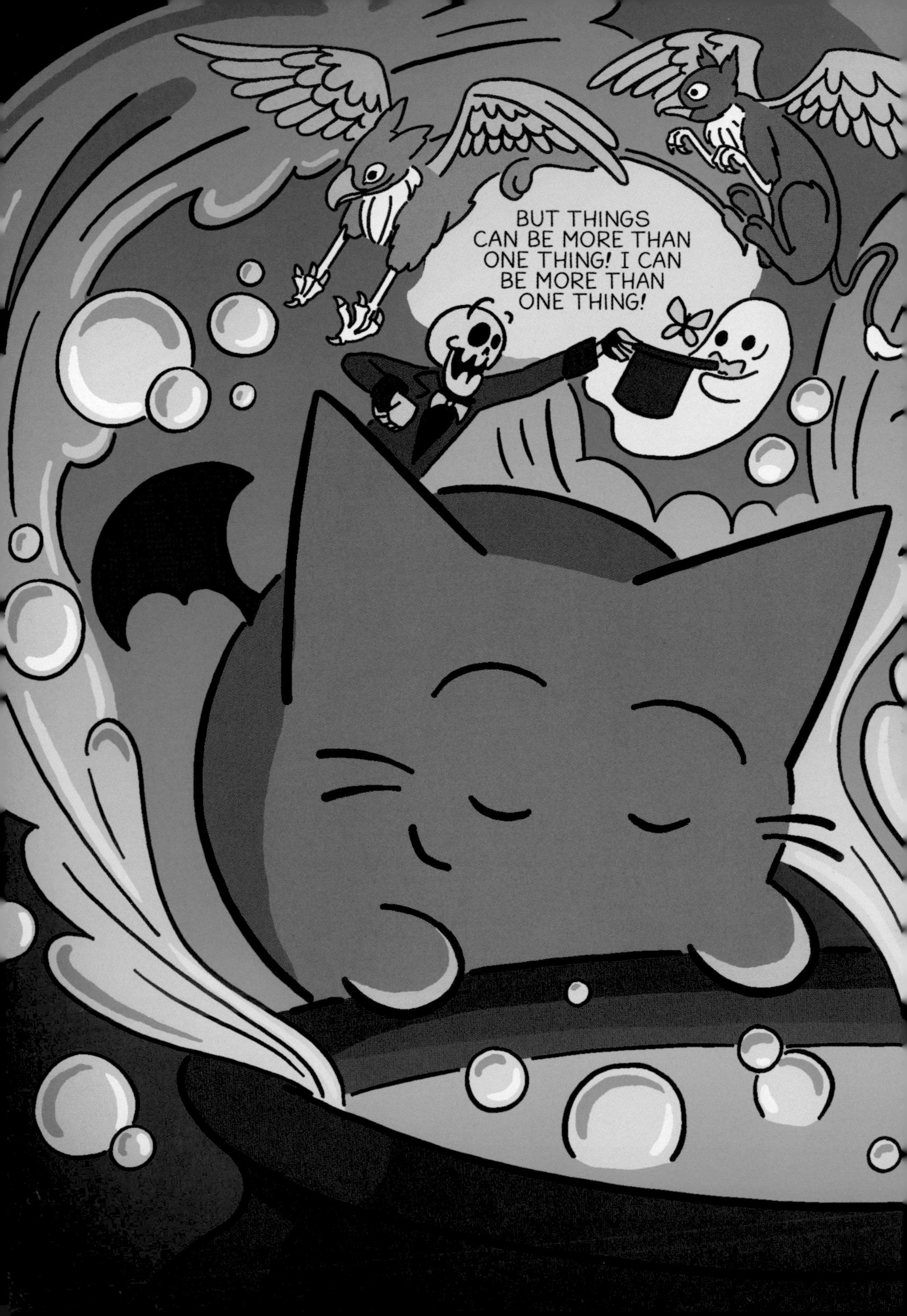
BUT THINGS CAN BE MORE THAN ONE THING! I CAN BE MORE THAN ONE THING!

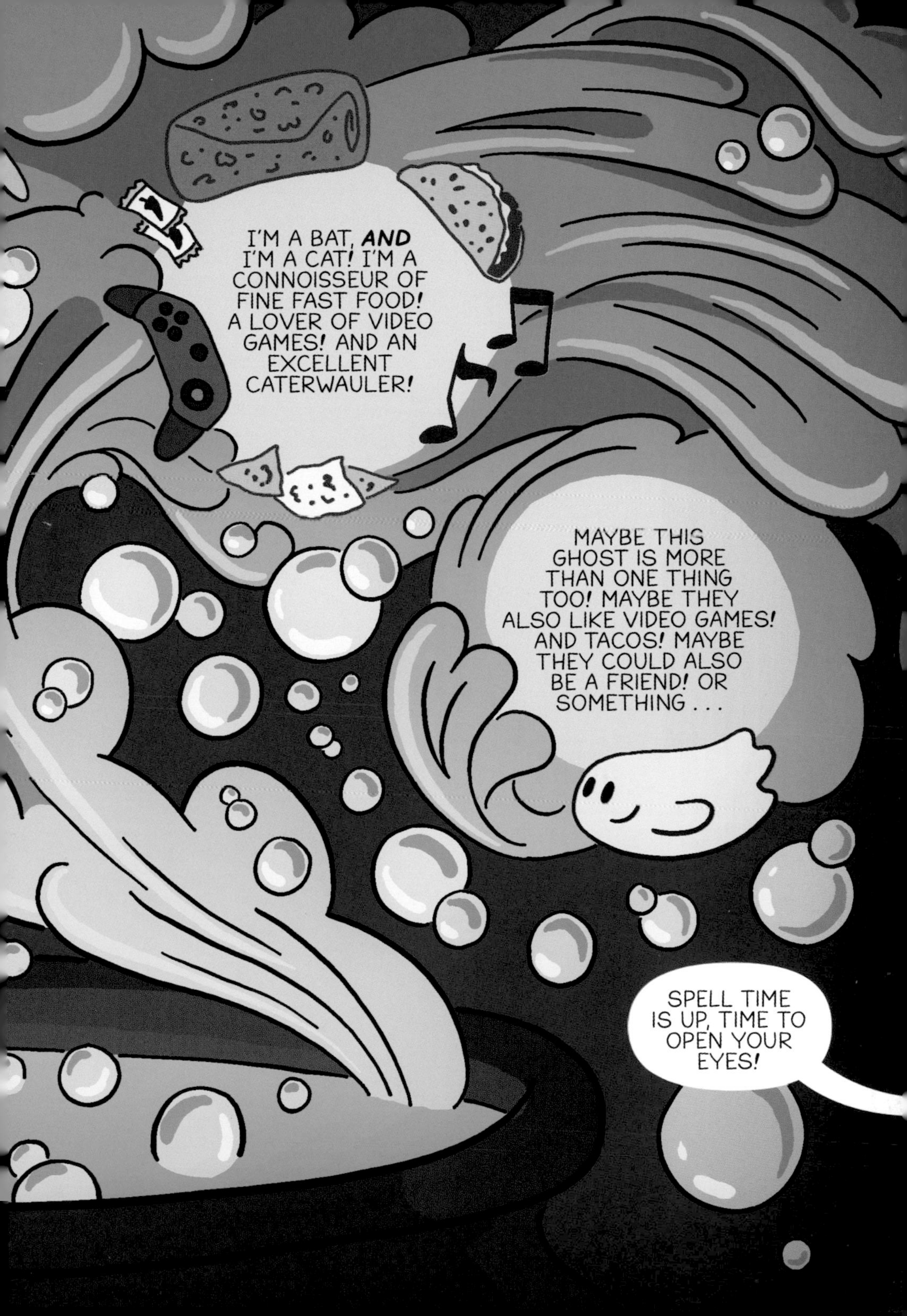
I'M A BAT, **AND** I'M A CAT! I'M A CONNOISSEUR OF FINE FAST FOOD! A LOVER OF VIDEO GAMES! AND AN EXCELLENT CATERWAULER!
MAYBE THIS GHOST IS MORE THAN ONE THING TOO! MAYBE THEY ALSO LIKE VIDEO GAMES! AND TACOS! MAYBE THEY COULD ALSO BE A FRIEND! OR SOMETHING . . .
SPELL TIME IS UP, TIME TO OPEN YOUR EYES!

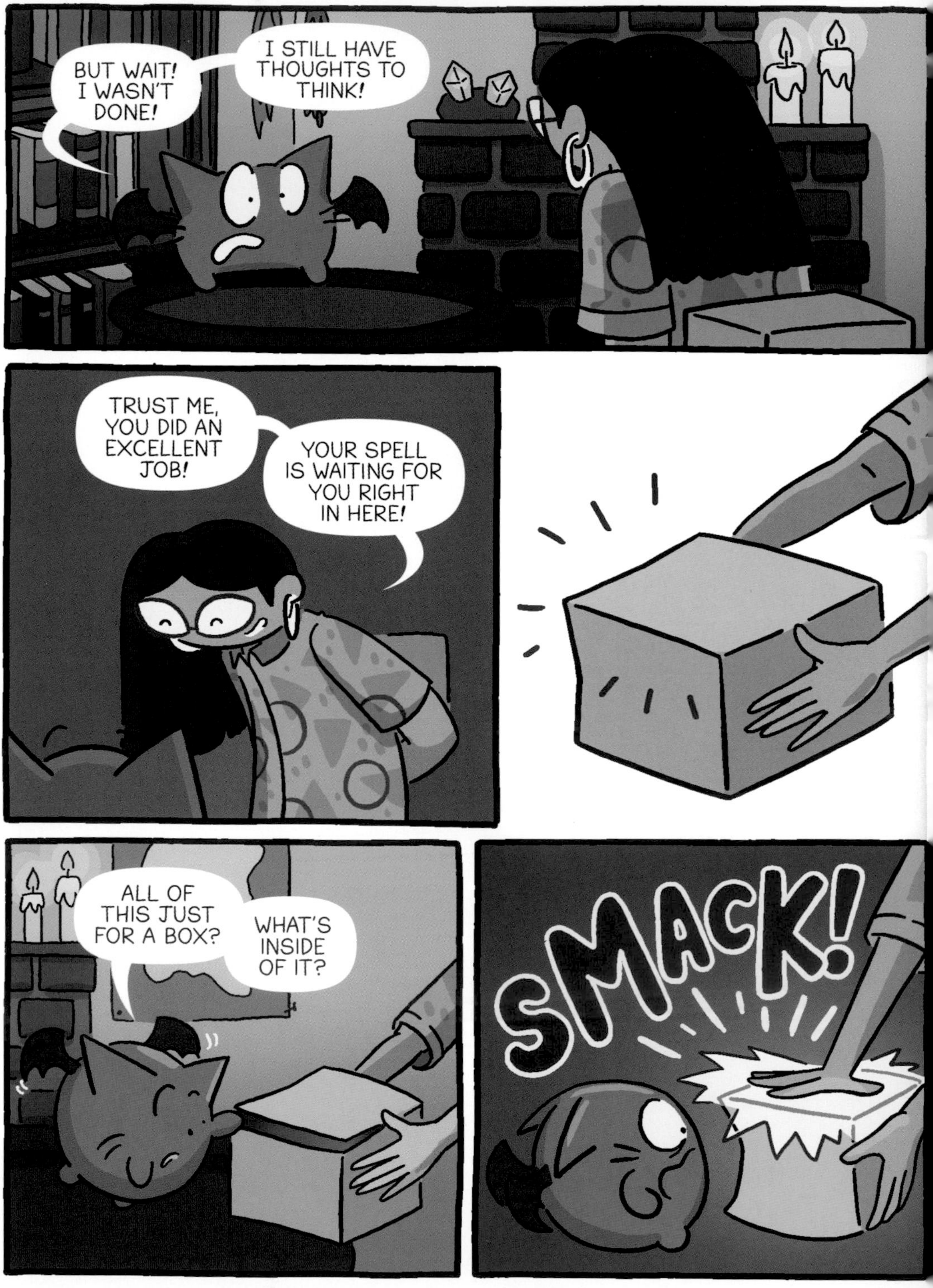
BUT WAIT! I WASN'T DONE!
I STILL HAVE THOUGHTS TO THINK!
TRUST ME, YOU DID AN EXCELLENT JOB!
YOUR SPELL IS WAITING FOR YOU RIGHT IN HERE!
ALL OF THIS JUST FOR A BOX?
WHAT'S INSIDE OF IT?
SMACK!

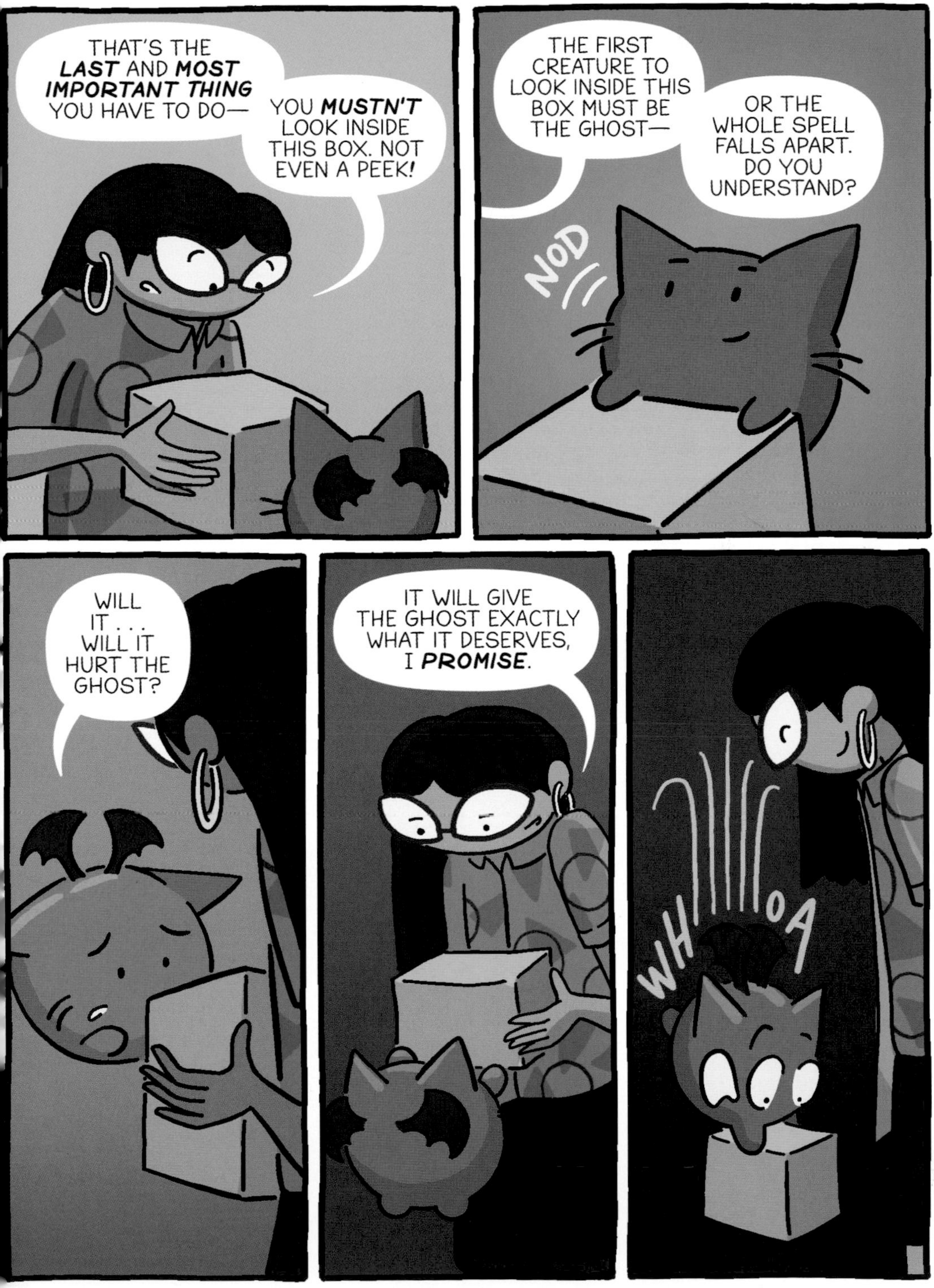
THAT'S THE **LAST** AND **MOST IMPORTANT THING** YOU HAVE TO DO—
YOU **MUSTN'T** LOOK INSIDE THIS BOX. NOT EVEN A PEEK!
THE FIRST CREATURE TO LOOK INSIDE THIS BOX MUST BE THE GHOST—
OR THE WHOLE SPELL FALLS APART. DO YOU UNDERSTAND?
NOD
WILL IT . . . WILL IT HURT THE GHOST?
IT WILL GIVE THE GHOST EXACTLY WHAT IT DESERVES, I **PROMISE**.
WHOA

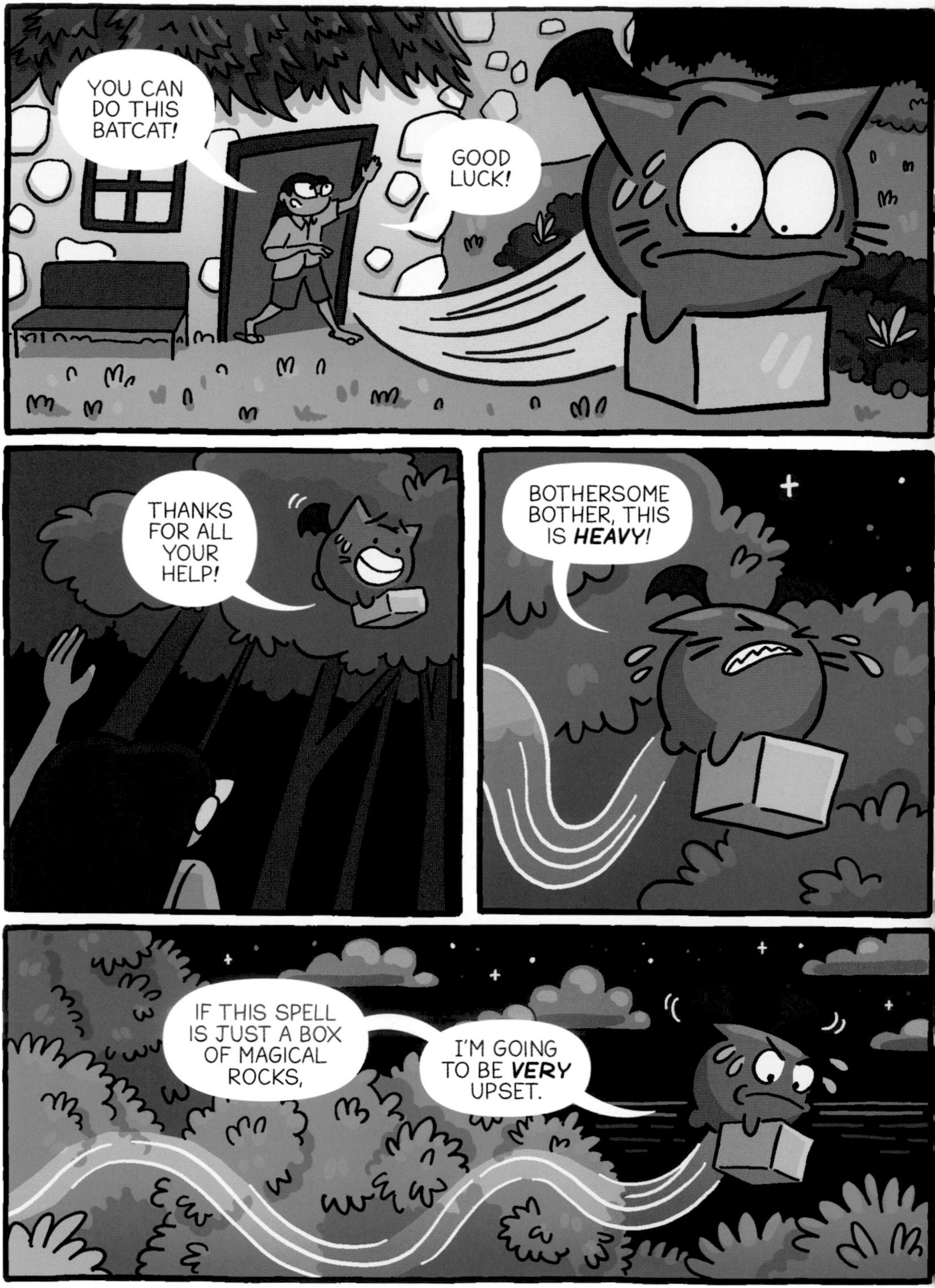
YOU CAN DO THIS BATCAT!
GOOD LUCK!
THANKS FOR ALL YOUR HELP!
BOTHERSOME BOTHER, THIS IS ***HEAVY***!
IF THIS SPELL IS JUST A BOX OF MAGICAL ROCKS,
I'M GOING TO BE ***VERY*** UPSET.

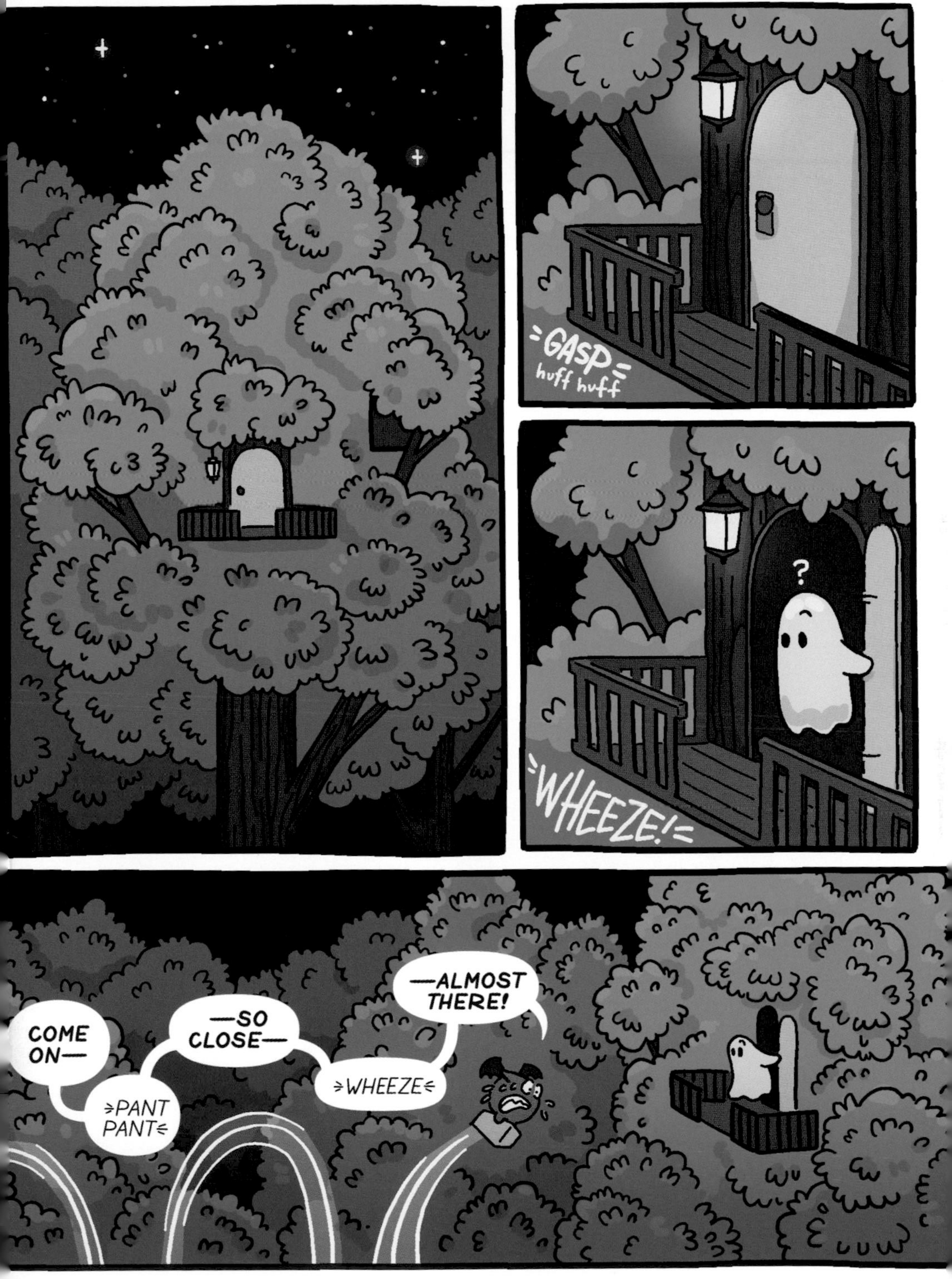
GASP
huff huff
?
WHEEZE!
COME ON—
PANT PANT
—SO CLOSE—
WHEEZE
—ALMOST THERE!

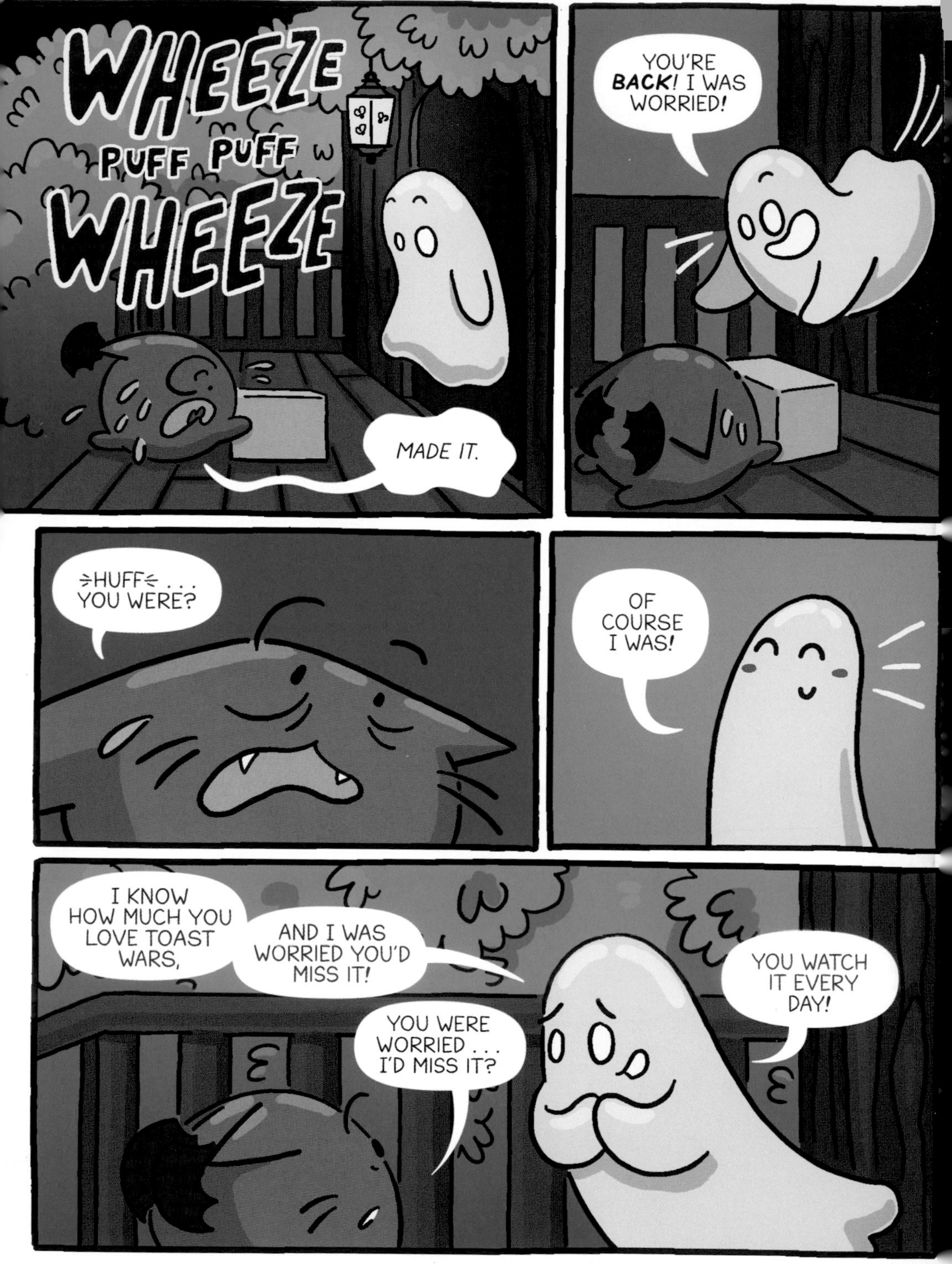
WHEEZE
PUFF PUFF
WHEEZE
MADE IT.
YOU'RE **BACK!** I WAS WORRIED!
⇒HUFF⇐ . . . YOU WERE?
OF COURSE I WAS!
I KNOW HOW MUCH YOU LOVE TOAST WARS,
AND I WAS WORRIED YOU'D MISS IT!
YOU WATCH IT EVERY DAY!
YOU WERE WORRIED . . . I'D MISS IT?

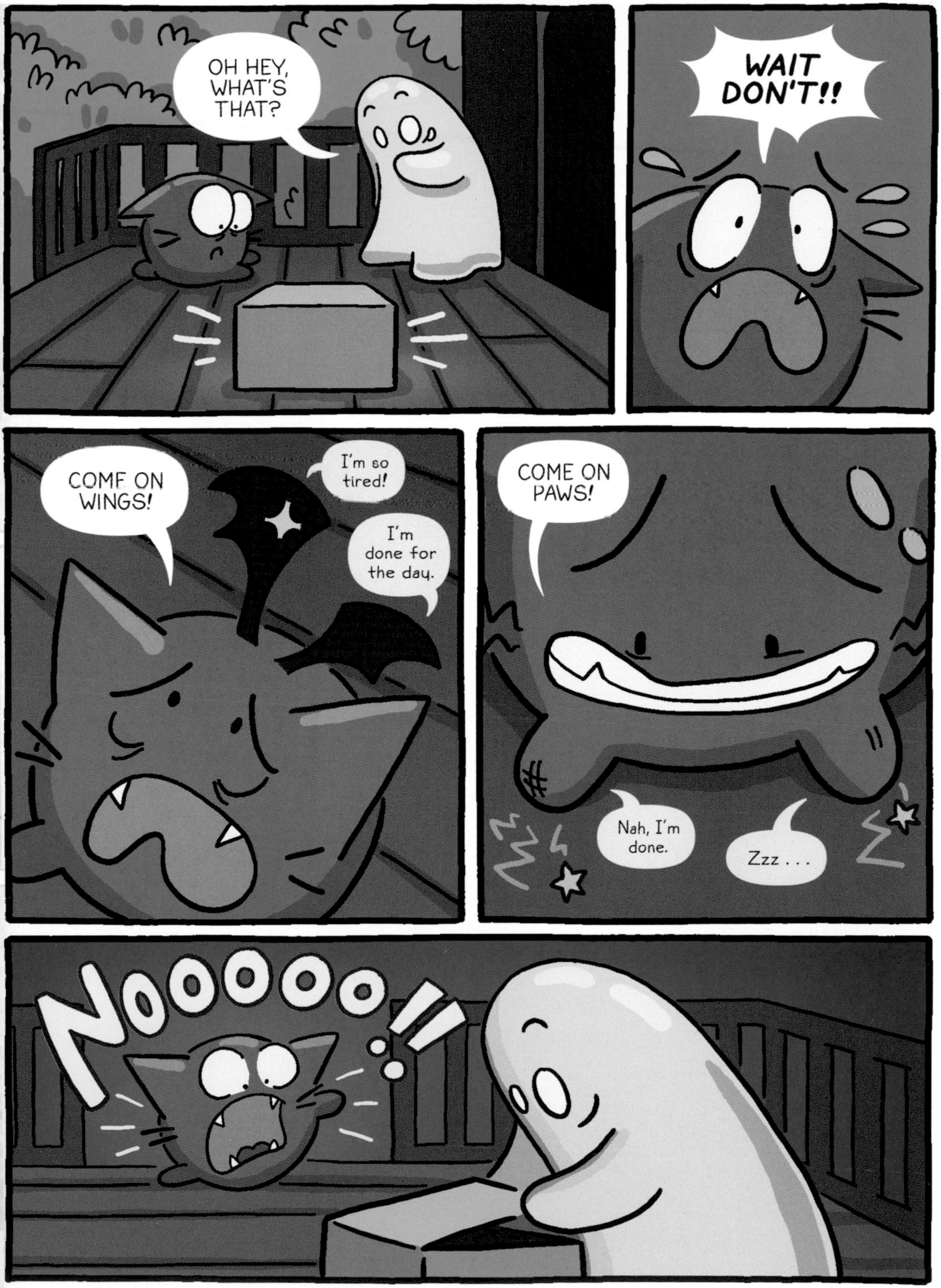
OH HEY, WHAT'S THAT?
WAIT DON'T!!
COME ON WINGS!
I'm so tired!
I'm done for the day.
COME ON PAWS!
Nah, I'm done.
Zzz . . .
NOOOOO!!

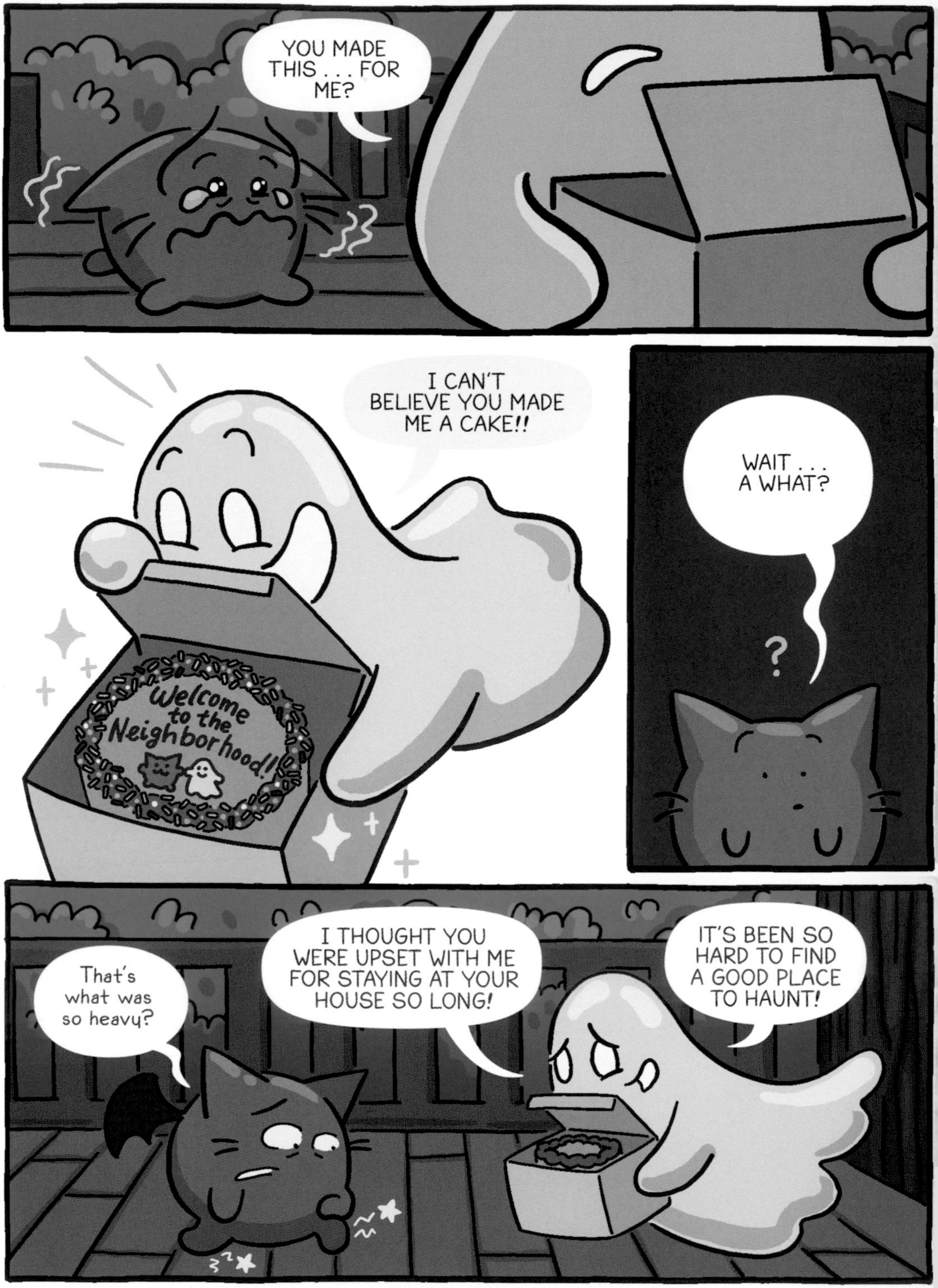
YOU MADE THIS . . . FOR ME?
I CAN'T BELIEVE YOU MADE ME A CAKE!!
Welcome to the Neighborhood!!
WAIT . . . A WHAT?
?
That's what was so heavy?
I THOUGHT YOU WERE UPSET WITH ME FOR STAYING AT YOUR HOUSE SO LONG!
IT'S BEEN SO HARD TO FIND A GOOD PLACE TO HAUNT!

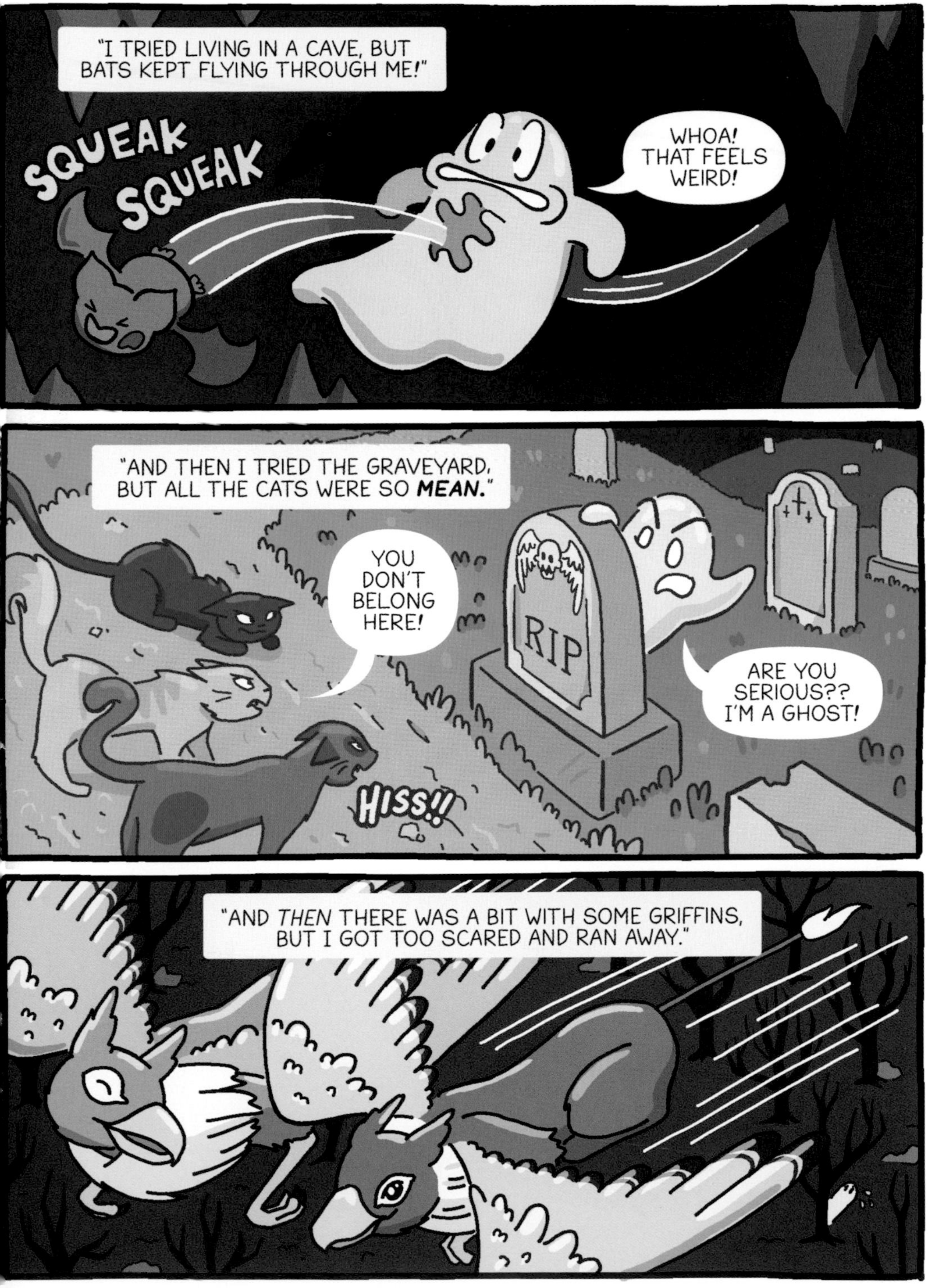
"I TRIED LIVING IN A CAVE, BUT BATS KEPT FLYING THROUGH ME!"
SQUEAK SQUEAK
WHOA! THAT FEELS WEIRD!
"AND THEN I TRIED THE GRAVEYARD, BUT ALL THE CATS WERE SO **MEAN.**"
YOU DON'T BELONG HERE!
RIP
ARE YOU SERIOUS?? I'M A GHOST!
HISS!!
"AND *THEN* THERE WAS A BIT WITH SOME GRIFFINS, BUT I GOT TOO SCARED AND RAN AWAY."

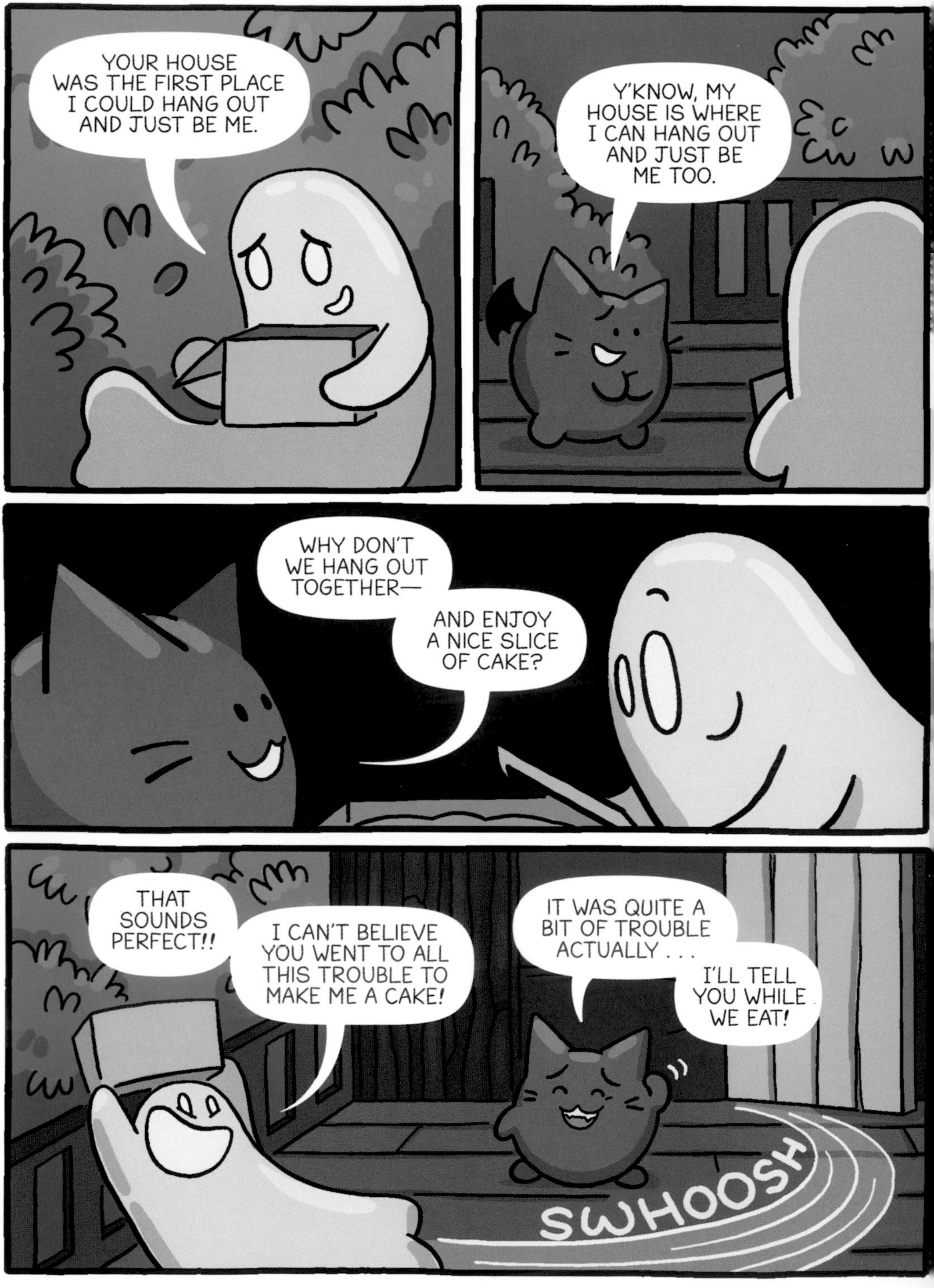
YOUR HOUSE WAS THE FIRST PLACE I COULD HANG OUT AND JUST BE ME.
Y'KNOW, MY HOUSE IS WHERE I CAN HANG OUT AND JUST BE ME TOO.
WHY DON'T WE HANG OUT TOGETHER—
AND ENJOY A NICE SLICE OF CAKE?
THAT SOUNDS PERFECT!!
I CAN'T BELIEVE YOU WENT TO ALL THIS TROUBLE TO MAKE ME A CAKE!
IT WAS QUITE A BIT OF TROUBLE ACTUALLY . . .
I'LL TELL YOU WHILE WE EAT!
SWHOOSH

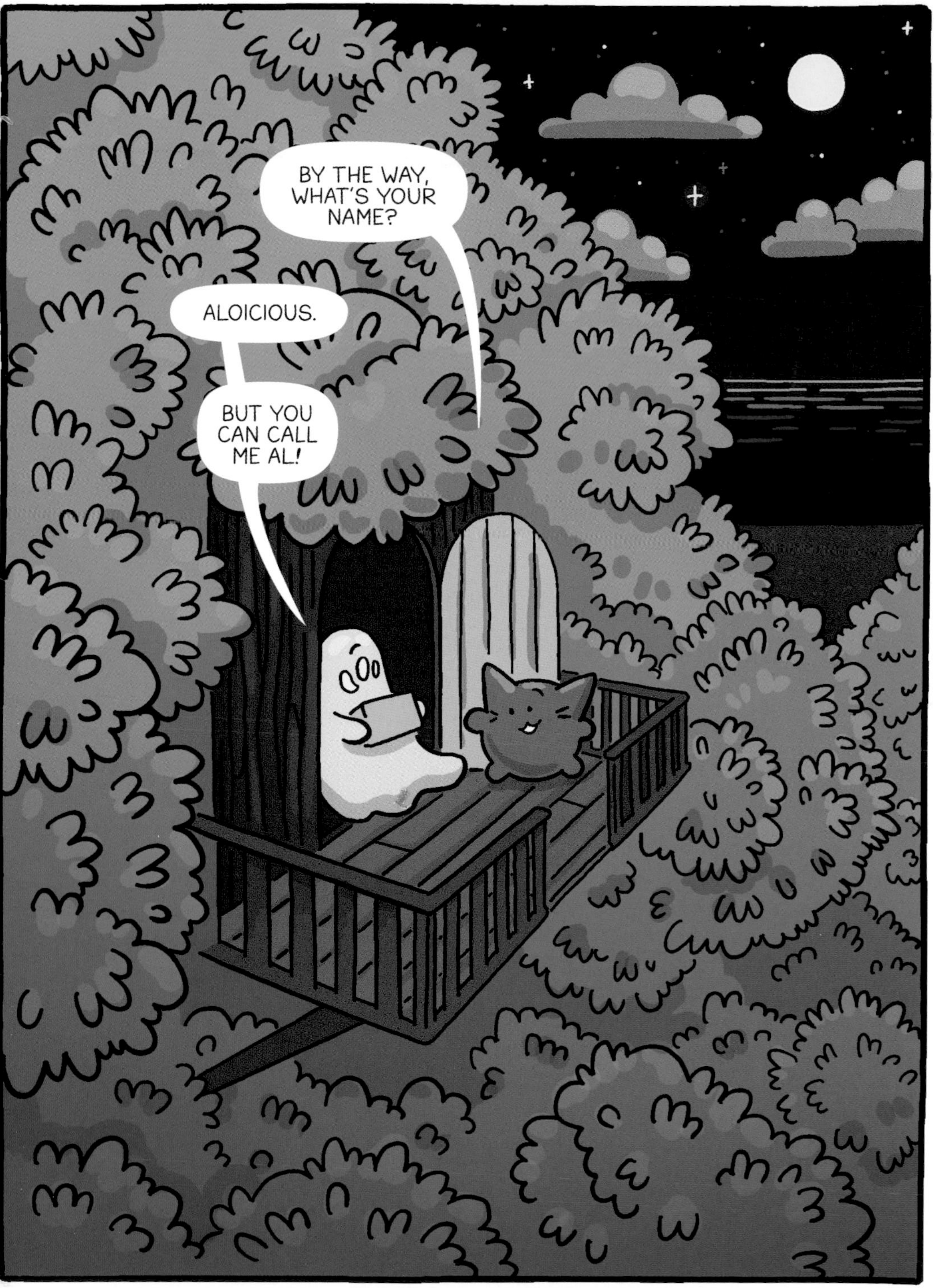
BY THE WAY, WHAT'S YOUR NAME?
ALOICIOUS.
BUT YOU CAN CALL ME AL!

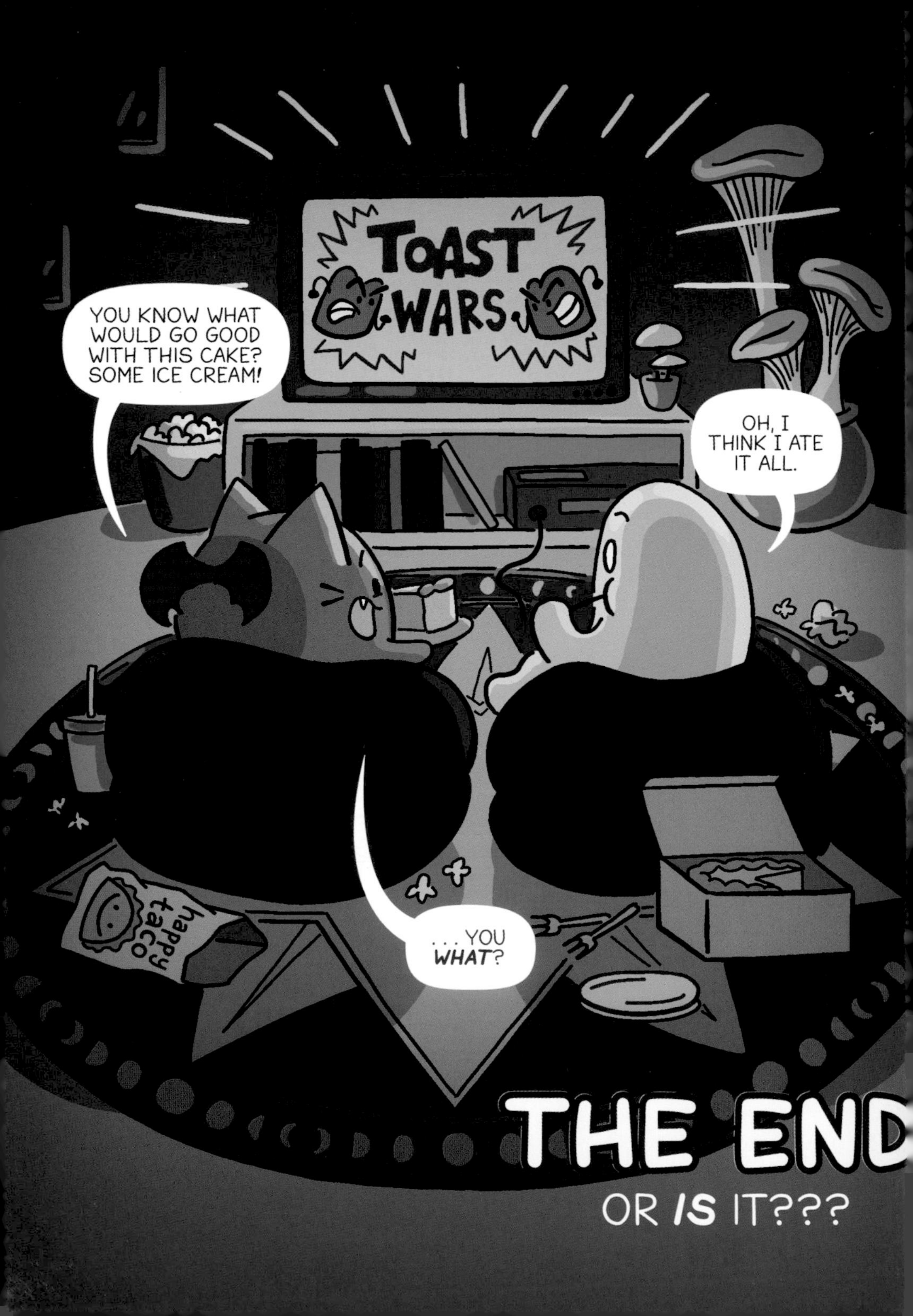
TOAST WARS
YOU KNOW WHAT WOULD GO GOOD WITH THIS CAKE? SOME ICE CREAM!
OH, I THINK I ATE IT ALL.
happy taco
. . . YOU *WHAT*?
THE END
OR *IS* IT???

ACKNOWLEDGMENTS

When I lived in California, I taught comics at elementary schools around the Bay Area. The last day of my classes was always the same: I'd make copies of the students' final projects, and we'd assemble them and trade them in a mini comic festival. Each semester I'd make a mini comic to trade with these students, and so Batcat was born.

It's thanks to Kate, Charlotte, and Andy that Batcat was able to move from copy paper to an actual book. They kept this book alive through a pandemic, which is a feat of strength unknown to mortal men.

Thanks to Lauren, Maia, and Patrick, who looked over early scripts and covers and assured me that I was sane when I was most definitely not.

Thanks to my students: Milton, Rowan, Wonder, Marek, Lila, and more. Teaching you comics was the greatest part of my life, and I hope you're still making them.

Thanks to my Batcats: Talulu, Ruby, and Squidget. I know you can't read, but I want to commemorate how much you mean to me on paper, because I love you all so much.

Lastly, thanks to Sam. Without you nothing is possible, and with you everything is. Thanks for believing in me.

**To anyone who was told
that they could only be one thing
and then decided to be something
completely different**

Library of Congress Control Number 2022940971

ISBN 978-1-4197-5657-3

Text and illustrations © 2023 Meggie Ramm
Book design by Andrea Miller

Printed and bound in China
10 9 8 7 6 5 4 3 2 1

ABRAMS The Art of Books
195 Broadway, New York, NY 10007
abramsbooks.com